MAX
PATCH
BEND

MAX PATCH BEND

A Novel

by

Nathan B. Tracy

A Todd Casey Adventure

YAV PUBLICATIONS
ASHEVILLE, NORTH CAROLINA

ISBN: 978-1-937449-17-9

Published by:
YAV Publications
Asheville, North Carolina

YAV books may be purchased in bulk for educational, business, fund-raising, or sales promotional use. For information, contact Books@yav.com or phone toll-free 888-693-9365.

Visit our website: www.InterestingWriting.com

3 5 7 9 10 8 6 4 2

Assembled in the United States of America
Published August 2013

Acknowledgements

My wife, Martha, spends many hours looking at the back of my head as I work at the computer. I know she would much rather that we be doing something else, or at least talking occasionally. She has read the manuscript several times, checking for errors. All nerve wracking reads. Now she is free to read it as a novel, and I hope she likes it.

I also want to thank Denise Loock for proof reading a printed manuscript. By design she mostly concentrated on my use of commas and involved herself only slightly with sentence structure and the larger aspects of editing. Please hold her harmless for any structural problems. Now I know how successful authors can knock out a book every six months. If you could afford a thorough edit of your manuscript, the labor of writing a book would decrease by 80%. I am going to try it on my next book if I become suddenly wealthy.

Special thanks to my publisher, Chris Yavelow, for his excellence, knowledge and unending patience.

TABLE OF CONTENTS

FOREWORD

The year 1783 followed closely the end of hostilities in the American Revolutionary War. The British surrendered, and were shipping their troops back to England, and mercenaries to their homelands. The Continental Army also slowly disbanded, sending the fighters homeward.

The foundation stones for the constitutional convention began to form amid constant verbal skirmishes between the leaders of the thirteen colonies. The post war era became a time of change and awakening.

During the war, our soldiers left their small towns, coves, hollows, cuts, or valleys, and isolated farms. They mixed with others from different areas and marched to places hundreds of miles from home. They returned with a wider understanding of their new country, and a desire to move westward awakened within them.

Before the Revolutionary war civilization virtually stopped at the east edge of the Appalachian mountain, chain. There were no roads westward. There were no bridges over rivers, no supply posts, and few people. In those days, there was no travel in wagons because the only way to cross the mountains was to follow game trails and buffalo paths. Travel was by foot or by horseback. The Appalachian Mountains are a series of many parallel steep ridges, and narrow valleys lying side by side and running north and south. It is said by sociologists that it took a generation to move to the next valley as the children grew and moved westward over the next ridge.

As the generations moved on, they left behind better trails, often wide enough for wagons. Occasionally there were bridges of logs over streams and gullies, and eventually men built barges to carry men and horses across wide rivers. Small trading posts began to appear.

The more rugged the mountains were, the more sparse the population. Communities were often so isolated they, of necessity, became a hundred percent self-sustaining. The language became a mix of foreign words and dialects. The dialect often changed within fifty miles or less, depending on the ethnic origin of the settlers.

The isolation and the lack of things except the basic needs of life drove the people into fierce independence and self-reliance. They willingly gave help to others, but found it difficult to receive.

In the United States, we have few poor today who are not a hundred times better off physically than a family living deep in the recesses of the mountains. The rustic mountain cabins of your dreams do not represent reality. Cabins were smaller than the average living room today. The few windows were small, with no windows of glass, only crude wood shutters. The single room was small, dark with a floor of mountain dirt, and only a rough fireplace for both heat, and cooking. The furniture was of axe-hewn tables, benches and stools, and few of those. Light came from candles and lamps. Oil being precious and candles few; the people lived mostly by daylight or firelight.

Clearing the land was difficult, but necessary before the planting of crops. Man tilled his soil with crude ploughs, pulled by a cow, the wife, or if lucky, a horse.

There were no sawmills or chain saws. You cut and split your wood with an axe, you made your boards with an axe; you made your shingles with an axe. If you hurt yourself during the process, there was no doctor.

Game was not plentiful or easy to kill. Your gun was a flintlock, undependable and required you pour powder and shot down the barrel and into the priming pan for each shot. When you pulled the trigger, there was a delay before the powder ignited, if it did at all, and in the rain, it seldom did.

The people ate anything, including coon, possum, woodchucks, squirrel, bear, or deer. Mostly they ate corn flour foods such as biscuits and fried breads. Their cooking oil was lard made from the fat of animals, especially bears.

They picked each kind of berry in its season, cleaned them, and dried them. They found and dried apples and gathered nuts, especially the abundant chestnuts would keep them, and their stock alive. They dried their beans and corn, buried their root vegetables, and cabbages in a dirt keep. The only refrigeration was the cold creek water, where they kept food in crocks and jars.

Water came from the creek in wooden buckets, carried by hand. Settlers heated water for bathing in an iron or copper pot nestled in the coals of the fireplace. They used it sparingly. Soap came from the fat of animals mixed with lye made by draining water through wood ashes. The soap was grey and rough.

Work began at sunrise, and ended after sundown. You made most of your own clothing, including shoes and boots. You worked nearly all the time, and children labored with their parents. There were no schools, and education was limited to what a parent provided by firelight.

The setting of this story begins in the Shenandoah Valley of Virginia in 1782. Driven from home because of an accusation of attempted murder, our hero escapes southward and westward into the mountains. The heroine, under similar circumstances travels from the Piedmont of North Carolina, westward into these same sparsely populated mountains.

The valley of Max Patch Bend does not exist. The author did have a particular example in mind. While on a trip to a western state, he stood on a high cliff, looking down at an extensive circular valley, ringed by continuous cliffs. A river flowed in a large circle, exiting near to where it entered. The river undercut the cliff on one side of the valley and the ruins of stone buildings remained in the cleft.

Creating the valley simply required mentally relocating the valley, letting the river cut through the small neck, leaving the valley high and dry. This imaginary place afforded the chance to populate the area with any tree, bush, flower, or animal desired.

The author lives just off Max Patch Road, in the Fines Creek Community of Western North Carolina. You will not find the mythical Max Patch Bend around there, except in your imagination, and mine.

Please call us at 828 627 3081
E-mail at finescreek@msn.com
Nathan B. Tracy

1783

SHENANDOAH VALLEY
OF
VIRGINIA

CHAPTER 1

THE AMBUSH

A HORSE GALLOPED TOWARD THE FARM of Gilbert Casey, a cloud of dust following. Jerking the horse to a walk, the rider shouted at Todd.

"I is Deputy Horace Snipe with a message for Todd Casey. Sheriff Grasty wants to speak to you at his office in town. Now!"

His voice was harsh. He jerked his horse back toward town, roughly spurring it into a gallop.

Todd was using his first day home in the field with his family planting potatoes. His shirt darkened with sweat, but he was feeling a deep satisfaction with life after graduating from the Virginia Military Academy the previous day. Then the voice of the deputy sheriff sounded an alarm. He knew Deputy Snipe and Sheriff Grasty. They knew him, making him wonder why their summons was so formal and abrupt.

Todd's father, Gilbert Casey heard the shouted message. As the rider wheeled away he said, "Snipe has no call to be rude like that. Something is not right. You better go, Son, but take your weapons with you. His attitude is not correct. Keep a steady hand on your temper."

"I will, Sir."

"Remember, Son, the Sheriff is in league with Lord Wellington Howe. Since we have not yet signed the formal peace with England, he still has power. It may have something to do with the threat his son Quincy made to you. I will clean up and be along shortly."

Todd nodded and started for the barn. He remembered the threat well. In his mind, he saw his dorm room. He remembered the door opening suddenly and slamming against the wall. He saw himself turning in his chair, then jumping to his feet, startled by the loud sound. He did not brace to attention as required of lower classman, but stood erect, ready to deal with whatever problem confronted him.

"I come to warn you, farmer boy—you are soon to die," Quincy Howe shouted with a high-pitched voice. "Your daddy is a traitor to the king, and he helped the colonial rabble steal this land from England."

The cadet continued with an exaggerated English accent even though he was born and raised near Richmond, Virginia. His round and fleshy face flushed with anger. He wore a blue and gray uniform with a scarlet sash covering his protruding waist; over it, a sword hung in a belted scabbard. A fat hand rested on the fancy hilt as he stood in the doorway of Todd's room in the military Academy. Standing behind Quincy were two cadets, Dills and Smathers. Both had round, ruddy faces and soft bodies, and both were sons of English Tories. Both were followers of Quincy.

"Don't hand me stuff, Quincy," Todd said forcefully but not shouting. "The only reason you wear blue is because wearing red would get you shot if you went off campus.

"You may think I am a farmer boy, but my shoulder boards show more rank than yours," Todd continued. "You only received your scarlet sash and sword because your daddy threatened to stir up trouble for the Academy. They stretched a few rules for you. They made you the cadet corps supernumerary and gave you a purple sash and a senior's sword."

"It makes me an officer, dirt farmer."

"It makes you a fool, Quincy. Do you know what a supernumerary is? The word means superfluous or extra, or an actor who only walks by and does not have any lines to say. Your daddy owns ships and should know what the word means, but you seem to think it is something special. I received my sash and sword for having good grades and four years of hard work."

"That is the trouble with this outpost you call a country," Quincy shouted with a sneer on his face. "You are a commoner, and think you have more rank than the son of a Royal. We graduate in one week, and as soon as we get home, you are going to die," he said as his face flushed red with rage. "Mark my words, peasant boy—you are dead meat!"

"If you try to kill me, Howe, be sure to bring your friends because you are not man enough to do it yourself."

"We will be at your killing," cadet Dills said.

"I plan to pound your face to mush before we kill you," cadet Smathers said.

"Out-of-my-room, Quincy," Todd said slowly and with menace in his voice. He moved one foot forward, his wide shoulders moving as his muscles tightened, his arms and rough hands ready at his sides.

"It is Lord Quincy Howe to you, farmer boy. My father is the Lord Wellington Howe. Your father is just Gilbert Casey, a lowborn dirt farmer. You cannot go any lower than dirt farmer, plowboy."

"Your father is no Lord in this country. He is suspected of being a traitor and lucky to be alive," Todd said, with disgust plainly in his full voice and on his square face. "Get out of my room!" he shouted as he leaned toward the doorway. Quincy looked up at Todd's face and jumped backwards. He jerked the door, slamming it shut.

Todd glanced over to the small painting of George Washington astride his white stallion. It gave him a measure of peace, knowing the great general had suffered so many indignities and earned so few of them. His mother gave him the painting the Christmas of his first year as an inspiration, and it always hung over his desk.

Todd heard and saw the encounter in his mind as it flashed through his consciousness. When he reached the barn, he whistled for his horse. He responded immediately. Todd put the saddle and bridle on the horse, mounted, and turned him toward the dirt road. His father waved as Todd rode from the farm.

As his large stallion, Eagle, trotted toward town with upraised head and tail, Todd relived the last few hours at the military Academy. He saw the seniors sitting on chairs on the outside platform to the left of the podium. They were resplendent in their dress uniforms. Their tight blue blouses were fitted with white button-in collars and white buttoned-in cuffs. White cross belts met in the center of the chest with a large brass clasp. Their hat bills and shoes glowed with polish and the trouser creases were pressed to a fine edge. Symbols of rank adorned their shoulder boards, and honor braid looped down from their shoulders. Each wore a purple sash and a sword.

As a matter of custom, the professors did not post final grades for the seniors until after the ceremony—no one was sure of graduating. When the Head Master called your name, you walked to the podium, made a crisp left turn, and saluted. If you graduated, he returned the salute, handed you a diploma, and shook your hand. If you failed, He did not return the salute and stood completely still. You made a back step, turned, and marched off the platform. How you reacted to either situation was a matter of personal honor and decorum.

Because of his high cadet rank, Todd was one of the first to cross to the podium to receive his diploma while the assembled parents and cadet corps cheered. Silence greeted Quincy Howe as he shuffled to the podium. He thought his father might have managed to buy him a diploma. Dills and Smathers did not even show up but sat in the Howe's carriage while it waited to take Quincy home. Quincy received no return salute, received no diploma, and no handshake.

Turning away from the headmaster, Quincy stalked across the platform with an upraised chin and haughty air, reminding Todd of cartoons of a haughty admiral. Quincy marched directly to the waiting carriage pulled by matched geldings.

A driver clothed in bright red livery sat stiffly, holding the reins. Quincy mounted and sat beside the driver, jerked the reins from the driver's hands, grabbed the whip from its socket, and cracked it near the heads of the horses. They bolted into action and galloped down the dirt road with Quincy still cracking the whip. His departure received notice only in derision. He failed his senior year. Todd felt embarrassment and pity for Quincy. America winning the war put an end to Quincy's royal lifestyle.

Todd shook off the thoughts of the Academy as he rode into town. A closed sign hung on the door of the sheriff's office. The deputy who delivered the message sat on the porch of the office, smoking a cigar in a leaned back straight chair. He jerked his thumb toward the end of town.

"Put your horse in the stable. You got to wait, college boy."

Todd was suspicious but did as the deputy ordered. He wondered why he had received an urgent message to come to town and then being told to wait.

He led his horse into the stable, but the stable master was not there, so after unsaddling Eagle he put him into a stall.

"It is good you unsaddled your horse, dirt clod, because you will not be needing him." The words came from the tack room. Todd started at the sound of the voice but recognized it immediately.

"I would guess the girly voice came from Quincy," Todd said as he stepped into the main room of the barn.

"You are done talking mean to me," Quincy said as he moved into the space between the haymows. He held a pitchfork with tines pointing forward, aiming at Todd's chest. Todd experienced a mixture of anger and fear.

4

"What are you doing with the pitch fork?" Todd asked warily. "You have never pitched hay in your life, judging by your puffy little white hands."

"It is hog sticking time," Quincy said with a sneer on his fat face, "and you is the hog."

"Where are your buddies? You never do anything without a backup."

"Right here, plow boy," a voice with a British accent said as a short youth stepped out of the shadows with a larger fellow beside him. Both wore a sword at their side.

"Well, well," Todd said, "Dills and Smathers backing you up like you planned it."

Todd said the words in a casual manner as he picked up a singletree bound with iron collars and hitch eyes on the ends, a swivel in the center. It was a wagon part used to equalize the pull of the traces—made from a fat piece of hickory three feet long. He found it leaning against the wall near the harnesses that were hanging from pegs.

Without warning, Quincy charged. The sudden attack caught Todd off balance. The tines of the pitchfork were only a few feet from his chest when he swung the singletree. The blow knocked the fork from Quincy's hands, sending the broken handle and the tines spinning toward the wall. Todd's hand dropped to the loaded pistol at his hip, but he did not pull it.

"So the farmer coward is going for a gun," Quincy said. "Why can't you fight like a man?" he asked, stepping back quickly beside his friends.

Todd did not intend to pull the gun. The threat was not yet sufficient, and his training as a cadet hardened him against taunts and insults. His fear subsided as the adrenalin quickened his senses, readying him for action.

Quincy's two friends crowded beside their leader with drawn swords in their right hands, smirks on their faces. Todd knew Dills was left-handed and up to something.

"Let me have him first," Quincy said as he drew his sword. He stood somewhat sideways with his left arm behind his body. "Our cowardly troops may have lost one war, but I am going to win this one. I plan to open your belly, dung heap, and string your guts from one end of town to the other."

He lunged forward with a long dagger held low in his left hand, ready for an upward thrust to Todd's stomach. He held the sword high in his right hand to distract Todd, and ready to deliver a chopping blow.

Todd sidestepped the lunge, swinging the singletree and landing a hard blow to Quincy's ribs.

Todd, still unbalanced, changed the force of his swing upward and then pivoted as Dills lunged with his sword now in his left hand. Todd swung the singletree downward, deflecting the sword, and smashing him high on the upper arm, shattering the bone and shoulder socket. Dills stumbled a few steps and then fell against Quincy, still staggering and gasping for air because of the blow to his ribs.

Quincy tripped in the hay, dropping his sword. Still gasping for breath, he fell because of the impact of Dills' body against his. His left shoulder struck the floor, driving the upraised blade of his dagger into his guts. Quincy screamed in fear and pain. His friend, Dills, fell beside him, also screaming and holding his broken sword arm.

Quincy screamed again and rolled to his back, the handle of his own dagger protruding from the center of his bloated belly.

"You stabbed him! You murdered him!" yelled Smathers as he lunged at Todd with his sword. Still holding the singletree, Todd ducked the clumsy slash of the sword and swung the heavy wagon part low, striking Smather's hip, sending him to smash against the wall.

"The Sheriff knows about this, and you are going to prison for attacking us," yelled Smathers, lying on the stable floor holding his damaged hip. He sobbed, tears running down his cheeks.

Todd backed away with his hand on the pistol butt, the pistol still not drawn. He glanced around to see if there were any more attackers. He was breathing hard and his eyes moved quickly.

"You guys best take yourselves and Quincy to the doctor," Todd said with a concerned note in his voice. "Dills has one good arm, Smathers, you may limp but you can walk. If you see the Sheriff, tell him he missed the whole ambush and should have trained you better. No wonder you guys flunked out."

Todd started saddling Eagle while watching the boys. He looked up to see the startled face of the deputy looking through the unshuttered window opening. They stared into each other's eyes. The deputy ducked and ran.

Todd finished saddling and led the horse outside, carefully looking around. He mounted, pulled his scabbard rifle, and after checking the priming, laid the rifle across his lap, his right hand near the trigger. The reins were in his left hand, but the horse did not need guiding. He rode Eagle slowly, watching the two youths struggling to support the wounded and sobbing Quincy as they staggered down the street.

Todd's father, Gilbert Casey, rode into town on his galloping horse, dust following him. They met in front of the still closed Sheriff's office. As they watched, the three wounded youths struggled toward the doctor's home. Todd told his father what had happened, watching the cadets enter the doctor's door with the help of the doctor and his wife.

The sound of boots on gravel behind the Caseys caused them to turn suddenly. As Gilbert turned, he drew his pistol. Deputy Snipe stepped from behind the corner of the office with his rifle in his hands, pointing their way and wearing a tied-down pistol sagging low on his hip. He was a scrawny man who tried to make himself look dangerous.

"Point your rifle at either of us and you are a dead man," Gilbert said, aiming his pistol. "You best go help tend to those boys."

The deputy took his time but lowered the rifle. The two Casey men wheeled their horses and galloped out of town.

CHAPTER 2

ESCAPE

LATE IN THE AFTERNOON, one of Gilbert Casey's friends learned Lord Wellington Howe and the Sheriff were forming a posse to arrest Todd for attempted murder of Quincy Howe.

Following his father's advice, Todd left the farm within an hour of hearing the news of the posse and the charge. Gilbert knew the Sheriff was corrupt, and Howe remained powerful with the local judge in his pocket. The political climate was unstable, and in Gilbert's mind, it was necessary for Todd to disappear until he was able to resolve the issue.

Todd knew nothing of the posse's arrival an hour after he left or of the threat issued by Howe. Todd took his colt on a lead line behind his stallion Eagle, both horses loaded with a few possessions his parents provided. The colt was too young to ride. It wore a distinctive blaze of a white tomahawk on his forehead.

Todd's faithful dog Anvil was too old to keep up with horses but her son, Hammer, eighty or more pounds of brains and muscle, was eager to travel. The dog earned his name as a pup by gnawing off the hickory handle of Todd's favorite hammer.

Before leaving, Todd hugged his small but hard-bodied mother, and his flat-chested teenage sister Nancy. He shook his father's rough hand and stooped to pet Anvil, a large bitch that had guarded him through his teenage years. His eyes were wet with tears as he scratched her throat and then mounted, Eagle, who had carried him during his years of military training at the Academy.

Once mounted he waved to his parents, and with Hammer ready beside him, he turned away, tears running down his cheeks. His hybrid colt trailing on a lead line he cantered out of the farmyard, guiding the animals toward the mountains.

Gilbert Casey and his wife Lucy watched Todd until he disappeared around a curve in the narrow dirt road. Gilbert knew the

Sheriff was involved with Lord Howe and passed the word to his neighbors, telling them he might need help. His military service in the war was well known, and he had many loyal friends.

Following his dad's instructions, Todd rode southwest, backtracking and zigzagging over several ranges west of the Shenandoah Valley. During the lonely night, his thoughts returned to the military Academy that was his home during four years of study and discipline.

He saw the old, well-used brick buildings in his mind. The campus consisted of the large timber-framed horse barn and three brick buildings, each three stories high, built like boxes with chimneys at both ends. Each building contained a wide central stairway to allow the cadets to enter and leave quickly. Each retained its distinctive smells and its unique creaks of stairs and floors.

The buildings were severe in their furnishings, decorated with flags and rough, functional furniture. An occasional portrait looked down from the walls. The entrance hall of each building, displayed a yellow flag with a coiled rattlesnake and the words, "DON'T TREAD ON ME" written across the bottom.

He loved the Gadsden flag with the coiled rattlesnake. Every freshman soon knew it as the first official flag of the newly forming nation, flown on its naval ships in 1775. Beside it stood the Betsy Ross flag of 1776, red and white stripes, with thirteen stars on a field of blue.

The stable for the Cavalry horses, their fodder, and tack emitted the strong smell of horses and hay with a hint of leather. Todd savored the smell of the barn and his daily task of caring for and grooming his personal Cavalry horse, Eagle. The stallion was a gleaming chestnut color, well-muscled, and standing seventeen hands tall—a horse of fine breeding. Eagle was loyal, smart, and loved Todd, who relied on him as a solid anchor of friendship through the hard years of the cadet life. Todd's young dog, Hammer, who had received training beside Todd and Eagle, lived in the barn with the horses.

All of the buildings smelled of heartwood pine used for timbers and flooring. One building served as a barracks which also smelled of sweat and shoe polish. Another, used as an academic building, smelled musty and somewhat moldy because of the library. The other contained the mess hall, administration offices, and the offices for the professors. It always smelled of food, usually the aroma of cabbage soup and braised beef. It stayed somewhat warm in winter because of the cooking fire, but in summer, it was hotter than the other buildings. Its cool, deep cellar was filled with supplies, cured hams, smoked meats, and slabs of side bacon and fatback as well as piles of meat buried in salt on long tables. There were vegetables home canned in glass jars, as well as vegetables in bins or covered in dirt.

A tall, wooden flagpole flying the stars and stripes stood in front of the Academy. Surrounding the flagpole was an area paved with flat stones, grass filling in on the edges and in the cracks. It served as the official station for making announcements, flag ceremonies, and the officer's gathering area. West of it lay four acres of flat field, kept mowed by a flock of sheep. Cadets from previous classes split the rails and built the fence surrounding the field. Beyond the flagpole, a wide gate opened into the field. The width allowed companies of cadets to march through as a unit.

No grass grew in the field around the fenced area. It was worn bare by the galloping Cavalry horses and thousands of footfalls of marching cadets. The first year students, known as Rats, were responsible for policing up the horse and sheep droppings before each drill session or parade.

Across from the parade grounds was a group of small homes where the professors lived. Near them was a large wooden building of one large room that housed the first year students, half of whom would drop out before the year ended.

The cadets wore gray woolen trousers with a tight blue blouse, decorated with woven gold colored cords on their shoulders and various symbols of rank and accomplishment. All of the cadets wore the same basic uniform and looked alike on purpose.

The students were a varied group from many economic, political, and social levels. Each went there due to the patronage of a wealthy or influential person. The uniforms made them equal except for distinguishing between academic years and cadet rank. The wool uniforms were thick, heavy, and itchy. They were warm in winter and brutal in summer.

The school proclaimed two main goals. The first goal was a classic education pointing to a career serving the colonies. The second goal centered on training men to fight for, and defend, the new colonies and the new nation emerging from England's rule. Many of its graduates served in the army, fighting against the British, some against the Indians, and all against whatever they perceived as a threat to their safety or liberty.

In 1776, the Declaration of Independence had brought a new fervor to the cadet corps, as well as a tighter vision of independence and the value of the individual.

> **We hold these truths to be self-evident, all men are created equal, and they are endowed by their Creator with certain unalienable rights, among these are Life, Liberty and the pursuit of Happiness.**

All of the first year cadets knew they would be stopped dozens of times, called to attention, and ordered to recite all, or part, of the Declaration of Independence.

A great experiment emerged from the war—"One nation under God indivisible with liberty and justice for all."

"All men are created equal." Quincy hated equality and refused to accept it. Todd recognized Quincy's basic problem. Equality was contrary to many generations of customs and privileges. He remained unprepared to accept or implement such a proposition.

For the first time in history, the people would establish and ordain their own framework of a country. No tyrant or king would impose his will—the will of the people would rule.

A deep and genuine animosity emerged between some of the boys, caused by the diametrically opposed political views of the fathers and patrons. Todd's father fought as patriot, proud of being an American and proud to help forge a new nation under God, where birthright and titles held no sway. The worth of a man was demonstrated by his abilities and his integrity.

TODD RODE until dawn, set up camp after hobbling his horses, and started a fire. He fried some fatback, boiled a mess of grits, and shared the food with Hammer. Then he sacked out in a large rhododendron thicket on a mountainside a hundred feet from his campfire, his freshly charged musket at his side. His black 'puppy,' as the family called Hammer, did not appear tired from the day's travel. Todd was exhausted and pulled the dog toward him, covering them both with his blanket against the mountain chill.

At dusk, he saddled up and headed for the farm owned by Sergeant McGinnis. Everyone Todd knew simply called McGinnis 'Sergeant.' Before dawn, he found the farm deep in a hollow of the mountains. He rapped the family signal on the door. It was opened a minute later by Judith, Sergeant's tall and sturdy wife. A small child in nightclothes hugged her leg. She patted the child's head with one of her large hands with unkempt nails. She looked like she laughed easily and often.

"We had word you was a comin' soon," McGinnis said as he loomed up behind his wife. He was tall and thick, his large muscular arms covered with scars. He had a long serious face with a slightly crooked smile.

"Your dad's old scout can find anyone, anywhere," he said in a deep voice rumbling from his chest. "He left out of here last evening. He brought a lot of new information you need to know. We have fresh coffee, so come in and set a spell while we give you the news."

CHAPTER 3

THE POSSE

BEFORE DARK on the day Todd had left home, Lord Howe and his corrupt Sheriff began to cause trouble. Even as his son lay grievously injured and near death, Lord Howe finished rounding up a posse of his few friends and their servants. The sheriff added a few of the local men from the bars and led the group straight to the Casey farm. Word of the posse had reached Gilbert and he was ready.

A successful tobacco farmer and experienced military officer, Gilbert Casey acted as an aide to the governor in the formation of the Declaration of Independence and in the politics of writing a constitution. He fought in many battles and rode with George Washington. He was with the Green Mountain Boys who stole the cannons from Fort Ticonderoga and turned them on the British at Boston. Confrontation did not bother him.

Captain Casey had no slaves but he employed laborers. He also had many friends, and they responded to his call. They stood as a formidable group in front of the Casey home, awaiting Sheriff Grasty and the group gathered by Howe.

The sheriff and his posse arrived at the closed gate to the Casey farm. It was only a chain between two posts but it sent a message. Lord Wellington Howe, who looked and dressed like a nobleman, shouted orders, demanding Todd surrender himself for arrest. He cited "Todd's unprovoked attack on Quincy Howe and his peaceful cadet companions."

"He is not here," Captain Casey answered. "Besides, we all want to hear about this attack. Did my son pull his gun and shoot somebody?"

"He stabbed my boy about to death," yelled Lord Howe.

"What with? He only carries a folding knife and it has a three-inch blade. And where were the others he is said to have fought?"

"We ain't answering no more questions except he beat them boys with a singletree," the Sheriff said. "We're taking him for attempted murder of three men." The sheriff sat erect trying to puff himself up but remained a narrow shouldered, weaselly looking man.

"I met my son in front of your office. He did not have a mark on him, not any blood or any torn or dirty clothing. He told a different story, and we all know Todd is not a liar."

"Are you calling my boy and them others liars, sodbuster?" Howe shouted out the words.

Casey stood at apparent ease, but he knew the mood of the men behind him. "Stand easy," he said over his shoulder to the men.

"Mr. Howe, it is clear by your actions you cannot claim relationship with the Howe who fought at Bunker Hill. He was an Englishman, but he was a real man—no kin, I am sure."

Howe bristled, urging his horse forward. The sheriff held out his hand to stop him.

"I plan to search the house, the barns, and the farm to satisfy myself," the sheriff said with an arrogant tone of voice. "Men," he yelled to his rabble, "Get ready for a scrap. I have a belly full of this bunch of farmers. Open this gate," he shouted.

"It is not going to happen," Gilbert Casey answered. "Get off my property or face the consequences. You are trespassing."

"I say it is going to happen," replied the sheriff. "I got the men behind me to prove I can do whatever I want to do. You just have a bunch of farmers."

"Form up," Gilbert shouted over his shoulder to his gathered friends.

The men behind him shifted into two ranks, the front row kneeling with rifles in shooting position. The second rank stood behind with rifles cocked and aimed.

"Pick targets and fire at my command."

Gilbert Casey stepped forward toward the sheriff's horse, ignoring the drawn pistol leveled at his chest.

"Sheriff," he said, "we fought a war for peace and justice, and we can do it again. Many of these men here were in those battles. Now, if I were you, I would turn my horse around and take my rabble back to town before one of these muskets happens to fire by mistake—because all of these men might then fire.

"You come back here with the governor and we will talk. Do not bring papers from judge McCoy. He is a drunk and addled to boot. The governor is an honest man. You come back without him and there will be trouble.

"By the way," Gilbert continued, "the man riding beside you is the one who told my son you wanted him in town. I heard the conversation. He shouted it like a command as he rode away real quick, but I recognized him as your deputy, Snipe. He is the same man who sent my boy to the livery stable, and the same man who witnessed the fight peeping through the window, and the same one who threatened us with his rifle in front of your office. It looks like you and he are involved in this frame up, and it is you and Snipe who need arresting."

The sheriff cursed, tightening his hand on the reins of his horse. The deputy rested his hand on the butt of his pistol.

"Men," Gilbert Casey said over his shoulder. "Keep your eyes on those two edgy lawmen. Fire if they aim a gun."

The sheriff quickly dropped his pistol into its holster.

"Mr. Howe," Gilbert continued as he turned to the man riding behind the sheriff. "I am sorry your boy fell on his own dagger. You should be home tending him and not out here trumping up charges against my son with a bunch of lies. Now get off this land! Take your king lovers and your bought sheriff with you. Get!"

The sheriff and the deputy stared at the barrels of twelve muskets aimed at them. The sheriff swore, wheeled his horse, and kicked him into a canter. The rest of the rabble followed, but Lord Howe lingered a moment.

"This is not over, Casey. Your boy Todd is marked to die. Until it happens, he better ride looking over his shoulder." He turned his horse and galloped away.

Not liking the situation, most of the men in the posse were happy to retreat in the face of superior odds and experience, and most were happy that the upstart spawn of Howe lay stricken at home. Only Sheriff Grasty, his deputy, Snipe, and Howe were infuriated. Their anger arose from their failure to kill Todd, not because of the well-deserved wounds of the corpulent Quincy.

One who rode with the posse later told Gilbert about the muttered conversations as they bunched up to talk on the way back to town. The sheriff, Snipe, and Howe had been riding out ahead.

CHAPTER 4

PROVISIONS

AFTER HEARING THE NEWS about the posse from the Sergeant, Todd leaned back. He tried to digest the importance of the information his father passed on by Scout who had arrived two days before. No one knew his actual Indian name, so they all called him Scout as if Scout was his name. He had no trouble relaying Todd's father's message word for word, as trained in the army. Raised in an Indian village, he was a lone wolf and a wilderness expert but dedicated to Gilbert Casey.

Based on the information from Scout, the Sergeant and Judith decided Todd would be in danger for a long time. He needed to disappear from the Shenandoah Valley until things changed. The reality hit Todd suddenly, and his eyes filled with tears. He wiped them away and turned his back on his friends, pretending to be looking for Hammer who sat quietly by the door. He said a few words to the dog to calm himself, turning back to Sergeant and Judith with a forced smile.

"Todd, you need to bed down in the loft of the barn after something to eat. We'll finish getting the stuff together. From up there you can keep a lookout just in case. I do not know why anyone would come this way looking for you, but it is better to play it safe.

"Let me tell you something so you will know. When we was discharged from the army, your daddy loaned us enough money for me and Judith to start a trading post down the road about a mile. We have most of the things you need at the store. We have a soldier who lost a leg in the war tending the store when we are away. We made a room for him so he lives there.

"Your daddy said in his note your packhorse is too high strung and too young to carry much stuff, so we are loading a big black workhorse with all the equipment you will need. He is about eighteen hands, and young but strong. His feet are as big as dinner plates. His name is Bill.

16

We do not need him because we have his parents here at the farm and another team we rent at the trading post in town."

"My dad will repay you for what you are doing for me," Todd said as he worked on bundling supplies.

"Todd, do not you worry yourself none. Your daddy will make things right, but we do not want or expect nothing. He saved me twice, and I saved him once, so this makes us even again—not that anyone is counting of course."

Before supper, Sergeant went to the house to clean up while Todd remained in the barn working on the supplies. As he worked, riders arrived at the farm, riding roughshod right up to the front door and pounding on it with a rifle butt. Both the coloring of the horse and the shape of the lead rider looked familiar. He watched the exchange and the negative shake of Sergeant's head and his wife shaking hers.

As they rode away, Todd slipped down to the house, staying in the shadow areas in case the riders left someone behind.

"Them is some of them," Sergeant said with a laugh. "It is not a real posse—no sheriff or deputy—only six men that did not look like much except for one wearing his gun down low. They asked if we noticed a rider going by on the trail. As I recall you did not go by, so me and the wife was right to say no. The boy they say you stabbed is still in bad shape and his father, a Lord Howe, has given these men money and wants them to hunt you down for a bounty.

"They are to take you back to the county seat where you will stand trial as an exhibit of the violence by patriots. They will try to implicate your father and seize his land and holdings.

"The one doing the talking, and saying too much, acted arrogant, like he is special or something. He jerked the head of his horse around rough like, and headed to the next farm."

"Tell Todd about them trying to catch him at his daddy's farm," Judith said.

"Before we talk," Todd said, "let me say that the man who did the talking reminds me of the deputy sheriff by the name of Snipe. Snipe called me to town, and he sent me to the stable—and it was him I saw looking through the window, after the fight with the boys. He is no doubt tight with the sheriff, and we know the sheriff is paid off by Howe and his buddies."

"Those facts changes things," the Sergeant said. "If the leader is a deputy, he has some experience and is more dangerous. We better set a watch. I reckon your daddy will have a thing or two to say about putting you on trial if caught. They is looking for any excuse to cause him trouble. Your pa, working with a government man broke up some of Howe's deals with the British when he tried to divert our guns and supplies to the British soldiers.

"Howe's ships were supposed to be working for us but he was double dealing. It is my opinion, and Judith agrees, this whole frame up is to get back at your father. The Howe boy may have a personal hate for you, but this here Lord Howe is behind it all to hurt your pa.

"Well," continued Sergeant, "if they still represent a defeated King they is in bad shape here in America. We do not take to intimidation. Your pa and I fought in the King's uniform against the Indians and the French, but we was in fact fighting for this country. Afterwards, we both fought for the Colonies. Now that we have the Declaration of Independence and have won a war we is a nation. I know you is a patriot too."

The posse riders only appeared to leave but stopped about a mile down the road. The sun had not set so the posse stretched out, passed a bottle around, and smoked cigars.

The leader returned to the farm on foot long after dark. Hammer nudged Todd awake. He appeared upset and a low rumble came from his throat as he watched through a crack between two boards in the loft of the barn. Todd watched with him and soon saw the shadowy form of a man.

The man moved to an open window of Sergeant's cabin and appeared to be listening intently. Soon he looked like he was about to climb in. From the darkness, Sergeant's voice boomed. He reached out and grabbed the shirt collar of the intruder. The man whirled around, drawing his pistol and aiming it at Sergeant's side.

"Is you peeping at my wife?" Sergeant shouted.

"I ain't a peeper and didn't lay eyes on your wife, but aim to kill you if you don't call Todd to come out."

"We told you we did not see nobody go by."

"Why is you out here skulking in the bushes if you ain't protecting the boy?"

"I is checking for skunks—found me one."

"No man talks to me like that. Two men what did is dead down by Savannah. Now you call the boy or it is your time to pay."

"He ain't aiming to call nobody," a voice said as the barrel of a Brown Bess jammed the deputy in the back. "And you sure ain't killing my husband."

"Lady, I can kill him faster than you can pull the trigger."

"It might be true but you would end up in two pieces 'cause the gun is loaded with heavy shot. Is you coming as the law?"

"Lady, I ain't the law today and you asking means the Casey boy has told you. My deputy badge is in the office. I want you to know I intend to kill both of you and the kid, but he is the one going back across a saddle because I got me a big reward coming. I know the kid is here 'cause I caught a glimpse of his pony in a bald up on the side of yonder hill."

The man appeared to relax as he spoke but he suddenly twisted, trying to aim his pistol at Judith. She expected his move and pulled the trigger. Blood squirted from several places in the ruin of his chest. He bled out and died with a grimace on his face.

"That was a close call," Todd said as he moved up to them. "I have been working around for a place to shoot without hitting you two. Snipe kept too close to you. This kind of fighting was easy when we were practicing at the institute, and killing seemed easy. Trying to creep around to line up a shot knowing he might make his play any time and kill one of you really scared me. I never had that feeling before."

"I- de- clare," Judith said. "I often considered whether or not I would be able to shoot a man if need be. The Sergeant said killing weren't hard if the time called for it and he is plum correct."

"I' m sorry you were forced to do it, Judith," Todd said. "It sure is not pretty up close. As much as I disliked the man, it is no satisfaction to see him covered with blood. The memory will bother both of us for a spell. Remember, you did not only save Sergeant, but yourself and me— three lives saved for one lost."

"What a wife!" Sergeant expounded as he grabbed her and swung her around. "But listen, horses is a coming. It is them others. Judith, charge your gun and go into the house to a shooting spot. Todd, you stay in the bushes and keep your dog still. Let me talk to them boys."

The riders galloped to the front of the house and pulled their horses to a stop. Sergeant stood erect, a Brown Bess held across his chest with the hammer back. "Let me say a word to save you some trouble," he said in a deep voice filled with battleground authority. "You are under three guns, which will take most of you the first shot because they are scatter guns. Now you stay bunched up while we talk. The man who was leading you was blowed in half trying to peep at my wife."

"Sir," the lead rider said, "we was not agreeing to this and are proud he got his self shot. He is, or was, a deputy and a mean man paid by the one who calls himself a Lord. Calling him a Lord just do not set well with us, no way. Some of us who rode the night we tried to take Todd at the Casey farm are of the opinion Quincy Howe tried to kill Todd, and afterward he tried to frame him for his own hurt.

"We know the sheriff is in it because the stable keeper is riding behind me. The sheriff paid him to stay away for a spell. Me, and them others behind me, work for some of Howe's friends so we needed to ride to keep our jobs. Besides, no one has an idea which direction Todd has went. He might be anywhere. The deputy decided to go south and we have not seen or heard any sign of Todd."

"You sound like a man of good sense," Sergeant said.

'Well Sir, here is the man's horse, so let us load him across the saddle and we will make ourselves long gone."

"Stay in a bunch. Over there by the house is the body. Two of you load it up and move on. In your report to Howe, tell him this is the way we handle men who trouble our women."

The men left, waving their hats and were glad that they were off the trail of the Casey boy, whom they admired. Sergeant and Todd remained outside listening while Hammer moved around the premises. Judith brought out bowls of food, and they sat on the ground discussing what happened. Judith shed a few tears about the killing.

They heard nothing. The dog appeared satisfied so they set up shifts for guard duty, and those off duty went to bed. The guard was concealed in the mountain laurel bushes near the driveway, cradling a shot-filled Brown Bess.

In the early morning of the third day, the animals were loaded. There were no more bounty hunters, so Sergeant now was sure that the posse had returned the body to Howe and been disbanded.

"Are you going to be all right, Sir?" Todd asked. "You have helped me, but I will not leave if you need me."

"You go on. This country will need men like you. Your pa and I will fight on, but one day your generation must step up to build this nation, if we ever get one started. We have won the war of bayonets and bullets, but now the political war starts. We have agreed on our Declaration of Independence, but now we need a government that listens to the voice of the people.

"It is important for you to live to fight another day, so start your horses and ride over a ridge or two as soon as you can. Watch your back trail, but I doubt those men will try to follow you. By dawn, trappers and such will start heading west and will cover your tracks."

"Thank you, Sir, and please keep an eye on my dad. He is going to have a lot of pressure because of me."

"That is what fathers and their friends are for Todd. Remember that what we give you today is meant for tomorrow."

CHAPTER 5

SARAH

WELL TO THE NORTH AND EAST of Todd's location, Sarah sobbed in terror because of what her mother, Pearl, kept telling her about her sickness—she was dying. Sarah helped her mother up from the bed, and together they knelt beside a large campaign chest. Pearl steadied herself with one hand on the edge of the chest.

"Sarah, help your ma by lifting up the lid of this here chest. When you get it open, start pulling out them guns what is in it."

Sarah took out a matched pair of pistols in a double holster gun belt and a scatter-gun with two huge barrels of 88 Caliber. It looked like two large caliber muskets with short barrels welded together to form a double barrel gun with two hammers. It fit well in a simple, well-worn, and stained leather horse scabbard.

Sarah looked up at her mother, tears still on her face. Sarah still had a look of youth and innocence. Her high cheekbones and wide spaced brown eyes complemented her full mouth. Her chin strong, but rounded, spoke of a handsome woman lurking behind the still somewhat immature face. She looked into the chest, away from the pain in her mother's face.

In a finely tooled case there lay a long gun with a long and heavy octagon barrel of 44 calibers. The stock showed tooling around the grip and light glinted off fine chestnut wood. The inscription on the barrel read, "Made for Judd Shipley, by H. Y. 1770." It was a long-range rifle made by an expert gunsmith.

"These are your daddy's guns. He worked as a government man helping the colonies to rid themselves of the British. Your daddy traveled for many years and then got hisself kilt. He did not come home, but some men brought his horse, his bedroll, and the guns. You saw all this at the time they brought his stuff.

"This is all we have of your pa except for the stallion and the young dog what came with his outfit. The man said her name is Chestnut, named after the color of our hair as a reminder to him of us. She is sure enough chestnut by color and a fine dog, too. You know about the horse being a fine animal but almost too high for a woman."

"I know all that Ma."

"You take them guns, Sarah. Get them loaded with shot and later put them on the packhorse with your things. Once the animals is loaded I want you to clear out riding on the stallion till this situation is straightened out."

"Why, Ma? What is to straighten out?"

"Big Red and his two gunmen."

"I do not understand, Ma."

Sarah's fingers fondled the guns as if to touch her father, then lifted them into her arms. The pistol belt looped over her head sagged on her shoulders. The weight of the guns made her wince.

"Listen to me, Daughter. Before we wedded, I worked in a saloon with a dance stage and rooms upstairs for the girls. I danced but was not interested in seeing men, only teasing them with the dance. I was a right comely looking woman with long chestnut hair and my body stacked up real good. Your pa saved me from the dance halls and moved me west and into this cabin, created you, and we lived real good on what he was paid by the government."

"Ma, you don't have to tell me," the sixteen-year -old said to her.

"Now is the time, Daughter. As you know, I went to dancing again after your pa died to make money for living, and you danced with me like a team. You know Big Red, well, he has a desire for me, and said he for sure is a'comin to rape you and me and kill us both. His men are going to take second visits. He has said it before, but now he knows about my sickness and is a'comin' for sure. One of the girls warned me of Red's plans—that's what needs to be set straight."

"You can get well, Ma." She stroked her mother's chestnut hair.

"No, Sarah, I am a'dyin and know it, and was told early this morning about Big Red coming this evening to have the two of us. Listen to what I'm a saying."

"But Ma."

"You keep quiet and listen to your ma. Saddle your pa's horse, put a lead line to my mare, the colt, and to the cow, and load your stuff. You need cooking pans, as much food as you can tie on, gardening tools, your schoolbooks, and a few chickens in a cage. The cow can pack stuff too. When things settle down, you study them schoolbooks. I do not want you to grow up ignorant as the likes of me."

"No, Ma. I will not leave you to Big Red! I will not let you die!"

"Hush girl, and help me up and into the kitchen. Keep them guns handy, and make sure them is loaded."

Sarah laid the pistols and long guns aside. She put a hand under her mother's arm and helped her up and into the kitchen.

"Now, fetch the powder and shot, and get them guns loaded now. Do a real good job of loading the double barrel gun 'cause I may need to use it. I am fixing to cook, and after you are through loading, we are a goin' to eat. Let me fry up some sow belly and pour you a glass of buttermilk."

Sarah learned from her dad to load and prime the guns, and they were soon ready. Her mother, called her to the table in the kitchen. She was only able to walk with help, but her tall full figure was only a shadow of what it had been.

"Child, lean the shot gun beside me and put a pistol in my lap. You keep next to the long gun and the other pistol.

"You is all is left of two families, Daughter. I is a Rogers and your pa a Tranthem. Plenty of both still alive but no direct kin of ours, and all of them back far in coves in the mountains. Our parents come over on a boat together. They was born with other names—they took those names to sound more American. They lived up near Philadelphia. Your pa moved us south and into the mountains.

"Now, after we is finished you go pack what's left of your stuff into bags and gather up cooking pots and the things you will need for a long trip. Do not leave me nothin'. After the animals is loaded and strung together, take them up on the side of the mountain a ways into the trees and hobble the big horse. Come on back but keep the long gun near you at all times and carry the other pistol. If Red arrives before you come down, sneak back up to the animals, and head away from here."

"I will, Ma, but why are you so worried-looking?"

"Because Big Red is unpredictable and may show up early."

"Now you are scaring me, Ma."

"Being afraid is a way of staying alive, Sarah, and I aim for you to grow up."

"Now you are scaring me more, Ma, but I will go and load the stuff and hide them animals up on the mountain. Then I will be a comin' back."

"Let your dog Chestnut watch for Red. She will growl as she do not like Red. If you is alive after this is over, you ride to my sister's place. Her man hates us, so lay off in a hidey place till he is not there."

"Yes Ma, I will do as you say, Ma, but I am a feared."

Sarah did as her mother said, more to humor her than because she believed what she said about Big Red. She knew Red often watched her and licked his lips when he saw her dance alongside her mother. The thought worried her as she made her way back to the cabin.

Chestnut barked a warning. Big Red arrived early. He was to come in early evening, but he rode up to their cabin in the afternoon. He called to the cabin without response and sat down on the horse trough in the front yard to wait. Chestnut knew him but never liked him, so she lay down in the shade of a tree watching.

"I know you is inside, and you know I is here," Big Red hollered. "Let us make this easy and you jest open the door and invite me in. I want to visit with you and with the girl and afterwards go away peacefully."

No one responded, but Sarah's heart pounded fast. She looked at her mother, who smiled.

After a few minutes, Red walked to the back of the cabin. He was a fat man, his stomach held up by his horizontal belt buckle. He did not waddle but swaggered. He carried two pistols on his hips and carried a rifle in his arms. His face was red and a stubble of whiskers covered much of it.

He saw that the window shutters were open so he made a small bundle of dry grass, primed his pistol, added some fine pieces of grass to the pan, and fired the lock. The spark ignited the gunpowder and the small pieces of grass and it ignited the bundle. The bundle flared up, and he tossed it through the window opening onto the bed linens. He reached for the lamp, pulled off the globe and the top of the oil reservoir, tossing it into the fire. The oil ignited and flames spread across the bed. Sarah rushed into the bedroom, but the bed linens were aflame. She backed into the main room.

"Ma, the house is afire!"

"Yes, child," her mother said, "the time is come. Set me in my chair in front of the door, for I fear I am too sick to move myself from this kitchen table. Hand me your father's double barrel and stand behind the door. When I say open, you lift the bar and jerk the door open. Stay back behind the logs while I handle Red."

"What are you fixing to do, Ma?"

25

"Listen to me, Sarah. You do what your ma says. Do not hesitate none; quick jerk it open when I tells you. Now peek out through a chink and tell me where Red is."

"He is a sitting on the stool in front of the water trough."

Pearl Tranthem straightened in the chair, readied the gun, and sighted toward the closed door.

"Now! Daughter," Pearl said sternly.

Sarah jerked open the door and her father's gun belched its load of buckshot, wadding, and smoke.

Big Red rocked backward with the impact of the shot but recovered enough to swivel the rifle in his lap and fire. Sarah's mother jerked back in her chair, sighted the shotgun, and fired the second barrel. Big Red took the heavy shot in his chest—blowing him against the horse trough. He slid to the ground and lay still.

Sarah's mother sat upright, smiled, and said, "Daughter, you did good. Take this gun, charge it, and mount your horse and head south. There is more a comin' behind Red."

"No, Ma. I will not leave!"

"Daughter, has you noticed the cabin is afire and both of us is about to burn? I is shot bad and is dying. You get, and get fast," she gasped.

"No, Ma. Let me help you."

"Your pa and I loved you, Child. Now leave and someday set things straight."

Pearl said no more, slumped over, and slid sideways from the chair, her bodice soaked with blood. Flames, smoke, and heat billowed into the room. Sarah threw up her hands and cried out in anguish before dropping to her knees and feeling for her mother's pulse. She knew she was dead. Gulping back tears, she closed her mother's eyes and touching her face, she broke down with racking sobs.

Feeling the intense heat, she grabbed the gun from her mother's limp hands, stripped off her ring, picked up the pistol and the other guns, and ran out of the cabin door. She ran into the woods, mounted her father's horse Thunder, and led the packhorses and the cow deeper into the forest, angling to intersect the trail south.

She sobbed and retched up her breakfast when the cabin roof caved in, sending up a spiral of sparks as two of Red's men galloped into the clearing. They had seen Big Red beside the horse trough, dismounting to run to him. While they were busy with Red, Sarah urged the animals behind a cluster of hemlock trees.

Sarah was no longer able to see the cabin. A few minutes later, she arrived at the south trail leading away from the cabin and away from town. She was walking her animals on the trail, stunned, and crying—not noticing the sound of hooves on the hard packed dirt.

"Sarah," a voice shouted. "Is your cabin burning?"

Orah Smith, a neighbor from a farm two miles away rode up, his son with him.

"Yes, Mr. Smith, and Ma has been shot by Big Red and burned in the fire after killing him. His two men rode in a few minutes after I went in the woods and I just now come out here."

"Quick, do as I say. Zeke," he said to his son, "take Sarah's lead line and take those animals up the old cut off trail. Sarah, you follow Zeke. I'm going to ride in and try to delay Red's men from following you."

"Oh, Orah," she said forgetting her manners and using his given name. He was a deacon in their church. "You ride careful because them is as bad as Red."

Orah nudged his horse with his heel and cantered up the trail toward the smoke. Zeke called to her, heading away from the road and up an old trail long grown over with young hemlocks and shaded by towering tulip poplars. Sarah followed for an hour or more, until they stopped in a small clearing under the shadow of a large cliff towering beside them.

She recognized the place where her family would come on hot days to rest in the cool shadows and have a picnic. Sometimes they came to spend the night camping. Remembering her father and mother sent a stab of anguish through her being. In her mind, she was able to see them.

Zeke dismounted and helped the sobbing Sarah down off her horse. The animals grazed on the tender grass, and the chickens clucked in their cramped cages when set down level. Sarah sat on the ground, her knees pulled up and her head cradled between her hands.

Two hours later Orah Smith appeared, coming through the woods but not from the trail.

"Some neighbors showed up," Orah said, as Sarah looked up. "We found your ma and has buried her fine. Red's men has took Red's body to town to stir up trouble. They is claiming he was ambushed by you and plan to raise up a party of men to hunt you down. They noticed the missing chickens and stock so figure you planned it out. I hate to trouble you with all of this but you need to know."

"It is not true. Let me tell you how it happened," Sarah said haltingly, her face still streaked with tears. She gave the details of the killings.

"Well, I believe what you say. Me and my horse went up and down the trail at the cut off to mess up the tracks, but I doubt any of the gang will be riding before noon tomorrow. Red's men found a wad of cash in his pocket and plan on a big party at his burying."

Orah left his son to help Sarah make camp. Later, Orah's wife Clovis came into the camp from the south.

"Orah told me what has happened and thought you needed a woman to talk with. I brung some food so we can rest up, and then you can start on your way real early."

"I am bad scared, Clovis. I need to be out of this land."

"I understand, Sarah, and agree. No telling what a bunch will do when drunk. The moon will be up in an hour. Rest a spell, and Zeke will take you through the woods by moonlight and lead you over the ridge. I reckon nobody can pick up your tracks once you are off this mountain. You have any idea where you is heading?"

"Thank you, Clovis. I got a need to head out of here to where my mother's sister lives about fifty miles from here. It is best I don't tell you to keep you out of trouble should the law or anybody come asking."

"I understand and appreciate it, Sarah," she said as she wrapped her ample arms around the thin, sobbing girl.

CHAPTER 6

THE SHIPLEYS

THREE DAYS AFTER LEAVING THE SERGEANT, Todd Casey, trying to avoid traveled roads, struck one decent trail following a fast moving river with steep rocky escarpments on both sides. It looked like a gorge or ravine with a steep upward pitch. The trail lacked good cover, and it proved impossible to travel off the trail. After several hours of watching and listening as he rode, he had not heard or seen another soul. The river took a sharp bend and the land leveled and opened up into a wide valley. The water of the river flowed smoothly, not like the boiling rapids he had passed in the gorge.

A small trail veered to the left leading down to the river and a sandy beach. Two covered wagons were parked near the river. Beside them were a canvas shelter and a tent, and near the shelter a cooking fire. A dozen hobbled horses were nearby eating the lush grass. Four of the large ones were wagon horses. All of the horses were fine animals.

A sturdy looking man of about forty stepped out from beside one wagon and flagged Todd down. Todd rested his right hand on a pistol at his side.

"Mister, it ain't my business but some men have come by two nights asking for a young man about your age with two horses—a young one with a white blaze on its head looking like a tomahawk. The rider is said to have a tall dark brown animal with no white at all. Your horses sure fit the description except they did not mention the workhorse with those huge hooves carrying a pack of stuff. I was born to horse traders and all I know is horses. You happen to have a mighty fine stallion and a well bred colt. Your black work horse is a good specimen too."

With his hand still resting on the butt of his pistol Todd replied. "Go on mister, I'm listening."

"Don't fret, son. I ain't no horse thief and we ain't fixin' to cause you no trouble, but is warning you them men may try coming back again tonight. They acted haughty, and smart-alecky, and they said the man they was looking for stabbed their friend who lay next to death up the valley near Richmond. A traveler mentioned to them he might have seen someone of the description I gave you camping around the river somewhere."

The man looked up at Todd and smiled. The smile stopped at a long scar on the side of his rectangular face. The hands holding his rifle across his chest looked large and thick. Todd studied the man and relaxed.

"Well," Todd said, "they are looking for me. Their friend is a bully. We went to military school together, and I had better grades and more rank than he did. His daddy is a king lover, and my daddy is all about building this country of ours.

"So you see there is bad blood between us. This man, Quincy Howe, and his English friends wanted to beat and kill me. Anyhow, after a struggle with his friends egging him on, Quincy pulled a dagger on me. I do not know much about dagger, fighting, but the fancy Royal people like to threaten you with a sword in one hand and at first opportunity stick you with the dagger. My instructor taught me the trick. I hit Quincy with a singletree and he tripped in the hay, fell on the dagger, and was bad hurt in the gut. He was hurt after he made the lunge at me. I am talking too much but have not said a word in days except to my horse or dog, and they aren't much for conversation."

"You keep on talking, son, it will do you good," the man said.

"They started the fight in the livery stables, and that was where I found the singletree by the harnesses and whacked him and his buddies real hard as they tried to poke me with their swords. I put my hand on my gun but did not pull it. They did not bother me more because they were hurt bad. I mounted my horse and told them to take the stuck one to a doctor, quick. I was watching to make sure they made it to the doctor when my father came galloping in and we rode home. An hour or so later Dad sent me away to a friend of his.

"In the evening a posse came by to arrest me but my pa, Gilbert Casey, and some of his old troopers ordered them away at gunpoint. They told them to come back with the governor who lives not far away, up the valley, and if they came back with only the sheriff, prepare to be shot.

"The sheriff is a friend of the one who calls himself a Lord. The governor is a fair man. My pa did some Indian soldiering out by the big river and served as an officer in the war. They knew not to mess with him. I wasn't there to see it but have been told."

"Well," the listener said, "my name is Eli Shipley. This here scar you has noticed is from a Redcoat cavalry sword in the war. I always tried to be shy of swords, but one cut me when I was looking somewhere else. I can understand how you was feeling with three swords against a singletree. I would have swung it mighty hard too.

"I believe your story," Shipley continued. "Now here is what I suggest. Do you see the rocky point back over there? To my thinking, you should take the horses and walk them through the field and behind the rocks. Try not to leave tracks and stick to the grazed area. My boy Putt will ride his horse back and forth a few times and mess any tracks you might have left coming in here or going behind the point. Keep watch. If the men come and leave without finding you, you are welcome to mosey on over and have some vittles. We got fried fish and biscuits planned for supper about sundown. We have plenty of fixins, but the kid needs to catch us a few more fish because you look like you have not eat much of late. Understand this, son. I ain't a lyin' any, but will not volunteer any information if the gang shows up."

Late in the afternoon three riders galloped into the camping area. Eli stepped out carrying his rifle.

"You seen the varmint we been looking for? He is the one who tries to kill folks by taking them in the gut with a dagger," the uniformed leader said.

"No sir, you are the only varmints I recall seeing all day."

No one smiled, and the one with a plumed hat and rank stripes on the sleeve of his cadet uniform urged his horse forward, smacking Eli Shipley across the face with his riding crop.

A metallic click followed as the traveler's wife cocked her Brown Bess and poked the barrel over the side of the wagon, lifting the canvas just enough to aim.

"You boys better ride on about your business," Shipley said as he wiped the blood off his face with his hand. "If my wife do not kill all three of you with her scatter gun, my kid with his short barrel will finish up. You ride on and leave us alone. I do not guess you see who you are looking for. It is best you go back home before some man kills all three of you just for fun. And you mister," he said pointing his rifle at the man wearing the plumed hat, "has best be careful who you whack with your crop. My finger was on the trigger and the gun aimed at your chest. If I chose, I would have killed you before your crop ever touched my face. The next man will kill you for sure."

The pimple-faced shrimp with the funny hat and the rank stripes moved his arm to strike with his crop again. One of the others spoke softly.

"If you is looking to get dead, Hundley, go ahead and whack. We sure ain't looking forward to taking your parts back to your mama in a grain sack. Lets ride out of here, go home, and send some of Lord Howe's scum out here. Except for what the old couple told us two days ago, Casey may not even be in these parts. The old coot did not even remember the colt that he is said to be leading. His woman was about to pee her pants and would have said anything if she knew it."

"Hundley Tarter," a heavy set youth said, "you may sit straight like a general but my saddle feels like a washboard, and my butt is sticking in the grooves. I bet yours has grown to your saddle too. I am for going home. I am taking Dill's place because his arm has not worked right since the fight. I do not much care for this manhunt so that you can curry favor with Lord Howe. Don't forget, our side lost and we ain't among friends out here way past the edge of civilization."

The uniformed Hundley, trying to look like something he would never be, swore, wheeled his horse like a general in battle, charged back to the main trail, and headed north.

"Thanks, Mr. Shipley," a voice from behind a pile of stones said. "If your family missed, I planned to back them up," Todd said quietly. He knew Hundley.

"I seen you move in," Shipley said, "and was hoping the big black dog of yours would keep quiet."

"If trouble started, you would have seen a flash of dog and the saddle of one horse would be empty. He took training along with me in college—he was a much better student. His name is Hammer."

"Do you know anything about the uniform the one who hit me was wearing?"

"Yes sir, it is from the military academy where I graduated."

"Come on in here, Eli," his wife Dorcus said. "Let me put some salve on your face. It is sure going to puff up soon. Our old hound is a guardin' us from under the wagon, but Hammer will let us know if there is any trouble."

Mrs. Shipley stood in the back of the covered wagon holding back a canvas flap. She was a full-bodied woman with a round face, most of which was involved with her wide smile and blue eyes. She spoke with a slight German inflection.

"Mr. Shipley," Todd said, "Before you go to be doctored, let me say a word. I admire you for standing still as you did. Most men would have pulled a gun and killed for a blow like Hundley gave you."

"I reckon it is part of being a man. It is a bad trade to swap a life for a whack."

During supper, they joked about Hundley's outfit as they filled their bellies. By the time dark came and things were put away, they sat around the fire becoming better acquainted.

Todd awoke at dawn and was soon ready to say his goodbyes, but the black sky filled with lightning to the west portended a stormy day. He sipped coffee from a burning hot tin cup as he sat across the cook fire from Mr. Shipley and his family. He had a deep respect for the man after the incident with Hundley. Hundley looked like a jerk wearing his cadet uniform years after graduation, but Todd knew from long experience that Hundley was twisted and dangerous.

"The one with the hat and the uniform is Hundley. He graduated a year ahead of me, and picked me out to give me trouble. He is a sadistic monster, and he has a hate for me."

"Well," Eli said, "I hope you two will never meet because only one is going to live. Do not hesitate a second or believe anything he says. He's one who deserves to die young."

"You can believe Eli," Dorcus said. "He has a way of reading people and don't make many mistakes. It's why he counts you as a friend."

"Well," Eli said. "I doubt Hundley will be back because he is a coward and not likely to face real guns. Just in case, we will keep our eyes and ears open. I do not fear much but I do fear a fool."

The sky darkened and a spatter of rain followed a gust of wind. Dorcus Shipley gathered up the pans and dishes from around the fire.

"I don't guess any of us will start moving today. With a storm coming we best bed down and wait it out," Shipley said. "Best you unload your horses and stow your stuff under the far wagon and pull a cover over it. Both wagons are ours and the boy sleeps in the far one. You are welcome to join him tonight. Today we can sit around in this wagon here. We move most of the clutter into the tent if we stop for a spell. We may could find ourselves holed up for several days by the feel of things."

"You are right about Hundley and his boys not liking the odds to be even, or against them. I do not think he will be back against your firepower, but I have caused you too much trouble. I will be moving out when the weather clears."

CHAPTER 7

THE HORSEMEN

"NO SIR, PUTTING YOU UP WITH A STORM a comin' is no trouble at all," Eli Shipley said. "I have been studying about your pa's name, Gilbert Casey. I have heard about him helping to organize the colonies to encourage them to get together. We have too many ideas right now to try to pull them all into agreement. Even the Resolve Agreement of 74 is not strong enough, but the 1776 Declaration did a good enough job so we pulled together and has about won the war. Cornwallis surrendered, but England has not yet signed no treaty."

"Yes, sir, we have yet to make our Constitution, but my dad and a lot of others are trying to smooth out ruffled feathers and start men thinking about working together toward a real peace. We have been so independent from trying to survive that we have not been looking forward enough."

The storm came with wind and rain and lasted for three days. Finally, the rain let up, but the earth, the grass, and the foliage were still wet and the air heavy. On the third evening, the clouds were breaking up as five men stopped on the main trail and checked the priming of their pistols. They talked together for a few minutes and then headed down the trail to the river.

"Them is mighty rough-looking men," Dorcus said.

"They is," Eli said. "Putt, take our dog and your shotgun and go to your wagon. Do it quick and keep out of sight. Todd, you need to go back to the rock pile with the double barrel of yours, your pistol, and your quiet dog. Dorcus, go to your hidey spot with your scatter gun."

The three of them said, "yes sir" and they all moved.

The five bedraggled men were draped with oiled rider's coats but their legs and boots were soaked. Their hats dragged down around their ears, and the horses were wet and mud splattered.

"Hello the wagon," the man in the lead hollered to hail the wagon occupants.

"Hello to you too," Eli said from the side of his wagon. His long gun rested on the top of a wheel, pointed in their direction.

"We don't intend no harm to you folk. For the past few days we has been a looking for someone, and for two of those days we has been squattin' under a ledge overhang in this rain. We is cold, wet, and hungry. We don't feel like much palaver, but we do want to ask some questions."

"Questions is cheap so ask away," Eli said. "But here is some advice. Do not try to spread out none. Stay bunched like you is and we will get along fine."

"A cautious man, but I don't see no backup. If a man gives advice, he should have some authority."

"I has plenty. If you try to make your move, you will end up dead real quick. Go on and ask your questions."

"We represent the men of the King from a town that had their boys roughed up and nearly kilt. Them's pals passed us three days ago and give us gold to find a boy. They was looking for a fancy pants boy thought to be riding around here somewhere. He has took a bunch of the man's things and has stuck his boy real bad. We is called to take him back dead or alive."

"Five of you to find one boy? Kind of unfair if you ask me."

"We rides this way, mister—not that it is any of your business."

"Of what town has this boy run from?"

"It is not any of youins business but it is up in the Shenandoah Valley. We is instructed not to tell about towns or places. It is enough his pa is a rebel against the King."

"To my understanding, the King's general gived up and we has won. If you is riding for the King, you is in a heap of trouble around these parts."

"We is riding for gold and do not care about kings and such."

"I hate to disappoint you, but I do not recall seeing no fancy pants kid. The fact is we have seen no one come by on the trail in the last three days. Besides, there are a bunch of ridges and valleys each side of the Shenandoah. He may be on his way headed straight west, or to Savannah to the south, or Charleston to the east, or maybe hiding in the crowd up north in New York. Why would he lurk around these wet mountains? Somebody give you an impossible job."

"We has not studied it out, and you might be right. No matter, we got half up front so if we are inclined to quit we have been paid good anyhow."

"You gents look tired, wet, and hungry as you first said. I happen to know a place about ten miles down the road what sells a good meal and homemade whiskey. They have a fire and a place to sleep, so my suggestion is you ride for it. The bottle your men is passing around looks about empty so maybe you need to buy some more and a belly full of bear meat stew."

"Your advice is good. By the way, while we is talking I seen some movement and know where one gun is. If I have seen one, there is more so we will start riding on to the place you mentioned. Much obliged."

The men gave a cheer, wheeled their horses, and followed their leader out to the main road at a canter.

Todd walked back to the wagon and joined the family. "You should go into politics, Eli." Todd said. "You are one smooth talker. I have the feeling they would have cleaned us out if you had not put some fear into them."

"Those guys are bad enemies to have. They are not too bright, but they are mean enough to make up for it," Eli said.

"Now here is my plan. Me and Putt is real good with horses. In an hour, we are going to take a ride down to the Inn and borrow them horses. We will feed them some oats and as they settle down, we will slip their saddles on, lead them over yonder ridge, and drop them off a mile apart. By morning, we will come back here and their horses will scatter over half the area. Some may even get stole.

"Come morning we all set off back a few miles and turn west over a gap. I has heard it is wide enough for strong wagons iffin you have a good team. I am also told there is a real nice camp near this same old river where it snakes around. We will set up there as innocent as mice. Not having horses should slow them down long enough for you to travel a long way to wherever you is heading."

"I should go with you tonight."

"First, me and my family do not intend to make a horse thief out of you, and second, you need to stay here guarding my wife and our stuff. Both dogs stay here."

At first light, Eli and Putt rode into camp, their horses lathered and thirsty. The animals were taken care of first before the men came to the cooking fire.

"We got it done," Eli said. "The way we scattered them horses will take the gang a long time to find them. We also found a lot of jewelry and cash in their saddlebags, and some gold dust and rough bars. Them were a gang of cutthroats for sure, and maybe bank robbers too."

"We will not be keeping much of it, Todd. We ain't thieves," Dorcus said. "We will try to give it back where it is deserved. An honest sheriff or marshal will handle it, and we hope to hear of a good one where we is going."

"Not keeping that stuff for ourselves is a fact," Eli said. "Well, Todd, you best saddle up and get going. Maybe we will see each other again. We plan to end up around a settlement they call Knox Town, so look us up. It is in flat land past the mountains near where two big rivers come together."

"Let me tell you something, Eli. There is a man who may know where I am heading. If you have need, ask around Knox Town; there is only a handful of settlers there in the flat land from what I have heard. It is kind of a code but tell anyone you is looking for a soldier named Max who fought at Aspen Point. The truth is, he and my dad fought a bear there but no one will know. Max is his first name, and most know him as such. soldiers is always looking for war buddies so it will not sound strange asking. He can tell you where I am holed up, and I would be proud to welcome you or do whatever is necessary."

As Todd rode past the wagons with his horses, he raised his hat to the family, turned north on the main trail, clattered over the pole bridge, and headed for the pass to the west.

Chapter 8

The Sister

SARAH FOLLOWED HER MOTHER'S INSTRUCTIONS about finding Rachel Wicks, Sarah's aunt, in Wicks Crossing, east and south about fifty miles. Pearl's sister married the second generation of Wicks, which Sarah's mother said were haughty folks who ruled the town.

She remembered her father said that Wicks' parents came from London about 1700. He laughed as he said they were sneak thieves let out of prison to be rid of them.

The sister acted nice back when Sarah was a young girl and her dad still lived. After he was killed under unusual circumstances, Wicks soon distanced himself from any hint of scandal, demanding all ties with the Tranthem's be broken. Pearl took up dancing again, and her dancing made excuse enough for Wicks to forbid any contact by his wife. She managed a few letters but remained afraid of her husband.

Sarah realized she had few options. She knew it would not be safe traveling as a single woman and creating a lot of attention. Her only chance was to contact Aunt Rachel and ask her advice or even her help. In the past, she and her family had made the trip to Wicks Crossing through the countryside, making it a family camping trip and a time together. She kept the imprint of the land in her mind, and leading the cow and the packhorse with her father's stallion, she made her way toward Wicks Crossing.

Sarah found the big brick house with white columns situated on a hillside with barns and outbuildings behind. It looked just as she remembered it. The buildings were located a few hundred feet from the edge of a dense stand of trees.

She remained in the edge of the woods, watching through the early dawn and the bloom of a new day. A colored man led a harnessed pair of black horses from the barn and hitched them to a carriage. Both horses acted high-strung, dancing and prancing as the servant maneuvered them into position. The servant hooked the traces to the singletrees and in turn, he linked them to the doubletrees so that both traces of each horse were pulling the carriage.

Wicks marched out of the house in a tailored suit of dark green velvet with white stockings to his knees. His head was tilted back, his large nose in the air, and his belly straining at the buttons of his vest. He did not even acknowledge the black man holding the horses steady. He mounted the buggy, snapped his whip, and the horses bolted down the driveway pulling the gleaming rig. The two black stallions leaned forward into the harness, heads high and snorting with pleasure, racing unchecked to the gravel road.

Sarah entered the back door. Hattie, the black housekeeper and cook, met her and recognized her. Little Tiny, a tiny black woman smiled but kept helping in the kitchen. When called, her Aunt Rachel hurried into the kitchen and embraced Sarah.

"Mom is dead and the cabin burnt," Sarah sobbed. Rachel gasped and tears ran down her cheeks. Hattie crowded around, hugging both women and cooing her regret.

Sarah told her story about her mother's sickness, and how Red set the cabin on fire. She told about Pearl killing Big Red, and being shot herself, and dying. She told her about how she escaped the burning cabin and about loading the animals and getting ready to escape as her mother instructed her before Red set the cabin on fire.

"You know you cannot stay here for the night, but tell me all about it again in detail. Afterwards, me and Hattie plan to fix you up with stuff while we think of something to do."

"I know how Wicks hates us and do not intend to cause you no trouble," Sarah said. "Ma gave me some money, two horses, a cow, and some chickens. If you have some old clothes and some corn meal, I will start on my way."

"My daughter, Hanna, is off to school in Savannah. She is about to marry some dandy in spite of me, and too uppity, to even come home. She hates her daddy and thinks he is nothing but a smooth-talking crook, but she sure likes his money and spends it like water."

"Aunt Rachel, you look and sound much like my ma. You is tall but more willowy."

"I believe you are saying I do not have as much chest as my sister. Thank you, Child, I know you intended it for a compliment. Your mother was a real beauty in her day. Now we have to start packing."

"I intend to give you a lot of Hanna's stuff that she will not be needing. Hattie, call your man and have him bring some grain bags and twine to tie things tight. We can pack a lot of stuff and load it on her horses or the cow. You find a ham, side bacon, dried beans, dried apples, and some sugar, flour and salt—also some pepper, herbs, and such. Give her some of Mr. Wicks' private coffee. He has plenty of it put away."

"Sarah," Rachel said, "this may sound like a real personal question, but since your mama has gone I feel responsible. Are you in the way of women yet?"

"Not really, only a few spots but ma said it was coming fast to be my time. My breasts are real hot and growing out and my body is not as square. Mama said curves is coming soon."

"You are near seventeen. My girl is going on twenty. She became a woman at about your age. Did Pearl tell you about pads and such?"

"Yes ma'am. She gave me some long strips of cloth and showed me how to fold them to fit, and about changin' the fold if one is too soiled. She gave me a belt and a cloth to keep the pad on my body."

"Well. We have lots of pads made up that Hanna left behind because the girls in Savannah all have little bags they stuff cotton into, then they can throw it away. They is too embarrassed to have their rags being seen on the laundry line."

"Now, this is personal too but do you have underwear like your ma used? She made some up like short and tight trousers so if her dress floated up while dancing her bottom wouldn't show."

"Yes ma'am. I have several pair and she showed me how to sew them out of whole cloth. I has some cloth in my load too."

"And she told you about the birds and the bees?"

"Yes, and we have animals so it learns you, and my girlfriends always whispered stuff."

"I-de–clare, I am proud of my sister and of you. She has made a fine woman out of you. Now I am going to tell you about the ways of men and avoiding babies and such. Afterwards, you will have to be on your way."

After they finished their private conversation, they went down to the kitchen where Hattie and Tiny served a heavy meal of meat and vegetables. Sarah ate her fill and said her thanks.

After the meal, Rachel Wicks made her final apologies with tears in her eyes as she clung to Sarah.

"You know we don't have any family left so there is no place to send you. It is best you go west and find a school-teaching job in some little town. I know you can read, write, and do figures. I notice you have forgotten your grammar. I know your father spoke well. Your mother was country as I was, but I learned my way out of most of it. You need to work on it and stop talking like a country person. I will give you a book about speaking.

"I am also going to give you some money I keep tucked away. It will hold you over a spell. Small towns do not pay teachers much but will put you up and feed you, most likely. I hate you should go alone but do not dare send a hand with you. Wicks would find out for sure, and it is hard telling what he would do. He hated your daddy real bad. We started out as friends. Later your daddy took a job with the Patriots or whatever—the ones rebelling against King George—and Wicks turned on him."

"Wicks is an attorney but has a hate for any kind of authority. He and the English officers worked things out with both sides engaging in a graft. He thinks he is the law. He has nearly ruined this town but still holds about every office and runs the ones he does not hold, like the sheriff. I must sound like a shrew and a terrible wife but have come to the conclusion that Mr. Wicks is not much of a husband."

Hattie's husband, John, loaded the horses and tied down the compacted bags of clothes, food, and a satchel full of girl's hairbrushes and cosmetics. He added a sack of corn and a sack of oats for the animals.

"Honey, it is the best I can do and feel real bad. I have a mind to go with you, but Wicks would turn out the men in the whole area and range out after us and would catch us for sure."

The cool air of evening signaled the day nearly over. Tate Wicks would return soon and Rachel grew anxious, knowing he must not see Sarah. The women hugged and cried. Sarah mounted, waving to her aunt while riding out the back way. Feeling both fear and determination, she turned west on a trail toward the sunset and the distant mountains.

CHAPTER 9

POTS RIDDLE

THE NIGHT AFTER SARAH LEFT the Wicks' home Todd was on the trail. He headed west toward Nancy's Pass, making out the dark shadow of a large mountain several miles ahead, silhouetted against the late evening sky. He still traveled at night to avoid being seen.

He guessed the time to be about midnight judging by the Big Dipper, bright in the moonless sky. Hammer stopped dead still in the trail ahead. Todd reined in Eagle. He waited a few moments and saw the distant flair as someone lifted a thin blazing stick from a small campfire and lit a pipe. As he watched, he saw the faintly lighted face of a second man as the first man shared the flame. It did not seem to Todd that honest travelers would perch up on the side of a rock-strewn hill. A copse of trees off the north side of the trail would be a better campsite.

Todd led the animals into the trees at the edge of the trail, dismounted, and wrapped Eagles reins around a low limb. He and Hammer went forward, climbing partway up the hill to overlook where he saw the two men lighting up their pipes. As he climbed higher, he saw another small campfire about fifty yards beyond the first.

As he neared the first fire, two men were smoking and passing a bottle. He and the dog appeared suddenly.

"Make no move for your guns, or the dog will kill one of you and I will kill the other," Todd said in a low but authoritative voice.

The two men turned their attention back from the other camp and their hands went to their guns. They saw the large bore scattergun in the hands of a man, and the pulled back lips of the dog exposing its teeth; they resigned themselves to having been captured.

The sound of a scream came from the other campsite as a large man grabbed a woman and tussled with her. The woman pulled a pistol from her clothes and the man backed away.

42

The two men turned their attention back to the other fire at the sound of the scream.

"Looks like Big Pots has him a wildcat," one of the men said, his arms raised in surrender but still watching the camp.

"She is Rose's daughter after all," the other man said with his arms raised too. "You remember how tough she was after her man got killed. She took to dancing but you need not touch the daughter, or her, or she would pull a gun on you. After her head was hurt and she started being dizzy, the men worked up enough courage to mess with her. Even sick as she was, no one ever laid a hand on her."

"I remember it all from our last trip up to see Big Red about joining with us and taking him a letter from Mr. Wicks.

"I guess I told you about the two years I hid out over there in the mountains—before I come this way, and you and me met up."

"You two men seem real casual and seem to know what's going on down there."

"We don't like what we are doing so it is easy to talk. Besides, you and your dog look like you can handle yourself and us. This job is not to our liking, and we sure do not plan to die for it."

"The dog and I have both received several years of military training and some recent experience, so we can have three dead men real quick if we want to." Todd was exaggerating to make a point. The truth was Hammer had attended school with him less than a year, but the dog learned fast.

"Listen, mister," the other man said. "You got the drop on us and have the big dog, but we ain't your problem. Me and my bud was talking about taking off. Pots Riddle, the skunk down there, is an animal, and one day he will kill us like he has others. We do not want nothing to do with his raping or killing a girl. We knew her mama who is a real nice person. I knew her daddy who rode as a patriot man— quick with a gun but real honest. He got himself bushwhacked, and I have a feeling Pots and his boss did it. They did it way up north to keep down the suspicion."

"Who is the boss? Todd asked.

"He is an attorney named Wicks in a town named after his family east of here—a real respectful looking man but trash. Me and my bud have us a belly full of it. This Wicks, has been bedding the house girl, a black one named Tiny. She passed word to Pots where Pearl's daughter was headed so that is how we found her. We do not mind hiring out to do a fight over cows, a claim for land, or something, but we ain't into killing and raping women. Me and my friend here didn't like getting shot at in the war and took off."

"Well," Todd said, "the girl has Pots sitting on a stone across the fire from her while she holds a gun. Let us make a deal. You drop your guns, your boots, and your trousers, and get on your horses real quiet-like and head east about ten miles. I will be keeping your saddlebags. At high noon you come back here and your gear will be waiting for you, except your long guns. The price of the guns will be in your saddle bags."

"Them is good guns Pots was gived by his boss. They is the best the Red Coats carried, but we will be glad to trade them for our hides. Besides, we will not need that kind of weapon from now on. You do as you say and we have a deal, if you will let me take some tobacco makings and a flint to make a fire."

"Agreed, out of your gear and get on your horses real quiet. Do not turn back. If I see either of you before noon, you are dead. I am a crack shot and my dog, Hammer, will tell me the minute you come within a mile of here. Take off your saddle bags, and your saddles real slow. Keep some makings and your bottle, then mount the horses and get gone."

"Mister, we ain't wearing much in the way of underwear."

"None, as a matter of fact," muttered his buddy.

"Well," Todd said, "Let us hope your shirt tails are long because the trousers are staying here."

Todd watched the two horsemen top the low hill and disappear into the darkness. He climbed higher and saw them in the distance as dark spots moving in the darkness. He kept an eye on the other campfire. The situation remained a standoff.

Edging down the hill with Hammer at his side, he crept up near the campfire. A pretty girl with long chestnut hair, wearing a full skirt and petticoats, sat on a stone with a pistol belt under her cape and one of the pistols in her hand. In her lap lay an open book, with the pages open.

Her chestnut colored dog crouched at her feet growling. The dog took quick glances back toward Todd and Hammer, but her main attention was fastened on the fat man.

The man began holding his gut and moaning, looking as if in terrible pain. She edged a tin cup of coffee toward him with a stick. He reached, picked it up, held it with both hands and sipped the hot fluid. Beneath several days of whiskers, his face was puffy and pock marked.

With a quick flick of his wrist, Pots tossed the coffee into the girl's face, jumped to his feet, and lunged toward her. His gun lay beside her in the dirt where she dropped it. He nearly reached her with his arm outstretched to grab her gun hand. The two dogs, shy of hundred pounds, each struck the man at the same time. He fell backwards with windmilling arms. His neck struck the spine of a rock followed by a cracking sound. His feet and arms fluttered. His head turned at an unusual angle and his eyes rolled for a moment, searching the darkness before they slowly rolled back into his head. With a final shudder, his body became still. The dogs sniffed and backed away.

Sarah dropped the gun, both hands flying to her face as she convulsed in fear and relief.

"Everything is okay," Todd said in a gentle voice.

She stiffened in terror at the new threat.

He went to her slowly, speaking softly and smiling. She was crying and did not know what to do. He gently folded her into his arms and held her. At first, she stiffened and trembled, but as he talked to her, she slowly relaxed.

"You didn't kill him; he killed himself with the help of our dogs. I ran off his two men and it is all over now. They told me the whole story and did not want anything to do with what Pots intended to do to you. You will be safe now, but let us take no chances, and pack up and start on our way soon. The mountain trail ahead of us should be safe, at least for tonight."

She pulled away as she wiped her eyes with the sleeve of her dress. "Who are you?"

My name is Todd Casey, and I am running away like you. The men told me some of your story. Some have accused me of stabbing a young man who really tripped and fell on his own dagger as he attacked me. Now his two friends, a deputy sheriff, and five hired thugs are trying to find me to kill me. A paid-off sheriff is probably looking too. The guy that was stabbed and his two friends were my classmates in military school. They hated me because they came from fancy Royal folks. My dad is a farmer."

"Why should I believe you is telling the truth? You may be another like them acting nice to capture me."

"Well, I had opportunity to do it while we were holding each other, you sobbing on my shoulder. Let me ask you something. One of the men said that Pots, the man who died here, worked for an attorney named Wicks in a town to the east. He received word from a black girl named Tiny where you were heading. That is how they found you. Does the information tell you anything?"

"My aunt's husband is an attorney named Wicks, and her house girl is named Tiny. She was in the kitchen on my arrival and again on my departure. She heard all the conversation between my aunt and me."

"You figure your aunt is involved?"

"No sir. She is my mother's sister, and all of us once was real close. It must have been her husband, a playin' around with a darkie and getting her to spy on his wife. My name is Sarah, and what is you called?"

"My name is Todd, like I told you. Will you come with me? The dog and I are headed over the mountains to the west, trying to find a valley."

"I will go with you, Todd. This night has showed me a woman alone don't have much of a future. Two have a better chance of surviving even if you is being chased. How far is it to this valley?"

"Well, I am not real sure but it might be within a hundred miles of here. It is a long story but to boil it down, Uncle Max, a kin of my pa, first saw the valley years ago. He was a young man when a gunshot Indian led him to the valley. We should find Max in about a week."

"You should know I am on the run. I left home fast before the posse came looking for me, accusing me of knifing a prominent man's son. I will tell you all the details, but we need to make tracks from this place in case those two men come back before morning. Their pants and boots is up there on the hill and they know not to come back before noon. They accepted things okay, but one never knows for sure, so we need to be gone soon—and need to keep an eye on our back trail. I put their long guns in some bushes, so let me fetch them. If you are sure about going with me, you are most welcome."

Todd decided traveling with a woman and several more animals made a good disguise. He let his whiskers grow and slumped in the saddle. He pulled his hat down near his eyes and folded the horse blanket over his finely tooled gun scabbard.

Sarah combed out her hair and put on a frumpy dress that looked filthy. She hid her fine rifle on the pack animal and the handguns in her dress. She slipped one of her mother's rings on the third finger of her left hand. They muddied the horses, tangled their manes and tails with burrs and rode on westward like dejected settlers moving west. The pace was slow. She studied the book and tried out her grammar on Todd. He responded with a smile and helped her.

Sarah finished cleaning up and sat on a log studying Todd as he worked around the camp. She smiled and called his name. "Todd, do you know you look like a splitting wedge for making firewood. You have wide shoulders and a narrow bottom. You have huge boots to hold it all up."

"They are big because I have big feet."

She laughed. "I do not think you are the biggest man I ever saw. I have seen big beefy men with broad shoulders, but they always have a big bottom from sitting in the saloon. Your shoulders are not as wide but sure not bony. You have muscles like my father and a fine build like him."

"Do you want to know what I have been thinking about you?"

"No, you cannot see enough of me with all these clothes. I am changing from a girl to a woman and do not know how I will turn out. There is no need for you to even think about it."

"I know about my sister who is about your age. When I saw her a few months ago, she looked mostly like a boy, straight as a stick and flat as pan bread."

"I am not like your sister, and it is not your business. All I want from you is to make me feel safe like my Pa did. The other is not your concern."

The next day at a crossing for a river the ferryman acted confused by first staring at the four horses, a colt, and a cow, and inspecting Todd and Sarah. On the one hand, they looked like stragglers, but on the other the horses looked like fine animals. Sarah saw him looking them over and spoke up.

"Them animals was give to us by them has borned us as a sending off." She was sorry about her partial lie, but continued. "We been a travelin' this trail a fortnight now. Not many of them folks is a moving west," Sarah said, exaggerating her country speech patterns.

"Not on this trail, ma'am. Most stick to the better trails. You cannot haul a wagon over this here mountain ahead of you. You all watch careful cause there is horse thieving going on around here." The ferryman was convinced by Sarah's sweet smile. He looked at her closely and studied her wide set brown eyes, her square jaw, and her white teeth. He glanced at her wedding rings but was not sure she was ready for marriage. In some ways, she did not look full-grown. He returned her smile and took them across the river.

CHAPTER 10

MAX PATCH MCBRIDE

ONCE THEY CROSSED OVER THE LAST MOUNTAIN, the land began to settle into rolling hills and large flat areas of huge trees and open meadows. Near a wide river they saw a cabin. On inquiry, the man knew Max Patch McBride and gave directions to his farm and cabin. Before sundown, they reached the homestead.

Todd introduced Sarah to Max and his wife, Claire, and after hugs and laughter, he handed Max a note from his father. The man grinned and welcomed them to his home.

Max looked the same as he had several years previously. He was built like a sawed-off length of log fitted with stout legs, huge hairy arms, a full head of hair, and black whiskers streaked with silver. His face was round and pleasant with sparkling eyes.

"Todd, your dad did not mention a girl. He said to help you on your way but no word of a girl. Is she your wife?"

"No sir, I met her on the trail some days ago. I will tell you all about her, but we both need your help. She is a Tranthem. Her daddy, Judd, was a Patriot and was killed or murdered."

"Could be the lady's father come through here a few years back—before the end of the fightin'. I was shot some and home on leave. He rode on a mission to contact me about some dealings I had with supplies over on the coast. He was a fine man and intelligent. He went on his way with my information. What made me remember is recognizing the rifle scabbard the lady has on the packhorse. It belonged to her daddy. The rifle should be on the horse she is riding."

"We are trying to look like discouraged farmers headed west in the state," Todd said. "We usually keep the gun under a blanket. Her daddy got killed, or hanged, as he rode as some kind of government spy. Her mother took to cabaret dancing, and later was hurt and her brain dying.

She shot a bad one named Big Red Suttles who set the cabin afire, and she died by his return shot.

"The mother forewarned the girl, Sarah, and she was all set to travel. She pulled out after her mother was shot and the cabin ablaze. Big Red's gang was about to set out after her, but were delayed by finding some money in Red's pocket so they had a burying party. They claimed Sarah murdered Red. Well, she made it out of those parts with the help of neighbors."

"Oh my," Claire said. "You is a young girl to have been through so much with this unfeeling boy beside you."

"Ma'am, he ain't a boy and he has even hugged me to make me feel better."

"I am funnin' you. I know this boy and often wished I had a son just like him." Claire hugged Sarah, pulling her to her solid body and holding her head against her breasts. "If you decides you does not want him, you come to me and I will be your ma."

Claire laughed. Sarah began to giggle and then broke out into the first laughter Todd had heard from her. He liked the fresh lively sound of it.

"I told you the first part of her story, so be ready to hug her again. We joined up after she was caught by three men sent to kill her by her aunt's husband, Tate Wicks. He hated her father. I come along, ran off the hired guns, and was about to shoot the man, Pots Riddle, who was molesting the girl. The dogs saw him make a move toward her and rushed him. The two big dogs hit him at the same time, knocked him over, and broke his neck on a spine of rock. Her dog, Chestnut, and my dog, Hammer, teamed up and hit Pots with about two hundred pounds of dog flesh. Afterwards we headed here to find the way to Max Patch Bend."

"Oh my, I do think you need another hug. You ain't even a woman yet and have seen hard things," Claire said, her arms still around the girl.

"Todd, you two have been through some adventures by the sound of it," Max said. In these days, with Red Coats and Patriot deserters still around, being travelers can bring you trouble, even a noose. We see an occasional maverick Indian and have some man-killing bears. This country ain't tamed yet.

"You sure look like your father—tall, strong, and easy of movement. You put me in mind of him with a square jaw that says "do not mess with me." I aim to outfit you with anything you do not have and give you some vittles to hold you over. I am sure you never intended to escape with a pregnant cow, several extra horses, a crate full of chickens, a new dog, and a beautiful lady."

"No sir, I did not even know the cow was pregnant, and life is getting complicated mighty fast. We took care of those trying to kill Sarah, but there is still a gang after me. We can talk about it tonight."

Max and Todd put up the horses and stock, unloaded the animals, and gave them feed. Claire fetched a hunk of bear meat from the smokehouse and put it into a heavy iron pot with a cover. She nestled it into the coals at the edge of the fireplace. Into another pot she put hunks of turnip, potatoes, and water. The pot had a flat lid with a lip, and later, when the meat was cooked, she placed gobs of biscuit dough on the lid, where it rose and browned. With the meal, she served fresh made butter and wild honey.

After the meal they sat around catching up on family and political happenings. Later Max became serious and called Todd aside.

"Now, let me draw you a map to press into your memory and you need to memorize it real good. It will show you the way to what I call Max Patch. Kind of egotistical of me but have held it in my mind for years. The Indian I found and doctored looked like a Shawnee, which is strange, because they is way out in western Carolina near the big river. At the time he was looking for game and land gived to him by the king. Someone did not like the idea. He called the valley a name that sounded somewhat like Maxpatch. It being sorta like my name, I changed it to Max Patch and stuck with it."

"What do you mean by sorta your name?" asked Todd.

"Well, lots of folks changed their name on coming over here. My birth name was McMillan McPatch McBride. How long do you reckon I would survive with a name like that? They would be callin me Three-Patch, or Patch a Bride, Patch McBride, Three Macs, or who knows what. I shortened it up to Max Patch McBride and made me a man's name what sticks. If you ever tell anyone my real name, I'll come hunting you for sure." Max laughed and went on with his story.

"I told her daddy, Judd Tranthem, the way if he needed to hide out but he said he needed to stay in the open and do his work, and he needed to see his wife and little girl. He never figured that one day his daughter might need the valley as a place to hide out. I never figured my own nephew might need it too."

"My wife knows all kinds of Indian things to eat, and cures, and such. She'll tell your girl about them and draw pictures for her."

"She is not my girl. We are helping each other out."

"I say she is your girl, and you is responsible for her. What you make of her is your business, but you owe it to her father to take care of her. He did much for this country and got kilt for it.

"This here is farming country with several rivers that has brought in good soil in the bottoms. Over in yonder haze of mountains is coal country. The mountain over there and to the right has thirty-one seams of coal. Most are too small for a man to dig into, and besides, no one wants the stuff. It burns for a long time but has a smell to it. Down lower are some better seams, and some people is digging into them for fuel to make fires in forges and such. The mountain land is part of Virginia.

"All the land and mountains you can see to the north is Virginia, and I guess you know it takes in about all the land clear up to the Great Lakes. Speaking of land, them in the capitol is talking about cutting off North Carolina on the west side of the mountains and calling the west part Tennessee. It is to go west to the big river. Therefore, we may be standing in Tennessee. Where I am sending you is sandstone on top and limestone down lower. Up higher is a trace of coal but mostly limestone with a band of sandstone on top. Up high is a hard, old cap keeping the mountains from wearing down. It is high country.

"Max Patch is a valley surrounded by cliffs and mountains. It looks south and west, has a natural bald area, and a stream that ends in a pond. I seen it about thirty years ago while out prospecting.

"I run into a shot Indian who knew the valley and called it something like Max Patch, like I said. We lived there several months with me doctoring the Indian, and he gave me a deed to the property writ in Indian marks. His tribe made a deal with England, or one of its nobles, and they gave him a deed. I do not know if it is worth anything but will hold on to it until you need it. You occupying the land is better than a deed. It is why he traveled so many miles east. He wanted to see the land. He was wounded after he rode his pony into the mountains, hunting and looking for the spot. Whoever shot him most likely did not like Shawnees that far east. I do not know if he ever made it home or not after he healed and left. Now I am giving the Patch to you.

"Gold is not found in limestone but I took a liking to the place. I seen Indian signs down in the valley, fruit trees and such. It must have been a village place once. It has some hot water springs and some cold water springs. It is a different kind of place. Like maybe where a volcano exploded a million years ago. I cannot say, but I have thought of it many times. I camped a few months and moved on because the Indian was gone, and it got so quiet of human sounds it spooked me.

"The valley is hard to get into and hard to get out of. The river on the west side is fast and treacherous, but I did find color in my gold pan at one spot. A lode is around there in the mountains somewhere if you was lucky enough find it."

CHAPTER 11

THE SHAWNEE

TODD AND SARAH WERE BOTH EXHAUSTED from the hard climb and the long hours without sleep. After resting for a while, they watered the horses in a mountain seep, clearing away leaves and twigs to make a spring about as big as a dinner plate. Sarah pulled a smoked ham from a sack, sliced off some pieces, and laid them out with hard tack biscuits. The meat needed cooking, but they did not want to start a fire. The dogs gulped down a share of the food.

They pushed on until they came to a wide flat spot on the trail where they tethered the horses and lay down on the damp ground. Todd awoke to full morning light. Hammer nuzzled him and kept glancing up the trail. Chestnut stood stiff- legged over Sarah.

Several days of constant travel were behind them since leaving Uncle Max. They were resting after climbing their way up a steep trail. With the clattering of hooves on the trail higher on the mountain and the nudges of their dogs, they awoke.

Soon they heard voices and the sounds of several horses coming down the trail from High Pass. They moved their horses farther back off the trail, rubbing their soft noses to keep them from whinnying to the approaching horses. The dogs moved upward through the tangle of rhododendron and a thick stand of hemlock.

Todd and Sarah followed the dogs, making their way to a position where a hundred feet of the trail coming down from the pass was visible. Men were laughing, and the horses' hooves clicking against stones.

Behind the lead horseman a rope stretched to the neck of what looked to be an Indian with copper-colored skin and black hair. At the trail cutback above them, the horsemen entered a small level spot where travelers rested their horses.

"Let's take our scatter guns and sneak up to see what is going on," Todd said quietly.

"Oh, I hope it is not more trouble," Sarah said. "But, if you think we better look, I will get the guns off the horses."

They found a spot where the low boughs of a hemlock reached to the ground. The man with rope around his neck wore the clothing of an Indian. The knot was a hangman's noose, and the young man's hands were tied behind him. He wore buckskin trousers and a loose buckskin vest. His elbows and knees were bleeding because of falling many times and being dragged by his neck until he was able to regain his footing. His face was a deep red from the tightness of the noose. He was not fully grown, but had a lean muscular body.

"Let's hang this Shawnee right here. I have me a special hate for Shawnee," the large man holding the rope tied to the youth said. He laughed and gave the rope a jerk. "Charley," he called to one of the men, "toss this end of the rope over a limb."

Charley tossed the rope and pulled up the slack. He did not appear to be enjoying his duties. The Indian stood beneath the tree, the rope stretching up and over a limb.

"I need your horse, Charley. Put him on it and we will have us some fun with him dancing at the end of the rope like the others we done."

Todd stepped forward with his double barrel musket aimed at the fat man in the saddle. Sarah covered the other two men, and the dogs watched all three of them, ready to move.

"Off the horse, fat man," Todd ordered.

"Who is you giving me orders?"

"The man with the double load of buckshot aimed at your body. The first barrel has a choke, so if I hit you it will leave a hole big enough to reach through. If I miss, the second will spread to hit you no matter where you move. Now drop your pistol real careful, and slide off on my side of the horse."

The fat man laughed and slid down to the ground.

"Drop the pistol like I said."

The fat man un-holstered his pistol and laid it near his feet.

"Good. Kick the gun away. Now loosen the noose from the Indian and slip it over your own head. Now we aim to have some fun at your expense."

"You is looking to die, fancy-talking boy. You sound like a college boy, but your woman looks like something the cat drugged in."

"Put the noose over your head, fat man, and if you keep talking about my woman we will not have time to hang you—at least not alive. Slip the noose over your head and mount up real slow or else this gun will cut a hole clear through your chest. You, Charley, as he mounts you pull the rope tight over the limb, and take a turn around one of those lower branches and tie it with three half hitches. You know half hitches?"

"I can do as you say, mister, but tell your black dog to take its eyes off me."

"I do not intend to call him off, and the big brown dog will keep watching your buddy. All we need to do now is decide the order of the hanging after the fat man dances his jig. Charley, tighten up your rope until Mr. Fat is standing in his stirrups. Let us see if it will make him more agreeable. By the way, Fats, what is your real name, so we can write it down in case anyone should ask?"

Todd was trying to act macho but his gut was cramping. Sarah looked at him, wide-eyed with apprehension.

"You ain't killing me. You is funning. I know your kind; you do not have the guts to hang a man. Let me down and I promise to keep going and forget this incident."

"Why did you want to hang this young Indian?"

"Cause he is Indian, and we kill Indians. Good enough for you, mister?"

"Charley, pull your rope tighter till the fat man has to stretch up to breathe."

"Do not do it, Charley. Do not you tighten the rope."

As Charley pulled the rope tighter and made up the half hitches, the fat man turned in the saddle, pulling a derringer from inside his shirt and firing both barrels. The two balls struck Charley in the center of the chest.

In the moment of surprise, the other man lunged for the fat man's gun lying in the dirt where the fat man placed it. He grabbed it, and pushing the barrel into his mouth, he fired as the dogs reached him. They veered away as the top of the man's head exploded, spattering brains on the fat man. His horse stood rock still through the gunplay.

"Sorry to disappoint you, smart boy, but this horse has been fired from many a time and will not spook. Them two killed themselves but you will not make me do it. You is going to have to chin up and do the job yourself—which you do not have the guts to do."

Sarah untied the Indian boy's hands. He stepped forward and faced the fat man. "This is my business. I will kill you myself."

He took several steps forward until he stood in front of the fat man's horse. "This horse will help to kill you."

Six Indians burst into the clearing howling like wolves. One screamed like a wildcat, whacking the fat man's horse with his rifle butt. The horse reared, the Indian screamed like a wildcat again, and the horse bucked and twisted. The fat man sailed upward in a sitting position and then plummeted down, the noose catching him eight feet off the ground. His neck broke with a snapping sound as urine soaked the front of his trousers and excrement from loosened bowls dripped out of his pant leg and off the tips of his boots.

Sarah screamed and Todd jumped back, raising his scatter gun. The six Indians stood unmoving. The young Indian walked to their leader, and they clasped each other's wrists. The older man began speaking in halting English.

"You did well, son. You also have made two friends who have helped you much."

"Father, I know not their names," the youth said in English. "Yes, they will be my new friends."

"Are these the men we hunt?" the father asked.

"Yes Father, from the top of the mountain they saw Indians following, but I did not know who it was. Seeing someone following is why they stopped to hang me. My walking and falling slowed them down and they were eager to go east.

"They killed three of our people and three of them have died. From their conversation this last day, they have killed many whites and many of us from several tribes. After this is told there comes a celebration."

"No! We will bury them. Then we will turn their horses loose after you tie the bridles on the saddle and remove the things from the saddle bags," the Indian who spooked the horse said. "No one is to know what has happened. This white man and his woman will have what is in the saddlebags and the guns. They will have peace from us. You will ask if we can help them."

The youth stepped forward to where Todd and Sarah stood with shotguns leveled at the group of Indians.

"Please lower your guns. I am your friend and this man is our Chief and my father. We are Shawnee from the sunset one white man month away. I am tested and have walked in the forest, not knowing my father followed with his braves."

"It is good we did not need to kill these men and am sure you agree," continued the boy. "You hesitated to spook the horse. I too hesitated to make the fat man's horse move and hang the man, but my father screamed his wildcat scream and frightened the horse."

Todd reached out his hand and grasped the extended hand of the boy. "We take hold of each other's hand to show friendship."

"Yes, this I know. I was taught by a missionary lady and learned the white man language, and many of his ways, and about his God. Now, the Chief has asked what we can do for you."

"We are grateful to you. I would ask if you know of what is called Max Patch. A friend of mine helped one of your people injured by a gunshot. This happened many years in the past. The injured man guided him to a large valley with high walls and a river on the west side. My friend did not speak your language, but the injured man gave an Indian name sounding like Max Patch. The Indian gave my friend a deed to the land in exchange for several months of nursing. I wish to go there."

"What is the name of your friend?" the Chief asked as he came from beside a horse and stepped forward to stand with them.

"McBride, Max Patch McBride."

Yes, I know this story and this name. The man who your friend saved still lives and is a great man. We will take you to this valley. My son, who you have saved, will stay with you until you are able to survive. Are we agreed?"

"Yes sir, we are agreed," Todd said, grabbing Sarah and twirling her around. The Indians smiled in spite of themselves, and the Chief's son stood with a wide grin, his arms clasped regally across his chest.

CHAPTER 12

THE BEND

AFTER TWO DAYS, traveling through rain, mud, and steep hills, the Chief said they were nearing Max Patch. The Indians left the main trail and started upward through the forest. The horses struggled up the steep mountainside, crowded with mountain laurel and rhododendron. The horses' hooves clattered on the loose stones and decayed matter covering the ground. They continued upward for several hours, crossing several ridges and stopping often to rest both man and beast.

The mountainside became so steep the pack animals came to a stop, no longer struggling—standing confused in a dense forest of rhododendrons. Each time they attempted to go up hill, they slipped on loose shale and wet leaves, struggling to keep their balance.

Todd dismounted, unhitched the pack animals, and called to Sarah to hold the lead line of the animals. He scrambled ahead of Eagle, pulling at his reins. Eagle hopped and slid, pawing for a foothold and finally topped the ridge. He let the horse blow, then using bushes as handholds he let himself down the steep hillside to Sarah's horse. After leading Thunder up the hill, he fell, heaving and panting on the ridge. Even Hammer and Chestnut were panting and lay in the leaves while saliva drained from the sides of their mouths.

The pack animals still stood on the steep mountainside, trying to hold their place without sliding downward. One of the braves stood beside each animal, whispering and calming them. Todd unwound a rope from his saddle, tied it to a saddle ring, and let himself down the hill, leaving Eagle standing on the ridge. He tied it off to the huge workhorse, Bill, given to him by the Sergeant. He gave a call and Eagle went forward, pulling the rope. With the help of the braves pulling, the scrambling black horse made it to the top.

Once on the flatter land at the top of the ridge, Bill easily pulled up the other packhorses and the pregnant cow. Todd rubbed Bill's soft nose and removed the light plowing harness. He snorted and tossed his head when Todd removed the pulling strap from across his chest. He ignored the activity of the men and animals around him and began foraging for grass.

Todd and Sarah walked hand in hand to the edge of the ridge and climbed out on a slab of cap rock that projected over the edge of the cliff. Both sensed a new life spread before them as they gazed into the large valley surrounded on three sides by cliffs, but neither of them grasped the full impact that the valley would have on their lives. Each wondered how they would survive in this wilderness—only the two of them in the wide valley below. Her hand was warm and comfortable in his. She leaned toward him in friendship, and he could feel the warm firmness of her breast. It stirred new feelings, but he tried to ignore them. He enjoyed being with her but she was, after all, just a girl he had picked up along the way.

The large valley became a reality below them as they looked down and studied the landscape. Their destination lay below, but it seemed only a dream after the many hardships of the trail. Conscious of holding hands, they released each other with a reluctance felt by the girl but ignored by Todd.

They saw the small stream, a pond, and the sheer face of the mountain behind. Below them spread a cleared area of several hundred acres with a small hillock in the center of the valley. To the north and east rose a vertical cliff with an undercut into the mountain. The evening sun lighted the face of the cliff, the deep cleft—the level space in front of the cleft and the boulder-strewn area at the bottom of the cliff overhang. They did not fully comprehend what they were seeing. The Chief and his son stood on the large boulder gazing into the hidden valley with more understanding. Their tribe told stories of villages built into such a cleft.

They made their camp in the trees, away from the cliff that dropped to the valley below. The Indians moved back deeper into the forest. The Cherokee claimed this territory, so the Shawnee did not want to be seen by them until they were ready.

Todd and Sarah celebrated with a slice of ham, and an egg each, and grain for the animals. The dogs ate a boiled hedgehog Todd had shot earlier in the day. They retired to their sleeping rolls, Sarah on one side of the fire and Todd on the other, as was their custom. Both were tired and eager to recharge for the day ahead.

Todd became confused whenever he thought about Sarah. He was twenty, in fine physical condition with his youthful libido in full awakening. She was a pretty girl, with growing breasts and slim hips appealing to him in a way he had never examined before. Her figure looked girlish—quickly maturing but still somewhat awkward. He reckoned she must be sixteen or seventeen. He guessed at much because her body remained hidden beneath the long and loose dresses she usually wore. He grinned when he realized he was not even aware she was growing breasts before she leaned against him a few hours ago. Until this minute, he had hardly even thought of her as a woman—only as a girl like his sister.

His only reference was his sister, and she only afforded a body to roughhouse with, as they often did when he was at home. Now, he inhabited a man's body with natural inclinations. A deep sense of honor and respect for womanhood, learned from his father, hedged his thoughts. He really wanted to hold her, feel her body, and kiss her lips. Even if he hardly thought of her as a sexual person, he now recognized her as being every inch a female. Honor and desire struggled within him.

To her, he had become a hero. He saved her on the road, befriended her, took care of her, and brought her to this wonderful, yet desolate place. He was tall and his body was thickening into a man. She found it difficult to take her eyes off of his face with its many slants and planes—looking as if it had been chopped out of a piece of oak. She felt her body warm and she yearned to be beside him. She slept restlessly on the opposite side of the fire.

WHEN THEY WERE VISITING in Knox Town, Max told him not to fear entering the valley but to find the most used animal trail and follow it down the cliff. "If big enough for buffalo and elk, it should be big enough for you," Max had said. The next morning Todd walked the rim of the valley looking for sign. He found an animal trail, but it ended at a large flat rock perched below the rim on a shelf of gravel.

The Chief joined him and showed him the scuffed rubble below the large flat rock. His eyes followed downward a few feet. From the top, it looked impassible but as he eased down, he noted the descent seemed easy and the path well trodden. The major drawback involved thinking about the sheer drop of two hundred feet into the valley.

Gathering the horses into a line, Todd started downward leading his usually frisky stallion. Eagle turned serious and carefully followed him, glancing occasionally wide-eyed at the drop-off beside them. Sarah followed with Thunder, the colt, and the cow, and the packhorse. Behind them followed the packhorses with the braves leading them, their own ponies obediently following. The dogs were scouting way ahead of Todd following the old game trail, tails erect and wagging. The chickens were cackling, no doubt thinking about juicy worms in the expanse of fields below. The lone duck quacked at the sight or smell of the pond.

Slowly and carefully, they wound downward with switchback turns and surprise flat spots to rest. In half an hour, they were at the base of the cliff extending upward above them.

"Todd, my men and I will leave you for several days," the Chief said. We have been on the trail for two of your months, but our mission is not complete. My son has passed his test, but our tribe also sent us to contact the Cherokees, just as the man your uncle saved was sent to do. It will take us quite a while for the ceremonies and the talks. We will leave two men down near where we left the trail and headed up the mountainside. They will erase the trail we made to make sure no one finds the way up the mountain as we did. My son and I will go to speak with the Cherokee chief and will come back for a visit. He will then stay with you until you have made a home. For now, we will rest, graze our ponies, and bathe in the warm pond we have heard of."

The Chief, his son, and the braves turned and headed toward the warm pool, easily recognized by the rising steam.

CHAPTER 13

THE HOMESTEAD

A SLIVER OF SUN GLINTED over the eastern wall as the valley mist thinned, revealing the land above. From the top, the trail into the valley looked impossible. The trail followed the face, descending into the long neck of the valley, cutting back several times, and finally reaching the bottom.

Todd and Sara went to the small, bald hill and took the bits out of Eagle and Thunder's mouths. They untied the other animals but did not remove the packs. The animals grazed hungrily on the lush green grass. One packhorse smelled the stream and moved toward it, the others following. They filled themselves and returned to the grass of the hillside. The duck found the pond and the chickens were pecking around its bank, finding worms and bugs.

Todd and Sarah lay back in the grass enjoying the warmth of the morning sun. They grinned at one another and gently touched hands.

You told the bad man I am your woman," Sarah said with an impish smile. "Did you mean such a thing?"

"Uncle Max said you were my woman to take care of."

"So what do you say?"

"I say I am glad you are here with me."

"That will do for now, Mr. Casey."

Later they climbed the gentle slope to the face of the cliff and the undercut area several hundred feet long. A rubble field of fallen stone lay under the high upper lip of the cleft. For fifty or more feet inside the drip line, the floor was of smooth, fine sand where nothing grew and rain seldom, if ever, intruded.

In his geology class at the Academy, Todd remembered the instructor saying that in the far west there were such places where cliff dwellers built cities into the mountain. The professors believed that the rushing water of a river cut into the rock cliff forming the deep cleft.

Todd tried to explain it to Sarah but stopped as he realized there was no river. He decided to give the matter more thought.

The Indians helped them gather, unsaddle, and unload the animals. They stored the goods and tack in the back of the cleft. The animals were glad to be free of the weight and returned to grazing.

Todd chose a spot behind a huge bolder that might have fallen from the overhead hundreds of years earlier. Smoke stained the backside of the boulder, and around it was a scattering of poles, dried hard in the arid sand. He buried them upright in the sand and fashioned the sailcloth they brought into a small room for Sarah. Todd made a smaller room for himself behind another boulder.

She put her clothing and private gear into her space, and he did the same. Their guns were handy but out of sight in their tent-like enclosures. Sarah still carried her father's big pistols in the folds of her skirts. They were cumbersome and heavy, so she took them off and left them in her bedding. She tucked the small gun Todd took from Pots body into her apron pocket. Todd kept a 58 Cal. pistol handy and his musket close by.

The Chief observed their camp and approved of the location. He nodded to his son. Their time to depart had arrived. The son used his best English to thank Todd and Sarah, petted Hammer and Chestnut, and mounted his pony. Father and son followed by three braves clambered up the trail and disappeared over the lip.

The sun warmed the face of the cliff and the sand in the cleft at its base. Todd and Sarah sprawled in the warm sand, relaxing for the first time in days. For the noon meal, they finished the parched corn Todd's mother had packed.

They wandered down to the creek and drank deeply of the pure clear water. They both lay on their bellies, laughing and sucking in the cold water. It was a small pool of about two feet deep held by a natural dam. Water spilled over the dam and flowed toward the larger pond.

"Sarah, this pool will serve well as our source of drinking water. It will be a long walk back to the cabin but will do until we dig a well near the cut. I will make a fence around it to keep the stock out."

"This valley is so beautiful that I will not mind the walk," Sarah said.

Filled with water, they followed the creek to the large pond nestled against the sheer wall of the south escarpment. The duck swam around the edge of the water, ducking its head to nibble things on the bottom.

"Todd," Sarah said seriously, "I really need a bath, and the Indians are out of sight and on their way to the Cherokee village. My plan is to strip down to my shift, and slip into the pond." Her cheeks burned with embarrassment, but her resolve was stronger than her pride.

"You can do what you please," she continued. "My father bathed without clothes in the creek near the house, so you cannot shock me. I was young at the beginning and adjusted to his nakedness. In the winter, we all washed in a tub near the fireplace. My pa died when I was thirteen, and afterwards Ma and me lived in the cabin and made do."

"My dad," Todd said, "and us kids washed in the creek or in a tub too, and no one was self conscious, Then my sister grew older and she became real shy and asked mother to hold a blanket around her. Mother always bathed alone."

"We have no blanket here," she said, "or I would have one too. Now turn around."

"Max said there is some hot water springs here. Do you want to find them before you take your bath?"

"No, I want to get clean now."

"Okay, it is off with my pants, so keep your eyes on the sky until I am underwater."

"I promise not to pay any attention to you," she said with a laugh, her blush deep red.

He did not believe what she said.

She stripped off her socks, her outer dress, some things under them all, and dove into the pond. She came up laughing with wet hair streaming. She massaged her scalp, rubbed all of her other parts and emerged to a sunny spot near the bank of the pool where she rested a minute. Her thin cotton shift clung to her, nearly transparent and revealing her body. Her ripe young breasts were outlined, and her pink nipples pressed through. As she stood to dive again, there was a flash of dark between her legs lasting for a second, disappearing as she submerged in the water, laughing and frolicking.

Todd stepped naked out of the water as Sarah averted her eyes. He sat down beside her, pulling his breeches across his lap. She leaned against him. He kissed her hair. She laughed, jumped to her feet, gathered her clothes, and ran up the gentle hillside and across the field to her canvas room. Todd sat there in stunned disbelief. Something new and strange continued to awake in him. He had never seen a real naked woman. He had seen his sister with her stick figure and tiny boy-like nipples, but this was exceedingly different. He had just experienced a sneak preview of womanhood. Now he had a good idea of what to expect, and he found it stimulating.

As they cooked their evening meal, she acted shy and reserved. They did not mention the swim, but he noted a smile pulling at the corners of her mouth.

The time to plant their garden was at hand. The soil warmed early in this protected valley, and spring came alive around them. The Academy always let the cadets off early to help their families with spring planting. Then they went back to school and in the fall, they were later released to help with the harvest. Todd was familiar with gardening.

He assembled a crude plow from parts Max had given him, attaching an iron sheer. He harnessed Bill with the work collar, hitching the traces to the plow. Bill ripped up the soil in the garden plot with Todd struggling to hold the handles controlling the plow. The furrows they cut were ragged, not at all straight, but the sod turned nearly upside down.

Todd went at the broken sod with hoe and rake, breaking up the turf and smoothing the furrows. Sarah followed Todd, picking up the larger stones and carrying them to one corner, outside of the exposed earth. Many of her fingernails were broken, but she smiled and hugged the rocks to her stomach as she carried them. Her apron and dress were filthy as were her bare feet. Her auburn hair became stringy and wet with sweat, but her comely face glowed beneath the grime.

After work, they needed to wash in the pond. This time she insisted they take turns, so each would swim alone. Todd was disappointed but recognized the wisdom of the plan. He elected to go to the hot pool to soak his distressed muscles. In the distance, he saw her swimming in the pond.

Two days later, they finished tilling the ground, making it ready for planting. The whole valley smelled of turned earth, and birds arrived to sample the worms. The chickens rushed with long strides, squawking with glee from one worm sighting to another. Each dog claimed a spot of cool earth and dug out a comfortable bowl to relax in.

They laid out the garden and planted the seeds that Todd's mother had sent with him. They planted many rows of corn seed, and rows of beans, squash, beets, carrots, cabbage, lettuce, parsnips, chard, turnips, and several carefully folded packs of seeds Todd did not recognize. They made mounds for the pumpkins and squash, seeds well buried with a bit of brush over them to discourage the birds.

Todd took special pride in three rows of potatoes. He cut the seed potatoes in quarters and the large ones in more pieces to create a big yield. He knew enough to keep at least two eyes in each piece and to dry them in the sun to harden the cuts.

His dad had included a pack of tobacco seed. Todd did not smoke, except for an occasional pipe full, but it would be good for trading. On the edges he planted sorghum but harbored no idea how he would squeeze the juice out of the cane to make syrup. First, grow the plant.

The garden plot looked small at first but by the time they had staked it out into rows and planted the seeds, they both realized they had planted much more, and created more to take care of, than they intended.

As Todd planted, he found he needed more room for squash, pumpkins, and gourds so he and Bill plowed more earth. Todd worked the dark, moist soil. He loved the smell of the newly turned earth. Around the circumference, he planted the gourds. They would be making a fence around the garden and the gourds could climb on it. He already had his eyes on some straight poles to make trellises for the climbing beans.

The chickens crowded in again to catch the worms and grubs that the plow uncovered. The chickens rewarded Todd and Sarah with firm eggs with deep orange yokes.

Both of them knew that it would be a long time before the garden produced, and thousands of bugs would to try to destroy it, so they searched the stream for ramps, lambs quarter, and 'salet,' as her mother had called the leafy greens by the creek. Sarah found emerging bracken, stinging nettle, dock, dandelions, and rock tripe lichens. Some of the plants tasted strong but their bodies knew what they needed, so they wolfed them down with thick slices of fried smoked pork. While plowing, they discovered a patch of artichoke tubers that they sliced and mixed with greens. They saved tubers to plant in a patch along the side of the garden. In the summer, the small sunflower blossoms would be welcome as the plant generated more tubers for eating.

With the vegetable garden planted, Todd turned to the serious work of making the earth ready for a large patch of corn and beside it an acre for wheat and an acre for oats. He and Bill would be doing a lot of plowing and stone picking. He already had plans to build a drag to smooth the soil rather than using his rake. Max has taken them to a trader that supplied corn, wheat, and oat seeds to the flat land settlers. Todd stocked up with what he needed.

On the warm side of the valley, they discovered an orchard of apple trees, plums, and pears, all in full blossom. Todd cut out some of the crossed and useless limbs and made a note in his mind to prune them heavily in the late fall or early winter.

They talked around the small campfire, went to bed early, and arose early to watch the new day come alive. They were growing closer.

The horses and the cow sniffed around the newly planted ground, looking interested. The new homesteaders gathered brush and poles and soon erected somewhat of a barrier around the garden. For real protection, it became a matter of educating the animals. Luckily, they had plenty of lush green grass to graze and plenty of cool clean water to drink. They did not need to raid the garden, but of course, they would try when the tender shoots arrived. They would train the dogs to keep the garden free of critters, large and small. All the dogs wanted in return was a patch of loose soil where they dug their holes and relaxed in the cool dirt.

Several weeks passed before the Indians returned, striding down into the valley. The son ran to Todd and Sarah, smiling as he shook their hands. He acted older and more reserved, but his love for them overcame his reserve as he smiled and gave each of them a hug, an unlikely thing for a Shawnee to do.

His father, the Chief, issued orders and his braves went to work, mixing clay from a bank near the stream, and laying up stone with clay mortar to build cabin walls under the protection of the overhanging cliff face. The chief had surveyed their canvas-walled rooms, and he knew they would be inadequate for the winter that would follow in five of the white men's months.

Before the Chief left, he and his men had laid up a cabin made of stone and clay. The Chief wanted to make the cottage round, but Todd laid out the corners for a square building. There was one common room and two small storage rooms. The Shawnee formed a fire circle in the center of the room and above it a vent through the flimsy roof for the smoke. Todd did not say anything, but after they left he started building a fireplace on one wall with a sleeping shelf on both sides of the chimney and a crude oven built into the chimney.

He opened one blank wall facing outward and added a wide window, framed with hand-hewed timber. He made shutters of thinly split beech that could be closed when need arose. The Indians left a small arched opening for a door to be hung with hides. Todd chiseled out a square opening and made a thick door with a cross bar on the inside.

When they moved into the new house, Sarah took one small storage room as her personal space and made a pallet on one side of the sleeping shelf built beside the chimney. She left the wider one for Todd, using what they had to make his bed comfortable.

CHAPTER 14

SMOKEHOUSE

THE RUTTING SEASON for the animals ended, and a small herd of elk made their way into the valley. The female limped badly, two arrows protruding from her front quarter and one low on her side—the animal was obviously dying. Behind her struggled an old bull elk, horns broken and shoulders scarred from the hooves of a younger male. He limped badly also, and his coat was shaggy. The old elk looked dejected, his head hanging low to the ground. Old bulls usually went off to die by themselves, but this one still followed his cows. The new leader was striding ahead, confident of his position.

Todd pulled the old shot from his rifle, charged it with new powder and shot, and primed the pan. Easing out into the field, Todd took his time and closed in on the herd. Both the wounded female and the bull were going to die, so he felt better about harvesting their meat. He sighted a clear shot at the female elk and fired. The animal fell heavily to the ground. The others scattered after the shot but Todd kept his place, well hidden in a growth of sumac that was trying to invade his field. He reloaded his rifle.

Minutes later the old bull came into sight, trying to gather the cows that no longer belonged to him. Todd sighted and fired. The bull stood, swinging its head in defiance. Todd reloaded and fired into the bull's brain. The animal fell.

Todd hitched up Bill and pulled the young elk up near the house. Sobbing, Sarah cradled the head of the female elk in her arms. She gave Todd a reproachful glance and continued to weep.

Todd tied off the old bull to the traces of Bill's harness and pulled the carcass up beside the cow. Sarah took one look at the dead eyes of the old bull elk and fled into the house.

Todd stood speechless. He thought he did a good thing by mercifully killing a wounded female elk and dispatching an old bull—

destined to lie down and die in the near future. He shook his head and approached the animals. As a kid he had watched his dad dress out many beef animals, sheep, and goats but had been detached, drinking tea and talking with the men. Now, as he sank his blade into the animal's neck and sawed the juggler and the windpipe he was feeling sick. Blood flowed but not with the heart-pumped gush he'd seen when his father slaughtered animals. The animal lay dead and the heart no longer pumped. He slit its belly and the intestines erupted out with a fetid smell.

Skinning and butchering the two animals took him the rest of the day and into the evening. He laid the parts on a large rock, telling Hammer to guard the meat. Todd handed him a large bone with clinging meat for his reward.

He did know how to skin an animal. That part had always interested him. After he had finished butchering the animals, he rolled the carefully removed skins and took them to the pond where he sank them, weighted by stones, to keep until he could tan them. He washed. Then he trudged home and crawled onto his side of the sleeping shelf exhausted. Sarah still quietly sobbing.

Now the problem remained to preserve the meat of the two animals. He wanted to show his appreciation for their lives by using them for a good purpose, extending his life and Sarah's . He did not sleep but he did make plans for a smokehouse. He knew the rubble of stones broke easily into flat-sided pieces. Building with them was much easier than building with round, hard fieldstones. He had learned a lot by working with the Chief and his braves.

He awoke at dawn. Sarah still did not talk to him, but she did fry him a thick slice of fatback in silence. He ate outside with faithful Hammer and shared some of his breakfast. They sat by the big table rock, looking at the pile of meat, Todd's mind working on a project.

When finished, he began gathering flat stones, piling them well back under the overhang. He went to the stream and dug in the bank of clay. He carried a large wooden bucket full to the overhang, stacking the flat shards of rock and daubing them with clay. By afternoon a six foot by sixfoot room with a low door opening was completed. He put poles across the top of the walls for hanging the meat He roofed it with poles and sheets of bark peeled from a felled tulip poplar. Finally, he daubed everything with clay. The roof needed to be tight enough to hold in a cloud of smoke. The overhang would protect it from rain.

Hanging the meat from the poles, he made a low fire in the center of the room. The smoke filled the area and seeped through the roof in a few areas. He daubed them until no threads of smoke seeped out.

The chief and his son returned from a long conference with the Cherokee leaders. They were surprised to see the smokehouse and the hanging meat. They were also pleased with the cabin. The Chief was not offended by Todd's changes. He was accepting that life was changing. The chief had shown him how to dry the meat on a rock to preserve it for winter. Todd considered doing what they suggested but thought of his father and followed his ways. The smokehouse stood finished and working. Without any unusual intervention, they had over three hundred pounds of meat swinging in the smokehouse for winter.

The exhaustion of a hard day of work upon him, Todd retreated to the hot spring, stripped off his filthy clothing and joined the Chief and his son. When they left to set up their camp, Todd heaped the warm mud on his tired body. He dreaded going back to the sound of Sarah's sobbing, so he put it off until nearly dark.

In the distance, he saw the flicker of a candle through an unshuttered window of his home. He rinsed off and pulled on his now clean but wet trousers. He heard no call to dinner, so he anticipated a cold slice of meat of his own preparing.

Opening the door, he smelled fresh baked bread and the sweet aroma of a pot of stew bubbling in the iron pot placed in the coals of the fire. Sarah smiled and touched his face. "Todd, put on dry clothes and we will have supper together." Her eyes were dry and a sweet smile lit up her face.

Sarah would not let him help clean up. Instead, she led him to his sleeping shelf. As he stretched out, she kissed him quickly on the cheek and fled from his reach, giggling. She stepped back toward him as he gazed into her eyes. He did not reach for her. They looked quietly and deeply into each other's souls. After only a few moments, she pulled a stool near him and sat down, reaching for one of his battered hands. Sleep came quickly to Todd, but Sarah sat in the firelight near to him holding his hand. She watched him for a long time.

CHAPTER 15

BUTTER AND EGGS

SARAH CAME FROM DEEP IN THE COUNTRY. Her father had taught her the basics of language, but after he was killed both she and her mother drifted into the vernacular. By day, in fleeting moments of rest, she studied the little book of grammar her aunt had given her. She was improving her speech.

Now she also handled the rough life of the wilderness with eagerness. She milked the cow that had recently calved and 'come fresh'—her udder and teats full of milk. She contended with the calf to take some of mother's milk. The milk was rich and the cream floated to the top. She skimmed the cream into a large jar, sealed the lid, and shook it vigorously until clumps of butter formed. She molded the lumps into a wooden form, and when it cooled she had a pad of fresh butter.

The day was still new as she poured the whey—that was left after the butter was strained out—into two cups. She made pan-fried bread in her iron skillet, and when done, she and Todd lathered it with her new butter. He gave a great smile as he carved a slice of his father's country ham and added two of Sarah's eggs.

They moved out to the sunshine, carrying their pewter plates to a large slab of rock that they used as a table, and devoured the meal.

"Todd," she said, "tomorrow I'll make some cheese. Right now, just hold me. This wilderness still frightens me, but I will learn to love this place and to appreciate you. I am sorry for the animals, but I know you did the right thing."

Todd did not understand the drifting emotions of the girl. She was so different from his stable and quiet mother. He did recall a few exasperated comments made by his father about no man understanding a woman. "They do not think like a man," he said. Now Todd understood—not understanding women was a universal problem in the world of men. Without further thought, he pulled her into his arms and held her tightly. She trembled, slowly relaxing, and smiled, nuzzling the side of his face.

The two dogs were jealous and attempted to climb the rock to nuzzle their humans. Both Todd and Sarah reached out and stroked their four-footed friends.

Todd was learning about this woman, even with no one to teach him. He understood protection, physical responsibility, honor and responsibility. He did not understand the nuance of the fleeting or unspoken needs of his mate. He did not understand that hidden area and wanted to know more.

Sarah was learning about Todd, but behind her was a million years of female instinct to guide her.

That night they slept alone as usual. Todd woke up with an urgent feeling that he needed more than sleep. He spoke Sarah's name in the darkness.

"I know, Todd, please go back to sleep," she said, and he did.

He awoke full of plans. He needed to make a shelter for the animals. The dogs slept in the cabin when it was cold, but the cow, the horses, and the chickens would need a warm, safe place when winter came to the bend.

The shelter of the overhang served them well, so he gathered clay and flat rocks and built three walls open to the back of the cleft. Nearby he stacked hay cut with a scythe on the lush field near the creek. He pitched it behind the low walls of stacked rock he had laid up near the stables.

He knew the animals would eat grass most of the year, but if storms came, they would need fodder. His dad often said cows would survive terrible cold if you provided something for them to eat, but horses needed shelter as well as food.

The chickens still used their crates, but Todd built a pen so they would have more room and protection from night-prowling animals. Chestnut, considered Sarah the top of her list of responsibilities, but chickens were number two. Nothing breached her perimeter of protection. Sarah and her chickens slept undisturbed. Even Todd received suspicious looks as he gathered eggs early in the morning.

Every day Todd looked around for a possible well site. There was a damp area only about fifty feet from his cabin. It was outside of the drip line of the overhang by only a few feet. He noticed it because the hooves of the horses sank in a few inches in just one small area. The grass was different, and greener and some weeds that generally grew near the creek were beginning to show themselves.

The professors had discussed dowsing at the Academy, and it usually provoked an argument as to whether it worked or not. His dad used it many times to find water. Todd took a forked branch off a willow tree growing near the pond and trimmed it like a large Y. He held a slim branch in each hand with the stem pointing out in front of him. Sure enough, the stem seemed to pull downward just as he walked across the damp spot.

He cut away the thick sod and began to dig. When he had a hole the size of a barrel, he was tired and moved on to another job after erecting a fence of poles and limbs around the hole.

When he looked into the hole a few hours later, it was half-full of muddy water. The next morning it was still half-full but the water had cleared. He laid down on his belly and watched and listened. He was sure that there was movement in the water and possibly a faint sound.

He paved around the well with flat stones and tied a rope to a wooden bucket weighted with enough stone to make it tip and sink. Later he would use a metal pail if he could find one. He also needed to dig the well deeper and line it with stones but was afraid to get into the hole without some strong help available. Sarah enjoyed the long walk to the pool but was glad to have water so near, especially with winter coming.

Firewood was not a problem but did require collecting and breaking up into burnable fuel. Near the river stood a copse of many acres of giant oaks, huge chestnuts, hickory, and black walnuts. The old limbs were shaded and died for lack of sunlight. They dried on the tree, and eventually fell to the ground, where Todd gathered them into piles, roped them and let Bill pull them into the cliff dwelling site.

Todd broke, chopped, or sawed them into manageable lengths and stacked them well back in the overhang. They were dry and dead to start with but became even dryer stacked out of the rain and mist. They burned hot and with little smoke.

As the cold weather approached, Todd and Sarah would keep a larger fire in the hearth. The stone sleeping platforms built into the mass of the fireplace, and the thick chimney would soak up the heat from a fire and radiate it back for hours.

The north wind never touched them, and the south rains fell at the edge of the overhang, so they would not have to worry about snow in the cleft. They should survive the winter.

During both summer and fall, Sarah remained busy drying fruit and berries on the large south facing slabs of rock. She started storing food in July as the blackberries and elderberries ripened and continued through months of various fruit to the winter apples. She dried peaches, blueberries, and herbs in their season. She dried everything that they did not eat. There were bunches of dried herbs, strings of beans, leaves of tobacco, and ears of corn hanging from the rafters of the cabin. One of the small rooms that the Indians had made was now a grainery with bins of corn, wheat, and oats. They would remove the corn kernels from the cobs and winnow the grains in their spare time when winter arrived.

She learned to use clay to make the rough pots that she used to store the dried fruit in her special room. Todd dug a deep pit and put the raw clay pots in, then carefully added firewood and kept the blaze going until there remained only a deep bed of coals. He let them die out around the pots which fused and hardened.

As they were harvested and the good fruit dried, Sarah crushed the deformed apples and peaches, leftover berries of all kinds, and the tiny fruit of the elderberry into large crocks and let them stand and bubble. The wine would last a few months if she put it into the coldest part of the creek and kept the top stoppered. She slowly learned the art of making pots fit for wine, dried fruits, and grain. Her wine tasted somewhat like vinegar but would bring a blush to the cheeks on cold winter nights.

By fall, they harvested corn, potatoes, pumpkins, gourds, squash, turnips, cabbage, collards, and other garden vegetables. Todd dug a cave in the back of the cleft, laid up rock around it, and daubed it with clay. The small door was heavy and well secured.

All that they needed required work, and preparing to survive remained their major concern. Both grew up on farms and in farming communities. Both understood the need to do first things first.

At the end of a long day, they found themselves holding hands and talking over their accomplishments. Sarah often leaned her head on Todd's shoulder, and he often encircled her shoulders with his arms. He was no longer a youth. His body had grown thick, his arms and torso hairy, his hands wide and strong. Her body no longer looked like a young girl, but was full and well shaped. Her breasts were larger, and Todd wanted to cup them in his hand and nuzzle his face between them. She wanted it too but neither would cross the line.

CHAPTER 16

DAY OF REST

THE WORK CONTINUED ENDLESSLY. Both were exhausted, their hands blistered and their nails broken. They were both ready for a day off.

Todd woke up thinking about another day of work. He climbed out of bed and dressed quickly, going quietly to where the exhausted Sarah still slept. When he touched her gently, she opened her eyes and gazed up at him.

"As king of this realm known as Max Patch Bend, I hereby decree this day is a day of rest and adventure," Todd said with a grin. "No work today. Today we explore the Bend, as we have begun to call it. I have something figured out."

"If you step outside, noble king, your humble servant will dress for the occasion," Sarah said with a giggle and a huge smile. "First, I will put some grits on, and you can fetch us two eggs and a slice of smoked elk from the smokehouse."

As they often did, they sat in the morning sun on a flat slab of rock outside of the undercut of the cliff and ate their breakfast off their pewter plates.

"I have been studying this valley and don't think a volcanic eruption formed it like Uncle Max thinks. This undercut of the cliff in which we have been living would be on the right side of any stream coming out of the mountains to the south. I noticed the big slide of rubble right across the valley on the southwest corner, and I also noticed a big tower of rock right near the river which matches the rock on the far side."

"Oh great king, such wisdom is beyond my comprehension," Sarah said with an impish grin. "This knowledge is too great for me and I cannot attain to it."

"Okay, let me put it real simple. The river on our west once ran through here and made this valley as it did the gorge over there where the river is now. The tall part of the cliff to the north west fell down and blocked the river and for a while—a few thousand years—this was a lake and caught lots of nice soil and sand as it cut down through the rock. The river found a crack, cut a gorge, and the lake drained out into the gorge which gouged out deeper, leaving this place higher than the river."

"How did the big undercut come to be here?" she asked.

"Well, this river flows from south to north, so as it came around this steep bend its current flowed faster on the outside of the turn. The water cut out the soft layer of sandstone and made our living space so we do not need a roof and are out of the wind—neat trick. It made all those cliffs over a million years ago as the river cut down through the rocks, like over yonder at the gorge."

"Okay, Mr. Geology. Let us go so you can show me all the good stuff. I have another question for you to ponder. I have been wondering about our pond. The little stream keeps running into our pond and the pond never gets bigger. If you check, you will find that no stream comes out.

"I haven't given a thought to why the water never rises but just stays the same. Usually, you and I go swimming without many clothes, so I always have other things on my mind."

"You mean thing. You only have one thing on your mind," she said with another giggle.

"Let's go," he said quickly and turned around to change the subject and cover his blushing face.

Hammer and Chestnut finished cleaning the plates and bounded ahead, shoulder-to-shoulder to clear the way. They were big dogs and growing bigger. Todd's dog Hammer was part Newfoundland and Chestnut came from the new breed called Labrador. They looked nearly the same except Hammer was jet-black and Chestnut a deep brown with red tints. Both loved the water and both loved to run.

Todd and Sarah started walking hand in hand at a brisk pace across the field to the far side where they seldom ventured. Todd estimated it must have been over half a mile to where the pasture-like clearing ended, thickening into a fringe of large trees, reaching up to catch as much light as possible. Behind them, the cliff rose nearly perpendicularly for hundreds of feet. They skirted the woods and circled around by following the cliff until they arrived at the pond. It was fed by the stream flowing in the field near the cliffs, and grew larger as small seeps flowed into it.

"Let's take a break and sit for a while. I need to study this thing out," Todd said.

"No swimming this morning, Todd. It is too cool to be wet and you need to keep your mind on geology," Sarah said with a broad smile..

"Okay, I've got it. The water has to go underground and probably go down to the river. Max said there are two kinds of rock here, sandstone and limestone. I happen to know limestone gets holes in it. Up in the Shenandoah Valley, we have many caves in the limestone. The rock must slant from north to south or else there is a fault, and one side is higher than the other is. Our cabin is in sandstone. Here at the pond the rock is limestone.

"To my thinking, there must be a crack or a tunnel or something to carry the water. I have been studying the cliff. Do you see the line in the rock slanting up to our right? It is a thin layer of something, and it shows that this whole area slants west, but there is a sudden change of strata over on the east side, so there might be a fault. There was a lot of earthmoving activity in this area, including a hard plug that I will show you. My theory also explains the hot spring. I think Max is partially correct about volcanic activity, except that I have seen no lava rock. The professor had a piece and it is very hard and black"

"Do you think there is a cave here?"

"The cliff is limestone so there might be a cave somewhere inside. Caves are found in limestone."

"My king, lead on. I am becoming chilly sitting in the shade of the cliff. Goodness, how do you like my English? Let us continue down to the large stand of trees and the gorge. I have not seen the river in weeks since the advent of the hard rain. Remember, it roared like a waterfall and we journeyed down to see it. The thunder of the rushing water frightened me."

Sarah hooked Todd's arm in hers and looked up at him with a wide smile on her pleasant face. He looked down with a grin and a nod of his head. "Dear woman, enough with this sophisticated talk. Let us amble to the forest."

A wide opening of perhaps a thousand feet led from the valley to the river gorge. Todd began to understand how the original path of the river carved the valley. A large stand of trees now occupied the area, filled with huge walnut, oak, and hickory trees plus an assortment of evergreens around the edges. Near the river, a brushy growth, mixed with dense mounds of Rhododendron, crowded the bank above the gorge. Beyond, a drop of fifteen or more feet ended at the rushing and tumultuous water of the river.

Uphill and toward the south, the river flowed through a cut with nearly vertical sides, and the land rose quickly. For several hundred feet, the land leveled and soon started uphill toward the mountain in the distance. The river gushed through another narrow cut with vertical sides, like the ones to the north.

They walked back to the north, following the gorge to a giant spire of stone. The rock strata looked quite different from the rock of the gorge upriver. It appeared to Todd that something had risen up from below, something extremely hard. It looked to him as if this large plug diverted the river, which in turn carved a large bend, forming the valley. The original outlet of the river was an arm of the valley, later plugged by a massive collapse of the mountainside. The lake formed and eventually the water found a crack, or an earthquake formed one, and the escaping waters cut the narrow gorge where the original river once flowed, bypassing the valley and forming the bend.

"Sarah, my knowledge of geology is limited but my ideas make sense. Anyway, no matter how it happened, it left us with a beautiful valley."

"Not just us, Todd. Do not forget the fruit trees, the buried jugs of corn and the hardened poles, the grinding hole in the rock, and all the other signs that Indians have used this valley for hundreds of years, but for some reason it has been forgotten."

"You are right, Sarah. Now let's look at the fruit orchard and afterwards, head back home."

"Let's not go home yet. Judging by the sun it is nearly noon, and the lake should be in the sunshine now. You said it is a holiday so let us go swimming, lie in the sun, take a nap, and later go home for supper. But, you have to promise to behave."

Before Todd and Sarah even arrived, Hammer and Chestnut charged ahead and, without slowing down, leaped into the water. The huge splash scared a flock of wild ducks and three drinking deer. Sarah's pet duck was paddling around, flapping its wings, and scolding the dogs and protecting the tiny brood of ducks swarming around her. Some wild duck had left her with a family of fifteen ducklings.

They laughed as they watched the dogs play, making a froth out of the water. Todd turned his back, stripped off his clothes, and dived into the chilly water. As he tussled with the dogs, he heard a splash. Sarah had joined them.

CHAPTER 17

THE POOL

THEY SPLASHED EACH OTHER AND LAUGHED but Sarah kept low in the water. As they tired of the game, the dogs headed for shore, pulling their bodies out of the water and shaking a cloud of spray.

"My clothes!" she shrieked.

Sarah lifted herself with part of her chest out of water as she worried about her clothes. Todd saw no straps or shoulders of cloth. She turned toward him slowly. He held his breath as he stared at the mounds of her breasts with occasional glimpses of her pink nipples as little waves moved over them.

She held him with her eyes, a serious look on her face, as she submerged to her neck. The current slowly moved her toward him, and through the clear spring water, he saw the slightly distorted form of her body.

"Todd, please don't touch me," she said softly. Let us just swim around. The current pushed her to him and their bodies touched. She threw her arms around his neck and let their bodies press against each other. She cried softly, looking him in the eyes, tears clouding her vision.

"No, Todd, not now. It is still too soon and it wouldn't be right."

They floated near the wall of the cliff, still clinging to one another. He felt embarrassed by his arousal and moved to pull his hips away.

"It is okay. I know about the birds and the bees. Mama worked in a dance hall, so I have heard and seen plenty. Hold me a minute longer."

She kissed him lightly on the lips and tried to pull away.

He held her to himself. "I feel real deep about you," he said with a catch in his voice.

"I feel the same, probably more. Please turn your back so I can go to shore and put on my clothes. When I have my clothes on, come out, and I will look the other way."

Minutes later, they were dressed and lying on the grass side-by-side and holding hands. The dogs stretched out and went to sleep, but Todd and Sarah looked into one another's eyes and smiled. They were experiencing a sweetness exceeding passion.

CHAPTER 18

THE SHOOTER

TODD WALKED BEHIND THE BIG HORSE, Bill, holding the handles of a simple plow. They were breaking the ground to enlarge the garden for next year's planting, turning the sod under to enrich the soil and discourage weeds. They did not own a harrow. Todd had made a drag, but the soil would still require hoe work to break up the larger clods. In the spring he would do it all again, including the original part of the garden.

A flash of light on the rim of the valley caught his eye, so he stopped the horse. Suddenly he recognized the reflection of the sun on the lens of a spyglass. Todd instinctively dropped to the ground and began crawling toward a mound of dirt thrown up near a large rock when he was plowing a furrow. A rush of wind passed near him and a ball struck the field behind him. A half second later he heard the sound of the shot.

He was in the center of the open field in plain sight with only a rock and a furrow of earth for cover. He wanted to move away from Bill, so Bill would not be shot. Somewhere above him, the shooter either reached for a second gun or reloaded the first. Todd gambled on the latter and sprang up. Bending low, he ran toward a boulder a hundred feet away. Before he reached cover, another slug struck the ground near him and sang off into the field. He pumped his knees frantically, finally throwing himself behind the boulder.

The next shot hit the boulder to let him know the shooter had the range. As soon as the bullet struck the rock, Todd launched into a run and headed to the rubble near their homestead. He did not see the muzzle flash of the next shot but heard the wind of the slug. Sarah saw the flash and her daddy's long gun answered. Todd kept running and slid in beside her behind the big flat rock. He lay gasping for air. His favorite musket leaned against the boulder, and she was charging her long gun.

The two dogs were leaping through the boulders and brush near the face of the cliff, headed for the path up to the rim.

"I'm going to the cabin for my pistol and head up there."

"No, Todd. Going up is too dangerous. Stay with me."

"He can't get a shot at me once I make it to the trail unless he goes below the boulder. If he does, you can take a clear shot at him. If we don't do something, he can keep us pinned down for days."

"Love you, Todd. Please come back to me."

"I love you, too, Sarah. This will only take a couple of hours."

They looked directly into each other's eyes. They had done it. They had both admitted to themselves—they were in love, both shocked by the enormity of their words.

Todd broke eye contact, gathered up his powder flask and shot bag. Gripping the stock of his musket, he broke from cover and ran to the cabin. From there he darted to the bottom of the cliff into the cover of brush and fallen boulders. He had no plan except to draw the fire away from Sarah and to work his way to the path up the side of the cliff.

A rattle of stones came from up ahead, dislodged by the dogs high on the cliff. He caught a brief sight of the dogs as they left the path—climbing upward on an animal trail. As Todd lunged across an open area, a slug splattered against a boulder near him and peppered him with shards of rock, followed by the sound of the shot. The shooter stopped to reload. Todd sprinted to the next area of cover. If the shooter carried two rifles, Todd would be an easy target for about three seconds—plenty of time for a marksman to take a shot.

No second shot followed as Todd scrambled upward behind a fold in the cliff. As he neared an open space ahead, he dropped to the ground to study the rim. Gun smoke drifted lazily from a clump of trees a hundred feet or more from the start of the trail, but near the jutting rock on the rim that the gunman used for his first several shots.

Todd would be in plain sight on the path if the shooter stepped closer to the rim. He took a deep breath, then ran for the shadow of the boulder marking the beginning of the trail into the valley. Todd heard twigs snapping as the gunman eased toward the top of the path. A musket ball whistled over his head and crashed through the brush and trees on the rim. The intruder muttered a swear word. Todd heard him as he lunged into the brush, away from the lip of the canyon. The sound of the shot arrived. Todd knew Sarah had fired her father's long gun as the man came into sight on the rim. The shot was close enough to put fear into the man.

Todd took the opportunity to run up the trail, intending to flop down below the rim but close enough to be in position to shoot if he saw a target. Instead, he heard a crashing of brush and a sharp pistol shot, then snarls and a scream. Todd was afraid one of the dogs had been shot. He kept running over the rim and into the brush, keeping low.

Looking toward the sound of thrashing, he saw the two dogs. One dog stood over a man and the other lay on its belly, its mouth on the neck of the prone man. They both appeared unhurt, but the man was pulling a knife from his hip sheath.

"One move with the knife and you are dead," Todd hollered as he shoved the barrel of his musket into the man's chest. "Hammer, back. You, roll to your stomach, arms outstretched. Not another move or you are dead." Todd barked the words as taught in military school.

"I'm Sheriff Grasty and has a warrant for your arrest."

"I saw no badge when you were on your back, and this is two hundred or more miles from your territory. Here you are a criminal trying to bushwhack a woman and me. Chestnut, guard! Hammer, bring horse. Bring horse."

The dog bounded away and in minutes returned snapping at the heels of the sheriff's horse. Todd pulled the rope off the saddle pommel and threw several turns around the man's boots at the ankles. He tied them tightly with three quick half hitches, forcing the man into a fetal position, then ran the rope to the man's neck and took a turn. Standing back he ordered, "Turn over real slow, keeping your arms out." The man obeyed. Todd recognized Grasty, but he was not wearing a badge. Using the tail of the rope, he lashed the man's hands and then rummaged through his pockets. He searched through the saddlebag on the side of the horse near him. He found no badge and there was no warrant for his arrest.

He turned back to the prostrate Grasty. "Why are you hunting me?"

"Telling you will not hurt much, Casey. Lord Howe is paying me as I am sure you know."

"How is Quincy?"

"He ain't worth nothin'. He will not try to do nothin' and is as useless as teats on a bull. He just eats, drinks wine, and is as fat as a pregnant cow."

"You know I didn't put his dagger into his belly. He fell on it while attacking me."

"I know it to be a fact."

"Why are you trying to kill me?"

"If I kill you I will be paid a lot of money when I take your head to Lord Howe."

"You don't mind killing an innocent man?"

"I have no druthers. I'll be right happy to kill the son of Gilbert Casey. This here situation ain't the end of the matter. You and the woman is both to die."

With a clatter of hooves, Thunders head came into view, then Sarah's head and body as her tall horse emerged—thunder, with Sarah riding bareback. She dismounted with one of her father's big pistols leveled at the man on the ground.

She slipped one arm around Todd's torso. "Thank God, you are not hurt. I really worried." Tears were on her cheeks in spite of the deep flush of excitement.

"Your shot saved my life. If he had kept coming there was no place to hide, and one of us would have been shot for sure."

"I'm going to see you hanged," the man said with a laugh.

"Not with me holding this horse pistol on you," Sarah said. "Todd has told me about skunks like you, and I am not squeamish about firing into you."

"Sarah, you keep your pistol on him, but not close enough for him to kick you. I will tie his arms behind him and loosen his neck and feet so he can shuffle. Right now his feet are tied too tight and his arms are over his head. I was unable to do better at the time. Now that you have a gun on him I can tie him up right."

"I don't want him near our home, Todd."

"Well, we cannot kill him like he would us. If we tie him to a tree or somewhere up here, the bears will kill him. The right thing to do is take him into the Bend. Once there we can think of something else to do."

"I know you are right. Tie his hands and put a noose around his neck, and we can lead him like the gang did the Indian boy."

As Todd tied the rope, he questioned Grasty. "Where is your badge?" he asked.

"Your daddy had it took. He went to the governor about our little trip to your farm, and the governor took my badge. Do not worry. Lord Howe is paying me good to find you and kill you. He knows he cannot have you hung. Quincy is living on his daddy's couch getting fatter and thinking of ways to torture you when I deliver you and the girl. He will pay extra for you alive."

"How did you find us?" Todd asked.

"I drifted for a long time after you ran, asking questions from town to town. I finally heard about a girl who an attorney named Tate Wicks was looking for. I heard in a saloon there was a bunch after her, and a boy of your description killed one and run off the others. I met Wicks. He hired me to kill a man down in Savannah, so it took some time. Then I did bounty work clear up to New York. Afterwards, I went back home and worked around there, and eventually Howe hired me to look around down here again. I started looking in the area where you killed the man Pots on the trail. I have been at it for quite some time.

"Pots was killed west of where I was looking, so I headed west and went clear past the mountains and then headed back into them. Today I seen two Indians in a camp looking like they camped there a long time. One went off hunting, so I sneaked up and took holt of the other and put my knife to his throat. I asked him about a boy riding a big stallion and trailing a colt with a white tomahawk blaze, and maybe with a girl. He got agitated. He made a move on me so I killed him. I took his scalp like some of them do."

Tears were rolling down Sarah's cheeks, but she held the gun steady.

"I knew I was getting close," continued Grasty. "I come up the mountain and found this valley with you in the middle of it. If I hadn't of missed my first shot, I would have caught me this woman for sure."

"Sarah and I did not kill Pots, who was about to rape her. Our dogs jumped him and he split his head on a rock."

"I knew Pots and I doubt it happened that way. I have my beliefs and I am seldom wrong."

"As many times as you say 'I,' you must have a high opinion of yourself."

"Well, before I leave this place I will have this girl, and I will have you dead over a saddle while I go back to grab me a piece of your daddy's farm."

Todd jerked the knot around Grasty's neck tighter. At the same time, he poked him in the gut with his rifle, gritting his teeth and wanting to shoot the man.

The dogs were sniffing around Grasty's horse, so Todd looked to see what interested them. Tied to the far side of the saddle was a fresh human scalp of dark oily hair, obviously recently taken from an Indian, the blood still sticky. Both Todd and Sarah sickened at the sight.

Sarah took off the two saddlebags, stripped off the horse's bridle and hung it across the saddle. She gave the horse a whack on the rump. It trotted into the woods clattering over the loose stones of the mountainside. In the distance, they heard the deep growl of an animal.

They stood beside the big boulder at the top of the trail with Todd holding the rope. Sarah's unsaddled horse did not have a bridle or halter, so they could not use Thunder for a place to tie the end of the rope. Besides, the animal acted nervous. The dogs were uneasy, too, glancing towards the woods and pacing back and forth.

"I'll go back and fetch Grasty's horse," Todd said, "and tie off this line to his saddle. He will try something to jerk you and me off the cliff."

"Be careful and take a loaded gun. Something is in the woods, and it sure enough might be bear. Something is worrying the dogs," Sarah said.

"You go on and check, Todd," Grasty said, "while I look over this fine valley. It will become mine when I kill you two."

As Todd glanced back towards the woods, he saw a brief movement, and his eye caught something traveling too fast to understand. A wet hunk against meat sounded next to him. The sheriff screamed as the impact drove him over the edge of the sheer cliff. The rope whipped through Todd's hands as he tried to stop it, but the end jerked through his grip, disappearing into space.

Startled, they leaned over the edge to witness the cartwheeling body as it bounced off a spine of rock and ricocheted into the rubble field below.

Todd and Sarah were speechless as they held each other. The dogs sprang into action, racing up the trail and into the forest. In minutes, they returned, panting but satisfied. Todd pointed down the trail and with authority said, "Go." The dogs took off running. Todd and Sarah headed down the trail, but Thunder was skittish and pawing. She spoke quietly, calming the animal and stroking its smooth nose.

They continued down the trail, finally reached the body. The corpse, broken and obviously lifeless, lay draped over a bolder. An arrow entered from its back and protruded from the chest. A short range shot from a strong bow drove the arrowhead through the body.

They found a sack of gold coins under his shirt and tied around his waist. Todd dropped the sack of coins into the saddlebag beside

Grasty's pistol and telescope. Todd was carrying the bags and Grasty's rifle when the sheriff fell.

The guns were like any other good weapons but not engraved or in any way special. The spyglass was of good quality but looked like many others of British issue. Todd remembered seeing one in his father's gear during the years he soldiered for the colonies. He decided to keep the guns and the telescope.

As they knelt by the body, they heard a yelp like a coyote on the lip of the canyon wall. Silhouetted against the sky they saw a man on a pony, leading a saddled horse with a body draped over the saddle. The man waved as he rode away into the forest, leading Grasty's horse.

"He looked like the big brave the Chief left to guard us," Sarah said. "It has been such a long time. I never thought he and the other brave were still nearby.

"One died for us," Todd said as he put his arm around Sarah's slim waist.

Later they returned with a shovel and buried the remains of the former Sheriff Grasty, moving a few large rocks over the shallow grave to discourage animals. They went home without speaking, hand in hand, lost in the horror of the day.

CHAPTER 19

TEARS OF A WOMAN

SARAH CRIED HERSELF TO SLEEP for several nights. She awoke with dark circles under her eyes and her eyes were red. Todd did not have any idea what caused the tears or what to do about it. He enticed her to the pond near the cliff but she refused to swim. He stripped down, keeping his back to her and plunged into the dark cool water. He splashed her, taunted her good-naturedly and finally pleaded with her to join him. In response, she gathered her skirts and started walking back to their stone house nestled under the overhang of the cliff. The afternoon sun shown into the cleft—washing their home with sunlight.

Puzzlement, dejection, and rejection rode roughshod through his masculine brain. It did not make any sense to him. They survived the assault by the ex-sheriff and he died. To Todd the occasion should be a happy one, not tearful, disapproving and sullen. What had he done wrong? To his mind, it all worked out fine. He did not kill Grasty; the Indian brave did it as revenge for his friend's death.

Returning to the house after seeing to the animals he found her frying Indian bread in an iron skillet, side bacon on one edge. She still sobbed, red-eyed and drawn. They ate wordlessly on the big rock and afterward he washed the pewter plates. Sarah went to bed still sobbing.

Todd sat by the small cooking fire in the fireplace, petting the two dogs that looked equally unhappy, needing her attention. He lighted a lamp and pulled out one of his geology books, studying the geological strata. Todd found it impossible to concentrate. He closed the book, extinguished the lamp, and went to kneel by Sarah where she laid, tucked into her blanket. "I love you," he whispered into her ear.

She uttered a loud cry as she threw her arms around Todd's neck, pulling him down beside her. She kissed him, her lips opening and her tongue exploring his still closed lips. They experienced feelings neither of them knew anything about, and their breath came in gasps as they broke for a second to breathe.

Todd crawled up beside her, throwing back her covers and pressing himself against her flimsy nightdress. She pulled him tighter and thrust her hips against him. His hands went to her breasts and she kissed him harder as he kneaded them and stroked her erect nipples.

They were lost in their desire for one another. He pushed up her nightdress with her help and kissed her nipples. She pulled his face up against a breast and pressed it into his mouth.

In only minutes, he shed his clothes and their bodies pressed against one another. He could feel the hair of her upper thighs against his member—his body and mind consumed with passion, desiring to make her fully his.

"No!" Todd said in a strangled voice. "No, we can't." I love you so much but I want to be married before we…"

"Thank you," she said against his ear. "Thank you! I love you so much. I would let you do anything. And want you so much."

Todd rolled off her sleeping shelf and fell to his knees beside her. His nakedness seemed awkward, so he pulled on his pants. She still lay there sobbing with her cover pulled back, her nightshirt bunched at the waist and pulled askew at the top to reveal her breasts. He kissed her lightly as he pulled a blanket over her body. Todd started to cry, holding her as they wept softly.

CHAPTER 20

FAMOUS VISITOR

TODD AND SARAH were tender with each other the next morning and for several days thereafter. Each looked toward the other continually and smiled each time their eyes met. They did not need words. Their relationship changed, and a deepening maturity infused both of them.

"You know what I have been praying, Todd?"

"No," he said. "Please tell me."

"We need to go and find a town, a church or something."

"You want to marry me?" he asked with a sly grin.

"Oh, yes. Do you want to marry me?"

"Yes, I do!"

"If it is so, you need to pray too."

A week or more passed. Todd was deep in thought as to how he might find a way to be married. The marriages he had attended as a youth were held in a church, with all the guests dressed up in their best clothes, and a big party afterwards. He had no idea where a church might be. They lived out in the middle of nowhere. He had no best clothes and she had no wedding dress. They could afford no party, and knew no one who would attend. For weeks, he mulled over the problem with no relief.

A "HELLO" ECHOED across the valley.

Todd looked up from his work, saw a figure on the lip of the cliff, and grabbed his rifle.

The figure was on horseback, wearing a loose rider's coat and waving his hat above his head.

"Who is it?" shouted Sarah from the grinding stone. "He seems friendly, and I have a good feeling about him. Take a horse and go up to the rim. I will keep my rifle handy. I think he hollered "Hallelujah.""

Todd rode up to the big boulder at the head of the trail. The two dogs went on ahead, and were wagging tails near the visitor as he waited.

The rider held back the tails of his coat to show he was not carrying a pistol. "My name is Francis Asbury; I'm a preacher spreading the good news of Jesus Christ."

"Welcome, preacher. I am Todd Casey and my friend Sarah and I have not seen a preacher for what seems forever. We are about to need one. We have been honorable, but it is getting difficult. In fact, we have been praying to find some way to be married."

"Well, I don't generally ride this way but had a feeling to come up here. I think this meeting is a matter of divine providence."

Arriving at the cabin, they found Sarah in petticoats with her hair brushed, glowing as if with an inner light. With her eyes and her face smiling, she gazed at her guest.

As Todd introduced her to Francis Asbury, she burst out sobbing. She knew the name and knew he was a famous preacher. She found it hard to speak as tears dribbled down her face. When the man shouted his hello from the rim, something quickened in her, and she knew he represented an answer to prayer. Emotion now blocked her speech as she stood before the preacher.

A faint sound came from the preacher's riding cloak. Asbury reached into a pocket. "I nearly forgot this," he said pulling a kitten from the pocket. "I don't know if it is a he or a she, but I found the kitten in the weeds next to a creek so named it Moses. Feel free to change the name."

Sarah took the small animal and held it to her bodice, cooing to it in baby talk. She sat the kitten on the warm sleeping shelf and gave it a saucer of milk. The kitten drank heartily.

As Sarah prepared a meal, Asbury talked to them of God and his mercy. Both Sarah and Todd were churchgoers in their youth, but neither had personally met God or committed themselves to Jesus. Asbury went on speaking and teaching, igniting their desire for God. Before they went to bed, the three of them knelt by the fire, and Todd and Sarah prayed the words that Asbury gave them and knew that something had happened within then.

"Tomorrow morning," Asbury announced, "about sunrise we are going to have a wedding. God and the animals will be our witnesses. It will be a new day, a new beginning, and a new life for you two."

After the ceremony, Francis Asbury mounted his horse, leaving Max Patch Bend with a wave of his hat. The lovers turned to one another, giggled, and ran to the cabin.

Chapter 21

Uncle Max

SIX MONTHS LATER Sarah was pregnant and showing. Her figure was changing, her usual slim silhouette filling out, her skin radiant, and her disposition excellent. She endured a few weeks of morning sickness, but remained healthy, strong, and active. She appeared and acted as a woman, not the girl she had been before Asbury's visit.

Todd had also changed since his marriage. He was far more understanding and caring, and his disposition mellow. He had always been serious about what he was doing, but now his priorities included his wife and he was more flexible. He still found it hard to keep his eyes, or his hand's, off his now always-willing wife.

Todd, and Bill, were plowing the garden late one afternoon when the sound of a shot from the area near the trailhead on the rim reached his ears. He quickly stepped from behind Bill and knelt down in the shadow of the plow. Looking toward the rim, he saw a man on a horse waving his hat and bellowing a 'hello.' He did not recognize the muted word but it sounded friendly. Todd ran to the house and fetched his spyglass. In the lens, he recognized the figure of 'Uncle Max.'

He shot his own pistol in the air, waved his hat, and whistled for his faithful horse Eagle. He asked Sarah to unharness Bill and turn him loose. Eagle arrived at a gallop, sliding to a stop. Todd mounted bareback and without a bridle, guiding the horse by knee or hand pressure, Eagle leapt to a canter. Todd rode with one hand lightly touching the horse's mane. Eagle slowed to a trot when they started up the trail to the rim. The two dogs bounded ahead.

Max dismounted as Todd rounded the boulder. Todd slid off the stallion, grabbing the barrel-shaped man in a hug. They looked each other in the eye, laughed, and chattered like women as they walked beside their animals down to the cabin.

Max reached to grab Sarah in a bear hug, but seeing her enlarged stomach he stood away, gazing down and laughing.

"I don't care if this kid is legal or not, but I am claiming it as my kin."

Sarah grinned broadly. "Francis Asbury happened by, and we married legal before this present came along," she said still smiling.

"Francis Asbury, about the most famous preacher ever to trod these mountains, or any other ground, since Jesus himself. You have done yourself proud, young lady."

"What brings you so far from home Max? Is the family in danger?" Todd asked.

"All is fine—your parents, your brothers and your sister, and even your old hound. What I come to tell you is news. You know we has won the war. Well, the British is about all cleaned out and is sailing home, and we is working on a constitution. Hallelujah! Your daddy and me fought French, Indians, and British, and has beat them all. Now it is a time to build our nation and settle down for some peace—except for politics—they will not be peaceful."

Max continued. "The good news is your daddy has been chose again to try and pull some of the politicians together. There are many ideas and many opinions out there. It is a confusing job. Your daddy is good at calming folks down and getting them to work together.

"I have got it all in a letter for you, but the outside was writ that I should read it too. The letter was brought by a man doing Indian business for our Continental Congress."

Sarah sat near the fireplace, tending the bread in the oven and the deer steaks in the iron skillet. She had intended on cooking a stew, but this being a special occasion, she was setting out a spread.

"Before I forget," Max said as he puffed on his pipe. "The sheriff causing you trouble was fired by the governor at your dad's suggestion. He disappeared and no one has heard of him or from him, so you need to keep your eyes open."

"Don't worry any about Sheriff Grasty," Todd said seriously. "He tangled with a brave up on the rim after scalping the brave's friend. Sarah and I caught Grasty after his firing into the valley, and nearly getting me three times. We did not know what to do with him. We tied him good and were about to start down the trail when the brave shot him clear through with an arrow. The impact knocked him off the cliff. We buried him where he fell and put rocks on his grave."

"Now that is good news. I have laid awake more than a few nights a worryin', and know you folks have too. Yes sir, Grasty being dead is real good news. I call it a deserving end for a skunk."

"Time to eat, men. Move up to the table and let me feed you as my ma did my pa. Todd gets regular fixings but you will have butter and honey for your hot bread."

"First," Todd said, "we say a prayer like Preacher Asbury told us to give thanks, and with you dropping by, we have lots more to thank him for."

"This here is a real civilized place," Max said as he bowed his head.

After the meal, Max leaned back on the bench and patted his ample stomach. Then he took his time filling his pipe and using a flaming stick and lit the tobacco. "I have a surprise," Max finally said. "Some supplies is comin' to you in a few days. They is on a string of packhorses, so do not go shooting anyone on the rim till you look them over good. Now, if you do not mind, your Uncle Max is heading for the pile of hay he saw in your shed. I put my bedroll in there so do not try to talk me out of it. I am all wore out, have a full belly, and is ready to say goodnight."

Max woke up the next morning with plans to build a summer sleeping place outside of the cabin that became stifling hot after a meal was cooked in the huge fireplace. He and Todd sank poles into the sand and made a rack about five feet wide and eight feet long. They made the bottom out of small poles, lining it with grass and clay. The sleeping area stood three feet above the sand, looking south across the valley. The two dogs claimed the shady spot under the sleeping pallet.

The pack animals arrived with one of Max's neighbors, Elwin Adams, leading them. Max had left the supply train at the bottom of the mountain with instructions for Elwin to take the long way around to avoid the steep incline. They unloaded the animals and stowed the food and the tools.

One package was heavy. Max unrolled the material and exposed twenty iron pins with one end mushed like a nail head and the other hammered to a rough point.

"Them is to make you a spike harrow," Max said. "I seen the drag you made. If you bore holes and pound these pins in and make two staggered rows, you can break up the sod a lot easier after you plow."

"Max, that is one fine gift. Sarah and I thank you. I studied harrows at school but had no iron to make the pins. I tried wood but they broke too easily.

Max brought a fresh ham, two fat turkeys, several geese, and a long string of sausage made up in hog gut. They packed the new meat in the smokehouse around the elk carcass Todd had shot, and the two deer Elwin had shot on the way. The small stacked rock-type building was full of hanging meat, and a low fire smoldered in the center fire ring, filling the room with smoke. The aroma of smoked meat seeped out, and the dogs spent time near it with their noses in the air. The smokehouse needed to be larger and more sturdily built.

Sarah kept working on the summer room, cutting tall grass and laying it out to dry for a mattress. When everything was dry, she covered it all with the Elk skins. She readied her sleeping blankets to spread out on the hides.

"Sarah, now we need to build two more rooms, one on each end of the cabin," Max said, "one for the children what is coming and one for your room. I believe you may need more space and you sure need a better roof to hold in the heat. Last winter was mild, but this one may be bad with lots of real cold days. This roof of youins sure will not keep much heat. Todd, me, and Elwin can lay up the walls and make the roof. Then make up shingles and have her done in the rough and Todd can do the rest. Then we will deepen your well some."

In a month's time, the three men and Sarah accomplished what they set out to do. Elwin proved to be an expert carpenter, and Sarah was always eager to help. Todd and Sarah were using the sleeping platform; Max and Elwin were enjoying the hay in the shed.

"Time for me to be getting back to my wife, and cold is a comin'." Max said. "It took more than a week to get here with the pack animals loaded, but we should make it home several days quicker with them unloaded."

He and Elwin saddled their horses, hitched up the pack animals to a lead line, and headed up the path to the valley rim. Todd, Sarah, and the dogs followed them to the rim, and then said their goodbyes to the man who had made their hidden valley possible.

CHAPTER 22

THE PRIVY AND THE KEEP

"TODD, YOU KNOW ME to be a woman not needing lots of stuff, but I am short two things I would like. You know we do have a chamber pot, but I dislike using it. With the baby coming, I must get up at night and go outside to squat behind a rock. Well, I would like a privy with a seat where I can do my business without fear of tipping over and falling into it."

"I had not given it much thought," Todd replied, "but it would be easier than taking a shovel with you each time you have a serious need. I reckon we can make one with three sides out of poles daubed with moss and clay. It will be under the overhang so it will not need a roof."

"You know best, but there is real deep sand down from our house, past the big rock to our west. I'll be glad to help you dig a pit if you can make the floor and the walls."

"Sarah, you keep to being an expectant mother and let me build the privy. A thicket of sassafras trees grows to the west where the old river turned to head to the gorge and down the mountain. They grow in front of where the big slide blocked it off. They stand straight—not too big—and have a nice smell to them. I can sharpen one end and drive them into the sand side by side like a stockade, and tie them off to a cross piece with rope, vines, or a nailed piece. I probably cannot make a door right away."

"We will not be needing a door if you face the open side toward the inside of the overhang."

"So what is your second desire?"

"My first and greatest desire is for my husband, but I would also like a place to keep our greens, cheese, and such. The springhouse you made me is nice, but we need a dryer but cool place. I noticed the cave way back under the overhang where it looks like the Indians kept stuff, but it is kind of a hole. The sun about never reaches back there except in deep winter. Maybe you should make thick walls of stones set in clay.

Build it up to the top of the cave so as not to need a roof. Add a small opening to get in and some kind of door to keep out skunks, coons, and such."

"You are right. We have rats, mice, skunks, coons, squirrels, opossum, and maybe even bear, all wanting to eat our stuff. We cannot keep all of our food in the house. Your idea of a root cellar is a good idea. My mother has a real strong walled cellar she calls a keep."

"First the privy—afterwards you can build the keep," Sarah said. They both laughed. Todd remembered his engineering classes at the Academy, opened his blank notebook, and sketched his plans.

The hardest part of the privy was making the hole in the seat without having real saw-cut boards. He cut down a wide ash tree, split it with the grain to make four thick planks and then smoothed them with his drawknife. He butted two together and sketched a hole, half in one plank and half in the other. He carefully chipped out the half circle in each plank, smoothed them with his drawknife and fitted them together.

Sarah sat on the hole with her dress on and needed more room. They laughed and joked, but Todd went to work with his drawknife and soon had a fit suitable to her. Next, she wanted a small one where she would train her baby.

The night Todd finished building, Sarah went to her new privy and used the facility. She returned to their bed giggling. Todd hugged her. She rolled to him, guided his hand to her growing breasts, and kissed him deeply. An hour of passion and bliss followed as she gave him her appreciation and love. They slept soundly until a late rising at the far edge of dawn.

Her job was to wear a thin dress, hiked up and belted around her waist while her bare feet treaded the shallow pit of clay. Todd worked in the back of the crevice, lying flat rocks slathered with the clay that Sarah made into a bonding agent. She brought him the clay in a trough made from the leftover planks of ash, pegged together into a long pan with high sides and ends.

By nightfall, they had made a keep six feet wide and ten feel long, ending in a wedge-shaped area at the back and six feet high in front. The next day they added a second layer of rocks and clay to the outside and then heaped sand against the walls, nearly to the top. On the third day, Todd split some more of the ash and fashioned a door, securing the planks with cross pieces pegged to the boards. The door pivoted on a rock, the leather hinges attached to the side frames.

Sarah liked it, and as usual, they celebrated every triumph, or most anything else, with their lovemaking.

CHAPTER 23

THE BEAR

THE NIGHT WAS COLD several weeks after Max and Elwin left. The smokehouse was full of game and the smell of the slowly curing meat filled the area around the cabin. The dogs were sleeping in front of the dying fire in the main house. Todd slept soundly on his side of the chimney and Sarah lay awake on her side, thinking about the baby to come.

The dogs leapt to their feet simultaneously, snarling and rushing to the door. Their ferocity startled Sarah and woke Todd.

Todd did not bother with his pants. Wearing just his nightshirt he grabbed his double barrel, checked the primer, cocked the locks, and opened the door. The hounds bounded out and around the cabin. A loud growl and a terrified yelp shattered the night. One of the dogs landed at his feet whining. The other growled fiercely only a few feet away. Todd raised the gun to his shoulder and stepped forward. A dark shape reared up, slapping the other dog aside while striding forward. Todd fired one barrel followed by the other. The shape moved on toward him undaunted. A huge paw swung in an arc, catching Todd's nightshirt and the flesh of his chest, slinging him to one side.

The animal moved to where Todd had fallen. Todd began trying to scoot away from the obvious intent of the bear to kill him. A wounded hound bounded in, only to be swatted away again. The huge shadow reached down toward Todd with a large paw, white claws picking up the light of the stars.

The loud explosion echoed around the valley as Sarah's rifle belched fire. The animal shuddered, swayed, growled, and fell.

"Todd! Todd!" Sarah screamed. "Are you all right?"

"I'm hurt some but I am alive, thanks to you."

She rushed to him but raised one of her daddy's huge pistols, found the head of the bear, and blasted a heavy ball into its brain.

She knelt next to Todd, feeling the sticky blood covering his chest. She helped him heave himself to his feet and guided him to the house. One dog lay still on its side, unmoving. The other was whining and licking its side.

"The dogs, Sarah. They are hurt. Bring them in."

She laid Todd on the stone-paved floor in front of the fire, checked the open wounds on his chest, sobbed quietly, and laid a fresh towel across the deep lacerations. She pressed down on the towel to stop the flow of blood.

Hammer continued whimpering and licking himself as he tried to crawl to Todd's side.

"Chestnut," Todd muttered groggily. "Get Chestnut!"

Sarah was torn by indecision—to stay by her man or to tend to her dog.

"Please, Sarah. I ain't hurt too bad. Bring Chestnut in and stop her bleeding, as I am certain she is clawed bad."

Sarah went outside, and in moments, she guided Chestnut into the house. The dog staggered and flopped down, panting and whining.

"Her is real bad hurt on the side and her belly too. Her guts is a comin' out," Sarah cried as she spoke in the vernacular.

"Push the guts in with your fingers and sew up the hole," Todd said, holding the bloody towel to his chest.

"I cannot touch her insides," she said.

"You must push them in and sew the wound."

"I cannot sew a dog like a pillow."

"Best try on the dog, wife, because you must stitch Hammer and then me. We all need a lot of stitching."

Sarah sobbed for only a moment as she rushed to her sewing kit and threaded a big needle with white thread. The dog whimpered as the needle went through its flesh. She pushed in the intestines, drew the stitches tight and tied them off. She cried softly as she slowly closed the wounds with stitch after stitch. When she finished with Chestnut, she sewed up a long wound on Hammers side. Her usual composure returned as she became accustomed to sewing flesh.

"Husband, I have been practicing as you said, but now it is your turn to try my handiwork. You pray and I will sew."

By morning all of the sewing was completed, the wounds washed with one of Sarah's mother's herb remedies for infection, and Todd's chest bandaged with several of her boiled menstruation rags.

The next day, with the help of Bill pulling from his plow collar, and a loop of rope over an oak branch Todd raised the body of the large male bear into the air, feet first. Todd first slit its throat and cringed as he gutted it, using his torn chest muscles—wetting his bandages with his own fresh blood.

"The guts, Sarah—you must shovel dirt on them and ashes from our ash pile. Animals will be drawn to us by the smell."

After Sarah finished, Todd staggered inside with Sarah's help. He lay down on the sleeping shelf, exhausted and shivering as his badly wounded body attempted to cope with the damage and the recent exertion. The stone shelf held the heat of the cooking fire but Sarah covered him with two blankets and later spread his riding cloak across the top. She squatted beside him sobbing, still mad at herself for not being able to keep Todd from gutting the bear. The extra work had taken a heavy toll on his body.

Todd was lying on the heavy elk skin, fur side up. The skin remained somewhat stiff because of their crude attempt at tanning it and the other skins. Weeks before, they had soaked the skins in a trough made from a hollow log filled with oak bark and fire ashes. The skins were still stiff, but Sarah used them to provide comfort for her husband.

The dogs began recovering, stitched up but alive, taking a little food and water from Sarah's hands. Two days later both dogs struggled to their feet, and Sarah let them out of the door. They trotted stiffly but excitedly out to the edge of the field, looking up to the rim. Something was approaching the valley. Todd rolled off the sleeping shelf with care, willing his stiff and aching body to stand. He took the long rifle Sarah handed him.

He was feverish from his wounds and unstable on his feet, but he limped to the door and saw horsemen on the rim.

"Hand me the glass," he croaked with a weak voice.

Sarah handed him the spyglass the sheriff had brought.

"Sarah, it looks like my father. It looks like my mother, sister, and my brother," Todd muttered weakly as he sank to the floor.

Sarah knelt beside him, calling his name, but he did not respond. She could not lift him. She threw a blanket over him and then called her horse, mounted bareback, and cantered up the trail to the rim. Both dogs remained behind at her command. She did not want their stitches to tear and open the wounds.

"Is you Todd's parents?" she cried, tears dripping off her chin.

"Yes," cried his mother. "Where is he?"

"He's been bad hurt by a bear. He has a fever and fell to the floor so I rode for you."

"Let's go!" called Todd's father. "Show us the way down. Hurry, girl."

"I' m his wife, married by Reverend Asbury, and pregnant with your son's child," wailed Sarah.

"Daughter, let us go quickly!" Todd's mother said.

CHAPTER 24

FAMILY VISIT

MRS. CASEY MIXED HERBS with her daughter Nancy, who was three years younger than Todd. Nancy had blossomed into a beautiful woman with light red hair in waves tumbling down her back, an ample bust, and curving hips. She had changed over the past year.

Lucy Casey tended the unconscious Todd after they moved him to the warm sleeping shelf. She prayed, as she worked over Todd, leaving the unloading of supplies to Gilbert and their other son Joshua. Lucy was slight, but straight, her top larger than her waist. Her dress fell straight down from under her breasts and if her hips were wide or narrow, no one knew except her and Gilbert. Her jaw was large and firm, her brown eyes flashed with energy, and she had permanent smile creases in her cheeks and around her eyes.

The Casey pack animals were loaded with household goods, food, huge copper cauldrons, a modern plow, jars to put up food, drying screens, sugar, flour, corn meal, salt, pepper, herbs, dishes, pots and pans, silverware, clothes, blankets' and a huge canvas tent.

Joshua and Gilbert set up their large tent and unloaded the supplies and their personal items from the pack animals. As soon as they unloaded the animals, they turned them into the field with the others. The tent fit under the overhang of rock and was soon occupied byGilbert's family. They were industrious people and worked from dawn to dark, building fences, a cattle shed and horse stalls. They worked with their axe and the long two-man saw they had brought.

"Son, first off we need to skin the bear, cut off the fat, and start it cooking in one of the big pots we brought. There is not room in the smokehouse to hang the meat, so we will quarter it up and put it on a rack near the floor. Being in the smoke will keep the flies off until we can build a larger smokehouse. We will make extra smoke to make sure.

"As soon as we take care of the bear, we need to check the garden and pick what is ready, put gourds to dry in the sun, and put squash, parsnips, turnips, cabbage, and green stuff into the keep."

They harvested the corn, kept some for eating, and lay the rest in the sun to dry. Later the family would sit around a fire shucking the corn so it would dry better and give them a chance to cut out the worms, intent on eating the kernels.

Nancy, nearly twenty, displayed an exuberance of spirit and vitality of body. She sang as she scurried from one job to another, keeping up a lighthearted, seldom stopping dialogue. Nancy's blue eyes, fair skin, and excellent figure attracted many suitors back in the Shenandoah Valley, but she had not found the right one.

Mrs. Casey carried herself with strength and determination in spite of her slim frame—the epitome of an excellent helpmate.

Todd's older brother, Joshua, had a chiseled and weathered face, his bright blue eyes startling in his sun-browned face. He busied himself cutting firewood and stacking it under the shelter of the overhang. Afterwards, he mounted and explored the valley. He graduated from the Academy three years ahead of Todd, joining the revolutionary army after his graduation. He was serving with George Washington when Quincy Howe and his friends attacked Todd in the stable. Todd left town and had not returned. Several years slipped by without seeing his brother. At present, Joshua was on leave from the army.

On a sunny afternoon, Sarah took her mother-in-law to the hot spring. Both shed their dresses and eased into the water in only their shifts. Lucy groaned with pleasure and slid neck deep in the warm water, and Sarah grinned with pleasure.

"This may be rude to say," Sarah said, "but Todd and I have often made love after being in this warm water."

"What you say being true, daughter, I may bring Gilbert up here after we have dinner." She laughed and patted her new daughter on the shoulder.

Gilbert and Joshua enlarged and reinforced the smokehouse, built a pen for the two shoats they brought, butchered and hung the bear, and rendered off many pounds of bear grease from the heavy animal. The huge copper pots they brought brimmed with fat, and chunks of fatback were stacked in the keep under a mound of salt. They had soap to make, dried berries to cook with sugar and can in jars—wine to be made from the late elderberries. They waited until evening to scrape the fat and meat scraps off the bear hide. After working on it each evening, they rolled it up and weighted it down in the spring pool. The water made it supple enough to handle and kept the flies from laying eggs in the flesh and producing maggots.

They cut enough locust poles to drive them in side by side to line the well down to fifteen feet. Gilbert rigged a metal bucket so that it would tip and sink, filling itself with water.

Todd missed most of the activities but aroused and sat up two weeks after the encounter with the bear. After awakening, he healed quickly as he drank the strange concoctions made by his mother, wife, or sister.

The dogs were fine except for fresh scars where Sarah had stitched their ripped hides. His mother cried quietly as Todd told her what Sarah had done—saving his life by shooting the bear 'just as it raised its paw fixing to maul me to death.'

During their first dinner after Todd had awakened from his coma, they sat together at the rough table, benches sagging. The family prayed, rejoiced and enjoyed the elk roast Todd provided. Sarah cooked him a mix of vegetable with a thin slice of meat. He soon tired and lay down on the shelf to listen and laugh.

The Caseys left a month after arriving. They had helped to make many improvements. The house under the overhang was chinked with moss and wind proof. Floors of sawn wood lay over the packed earth, except for the stone paving in front of the hearth. A new bed stood waiting in the extra room. The shutters on the windows were now made of plank and fit tightly against the new frame, secure against cold and wind.

"Daughter," Lucy had said, "I would have you at my house for the baby, but know without asking that you will not leave my son here, and he sure cannot leave with all this stock.

"I spent some private time with Todd and talked to him as I would a woman because he will deliver your child. I told him all I know about birthing. He can do what needs done, so trust in him. I will be back as soon as the roads get better in the spring to see the new Casey you are giving us. Daughter, I am proud that you are my son's wife. We are blessed to have you in the family and will pray for you every day."

CHAPTER 25

NEIGHBORS

SEVERAL WEEKS LATER, a rider called a hello to the valley from the rim. Todd checked him with the telescope and waved. The man waved back, so Todd rode up the path to greet him at the rim.

"I is a huntin' and happened on this place. I seen your smoke and them fences, stock, and such, and figured I had me a neighbor. I live in a settlement past the wide valley to the southeast. My name is Sam, Sam Lancelotta from up above Washington. Been down here a year or so with my wife and two small children. Politicians, claiming we was squatters on the land, ran us off. Of course, they didn't mind our clearing it for them."

Sam paused for breath after so long an introduction.

"Pleased to meet you, neighbor. My name is Todd Casey. Other than my family and a few Indians, you are the first person we have seen in many months. Come to think about it, other than Preacher Asbury you are the first person, except family, we have seen."

"Well, sir, me and some friends rode into the area south and east of here and found us a nice high ridge in the middle of the mountains with pastures and a river. I ain't no farmer and would like to open a small store. We has four other families settling in our village and hear that now the war is over others will be looking for land in the mountains."

"So, you mind if I was to get down off of this horse? I has been riding for several hours a huntin'."

After Sam dismounted, Todd shook his hard and calloused hand in welcome. Sam was nearly his height but heavier. His complexion was light, he had a heavy shock of red hair, and his grin was wide.

"Well," Todd said, "We would surely welcome some neighbors. I have a lot of new fences, outbuildings, smokehouse, and such because of the help of my uncle, my father and my brother. My big worry is that we have a child on the way, and I am not looking forward to the job of birthing a baby."

106

"My wife is good at midwifein'. She has delivered children for folks plus two of her own. She would be proud to come up here and help out if you was to need her."

"That sure eases my mind. How far is it to your town?"

"It ain't much of a town, only five cabins so far, and it is about five miles after you get off this mountain. Down in the valley is a right fat creek and if you was to follow it, you would come to where we is. My wife goes by the name of Lois. My Lois is a fine woman. I do some Bible studying and preaching as we have meetings in a barn if it ain't too cold. It is a small log barn not yet chinked so it is a might drafty."

"I can suppose you are a Christian, preaching the Bible like you do."

"Yes, sir. We got no real minister, so it is up to me to do the preaching in the barn we use for a meeting house."

"We would be proud," Todd said, "to hear you preach and meet your Lois."

Sam nodded. "We need to get the women together to talk birthing, babies and such."

"Sam, I agree. Follow me down to my place and have supper with us. It is too late for you to make it home today. Stay with us and you can get an early start tomorrow, and hunt as you go home."

'That is right kindly of you and I will accept, Mr. Casey."

"Call me Todd, Sam. I think we are going to get along fine. Let's go down and meet my wife Sarah."

The dogs went ahead as they descended into the cut.

"I is glad to set my eyes on neighbors like youins," Sam said after the introductions in the cabin. "Some a comin' into the mountains is plumb rough. Excuse me for saying so, but us folks in the village would be proud to have the likes of you visit. On Sunday we have church and a meal afterwards. Besides, my wife Lois says we is overrun with cats and has a batch ready to be weaned. We would be proud to have you take them."

"We have us a cat that Preacher Asbury gave us but fear there are more things after our grain than she can handle. Besides, she has not grown big yet. We would be proud to have your litter. We will come to your village in a fortnight," Sarah said.

"You can see I am big with this child. I need to talk to Lois and the other women about this birthing."

"Come anytime and you will sure be welcome," Sam said. "I know the women will be glad to give you an earful." Sam spoke with a broad and honest smile on his face.

CHAPTER 26

FRIENDS

TODD WENT TO WORK on his farm, but his thoughts were on the pond and why it never overflowed. Hammer growled and stood stiff-legged. Todd noticed the stance of the dog and heard a distant hail. Scanning the edge of the cliff, he saw the tops of two covered wagons and three people waving their hats. He was puzzled a moment, but suddenly recognized the shapes of the people, even at the distance, and connected them with two covered wagons. The names came to mind, Eli Shipley, his wife Dorcus, and their son Puttman. He hoped that he was not seeing things because no wagon had ever been on the lip of the Bend. It was impossible to get to it with a wagon.

He calmed the dog and waved his hat in return, then whistled for Eagle who responded with a whinny and a toss of his head. He gathered his legs under himself and launched into a full run. He slid up to Todd, who grasped his mane, leapt on his back, and with a nudge of his heel urged him toward the cabin while shouting for Sarah.

She heard the hail from the cliff and knew by Todd's response that the visitors must be friends. She heard him whistle for the horse and called her own. He hardly arrived before she stepped up on a block of log, mounted, and was ready.

"It is the Shipleys I told you about. They ran off two of the groups of thugs who were after me."

"I will be proud to meet them, Todd. You notice I put a bridle on Thunder as you have been telling me because of the baby. I used the mounting block to mount because of the extra weight of our child."

"Well, it is for the best. You stick to a horse like a burr, but Thunder is a mighty tall animal," he said. "Let's ride."

Todd held his horse back as they made their way up the steep path. He did not want the two horses to start to race as he and Sarah often urged them to do. Things were different since she had become pregnant.

Todd called out the names of the Shipley family as he hauled up to them and swung to the ground. He reached up to Sarah whose horse crowded in beside him. She slid off into his arms.

"This is my wife Sarah," he said with obvious pride. Before he said anything else, Dorcus rushed up and embraced Sarah.

"Todd, Sarah is beautiful," Dorcus said as she turned to gave him a hug.

Eli and Putt stood there grinning. A dark haired girl pushed by the men and joined the women.

"This here girl is my daughter-in-law," Dorcus said. "Her name is Dare and we are proud to have her as part of our family. Dare, this here is Sarah Casey, who is a surprise to us like you is a surprise to Todd. We have us two new women and it's a good thing.

"Glad to meet you" Dare said. "Them two gawking men over there is my-father-in law, Eli Shipley, and my husband Putt."

The men finally stepped forward and grinned, nodded to Sarah, and touched her hand. The men shook Todd's hands with a lot of vigor and added slaps on the back.

Eli rubbed Thunders nose and stroked his neck. "I am mighty impressed with this stallion your wife is riding. I see that you still have the quiet black dog and you added a beautiful chestnut hair dog. I watched them race the horses up the trail, and they did not even pant after reaching the top. Them is fine dogs!"

"The amber one is Sarah's dog, Chestnut. The story goes she was born near a battery of cannon and fetched from the battle by Sarah's daddy. Chestnut and Hammer guard the whole place, watch the rim, and listen. I recall your dog Shadow is good with stock. We have plenty of dogs now and will surely know if we have visitors. The stallion, Thunder, was her pa's horse and is one smart animal."

Todd stepped back to look at the wagons. "How in thunder did you get those wagons up here?" Todd asked.

"It weren't easy," Eli said. "We cut a bunch of trees and rolled more than a few rocks. We hitched about half our horses fan style to each wagon and jerked them up. With so much horsepower, it didn't much matter how good the path was."

"We been at it two days not counting this morning," Putt said.

"Your friend Sam at the trading post rode with us the first day to keep us out of the wet spots down by the creek and to see we was pointed the right way. He is a fine man. He needed to go back to his store—I guess you would call it a trading shed. He is just building it a little at a time. He needed to get back to work or he would have helped us until we arrived. He said to tell you he is doing better and getting some pelt trade and customers from the Cherokee village."

"Sam is a true neighbor," Todd said. "Now we need to guide you down to our place. You must be plumb wore out. Fetch some of your stuff together because there is no way we can get those wagons down the trail into the Bend any time soon."

"Me and Putt have been figuring on the problem. For now, Putt will stay with the wagons and keep his horse and Dare her Indian pony. We will take the rest of the stock down into the valley where they will be a lot safer. We will worry out what we will do next. We hate to impose on your hospitality but we need to lay low a spell."

"We ain't done nothing illegal," Dorcus said, "but all them horses of ours make us look like horse thieves in some eyes, and the real horse thieves have their eyes on our horses too."

"It is true," Eli said. "If it weren't for your Uncle Max, we would have been in trouble. He talked to an old Union officer who considers himself the law and then snuck us out of town. Some friends of Max covered our tracks till we was into the mountains. Still, there is some cutthroats no doubt a lookin' for us. A new man in the settlement has opened a drinking place that is attracting rabble from out of the woods, or wherever them type live. We hid our tracks best we were able by keeping off the roads, but most any tracker would no doubt find us. Two wagons and all those horses leave a lot of tracks to follow.

"Todd, believe me—I sure never intended to cause you no trouble by coming here."

"Eli, you will be safer here than in most places, and you are welcome to stay as long as you want."

"Me, Dorcus, and Putt was a lookin' at your valley and noticed you have a neck of land to the north fenced off. Looks like about ten acres of tall grass there."

"Yes sir, my father and brothers fenced it off last time they visited. We have seen panthers, bears, coyotes, and such up in those rocks and in the thick woods up above where the slide comes down. We have plenty of pasture within sight of our cabin so decided to keep the stock out where we can keep track of them."

CHAPTER 27

WAGONS

THE THREE WOMEN made a fine dinner of elk roast, with onions, carrots, and potatoes cooked in a Dutch oven, snuggled in the coals of the fireplace. Dorcus whipped up a batch of biscuits, baking them in another heavy iron pot with a flat lid made to keep the biscuits warm after baking.

After pushing away his plate, Eli started talking.

"We was talking with Sam at the trading post. Sam told us about your valley, the cliffs, and only a horse trail down from the settlement. We talked about the wagons, and he mentioned some folks that come into the store talked about using ropes and tackle to lower their wagons over the steep places and even down some cliffs. For reasons of their own, they were traveling through the woods and not on trails.

"Well, sir, Sam swapped supplies for some rope that come from a ship up in the Chesapeake Bay area. Them folks were not aiming to go no farther into the mountains.

"You know I trade some, and Sam needed a horse for his wife. I happened to have a gentle soul of a horse with a good spirit and not much breeding, but sound. She come as part of another deal, or I would not have owned her. Now Lois wanted a horse so she has one, and we now have eight hundred feet of good rope. It has been tarred for use on water. It is messy and smells like tar but it is strong."

Todd leaned toward Eli. "I took mechanics at the Academy and understand mechanical purchase, fulcrums, multiplying the force and such by using blocks and sheaves. So keep talking."

"I figured on you knowing such things. It is simple. We take the wagons apart and lower them parts down. If need be we can haul them up the same way. We figure we take off the wheels and axles, take the beds apart as much as we need, and lower it down a piece at a time."

"If the rope holds, we can do it," Todd replied. "I even happen to know how to splice in case the rope does break. My pa taught me."

"If it sets with you, we can start tomorrow. I would like to move Putt off the ridge. Figure we can set his wagon in the ten acres, and he can live there to keep an eye on the stock. We can put the other wagon there or wherever you would suggest."

"How about putting it under the cut at the far end?" Todd said. You will be out of the wind and wet. Then we can make you a tight cabin of logs or stone to keep you warm come winter. It would be safer than a wagon from gunshot if we have unfriendly callers. We will need to get at it soon."

All agreed, and while Eli and Putt started disassembling the largest wagon, Todd scouted for the best location to lower its parts down the cliff. He needed a strong tree near the rim to anchor the ropes and a place without rocks at the bottom to land the parts.

He picked his place, and with the help of Eagle, he pulled the long rope and pulley blocks to the tree. He used a stout chain to wrap around the tree into which he hooked a large two-sheave pulley block. He tied one end of the rope to the ring beneath the block, passed the line through another block, and up to the first one. He repeated the process until the four sheaves had a line over them, dividing the eight hundred foot rope into four parts of two hundred feet each. His hands were black and sticky from the tar used to preserve it, and the smell permeated his clothes.

They set the tackle to handle two hundred feet of cliff. Between Todd and Eli's supplies they found at least fifty feet of chain. If they needed more length, they would attach it to the tree or to the hook of the last pulley block.

Todd picked the lowest part of the cliff and hoped it measured no taller than two hundred and fifty feet. The place he picked was a low place on the rim where a loose area had fallen away, creating a mound below. The men figured the two hundred feet between blocks should reach the mound with some to spare.

By noon the larger wagon was disassembled and the parts dragged to the lip of the cliff by Bill. They shortened the falls, pulling the two blocks close together and attached a wheel to the last block. They eased it to the edge, and Todd took a turn around another tree to take the initial weight. Eli pushed the wheel over while Todd tended the line. It hung above the vertical drop. The friction of the rope through the four sheaves let the weight pull the rope through the sheaves without much effort to check the fall. It lowered away smartly and settled on the mound with some rope to spare. Putt stood below, unhitched the wheel, and rolled it away.

The two men handed the rope until the bottom block reached the lip and was ready for another load. Another wheel went down, and following it the other two went down tied together. The heavy axles made of oak timber took two men to handle but overboard they went, requiring more hold back to check their fall.

The heavy oak falling-tongue, was the beam between the horses, attached to the wagon axle, and turned the wagon. The singletrees and doubletrees were attached to it. The bundle was heavy and awkward but went over the lip with no trouble. The bundled boards of the sides followed, but the floor of the bed proved to be too heavy for the two men to carry in one piece to the launching point. They finally hooked the block and tackle to Bill's harness, dragged it near the lip, and used pry bars to move it over the edge. Before it went over, Todd took a wrap around a tree to help take the strain. As the bed went over, the rope tightened around the tree, stripping away some of the bark as it paid out.

One wagon made it down and the three men were exhausted. Below rested a pile of parts that needed to be reassembled and moved to a final location. The women would do the canvas work and give the wagon a good scrubbing.

"Eli," Todd said. "I for one am done in and ready to quit. Therefore, before the sun goes down you can have your choice of soaking in our hot spring or swimming in our cold pond. If you try to soak in the cold pond, you will shrivel up, turn blue, and sink."

"I choose the warm spring, but have no bathing outfit."

"We bathe in just skin and chuck the modesty," Todd said. "Today, no women allowed."

CHAPTER 28

COLD SPELL

AFTER TWO DAYS of intermittent rain, the temperature began dropping as the cold air rushed down the mountain and poured into the valley. The water dripping down the cliff above was forming into icicles. The low clouds were breaking up and patches of blue shone through. The afternoon passed with constantly falling temperatures. The hazy, heatless winter sun settled toward the mountains, shining its last feeble glow on the hundreds of ice spears hanging from the rim of the cut. Several reached downward ten feet or more—most of the ice had accumulated since noon. Todd stood in front of the door to his cabin gazing upward, wondering how safe it would be to walk under the long, icy daggers.

He called Sarah to come to the door to see the many colors of the rainbow reflected in the dangling ice. She clung to him, looking up.

"I marvel at the beauty of the hand of God," she said. "I am glad the firewood is in the back of the cut so you don't have to go under those huge icicles."

"I may try to shoot several down to make a safe passage to the outside."

"No need, husband. All of the animals and all things we need are right here under our rock roof the Lord has given us. I fear I must sit as the baby is pressing down, so please get an armful of wood and come back inside to be with me." She blew out a breath, clouding the frigid air.

The cold penetrated Todd's shirt, and he wished he had put on his coat. Checking the animals, he found the cows and horses crowded together in the lean-to, contentedly chewing hay, their heavy breath freezing on the posts and the underside of the roof. A thin coating of ice adhered to everything.

The pigs squealed and bumped one another as they dug into the sand in the back of the cut, and the chickens and ducks crowded together in their pen, nestling down into the hay. Both dogs accompanied him on the inspection trip, stopping to relieve themselves. Todd visited the privy as briefly as possible and went for a load of wood.

By the time he reached the cabin he was shivering, and the warmth of the cabin soaked into him, driving out the intense cold. He stoked up the fire, raking the hot coals around the new heavy chunks of wood. They needed a long burning fire to keep the massive fireplace and the sleeping shelves warm. They would not be using the bed in the cold bedroom. The cat purred softly in her nest of hides and blankets. Sarah rested on her side on her warm sleeping shelf, her belly propped up with a pillow.

After a few minutes of warming himself, Todd put on the long rider's cloak, pulled his rabbit skin cap down over his ears and opened the door for the dogs to join him. Chestnut lay down, declining another walk. Hammer got up slowly, looking back at his spot near the fire.

Hammer stayed near to Todd as he lugged several armfuls of wood and stacked them near the front door of the cabin. He looked up and saw the gray sky breaking up, and in its place a clear sky studded with stars.

The wind completely died. Intense cold flowed into the valley, a silent force, drenching all that it touched with silent, penetrating chill.

He listened for the ever-present sound of the rapids in the gorge. The sound, muffled by ice forming on rocks and at the shallow edges, belied the strength of the river. In the distance steam rose from the warm pond, and a sheet of ice on the cold pond reflected the bright, cold light of the rising moon. He and Hammer retreated inside the warm cabin.

A doe and her fawn made their way down the entrance path and edged toward the lean-to, mingling with the cows and horses. Swallows and bats crowded deep in the back crevice of the cut while a bear pawed a hole in the sand near the warm pool and curled up.

Hammer stirred and went to the door—then came a knock, and the voice of Eli was plain. Todd took the bar off the door and welcomed both Eli and Dorcus into the room. They carried a pile of hides and blankets.

"This is a deep and terrible cold," Eli said. "Dorcus is worried about Sarah being so big so we has come to stay and to lend a hand with the fire and cooking, and be closer to the animals in case of any trouble. I seen a bear dig a hole by the warm pond but doubt he means any trouble. It must be fearsome cold up on the mountain.

"We does not want to intrude, so we will go if you say the word," Dorcus said.

"You are welcome, my friends," Sarah said. "What about Putt and Dare?"

"They has moved into our cabin and under a pile of hides. They will be fine, hugging and all, and keeping the fire a goin'. Our old hound is there to guard them if he happens to wake up in time."

"I aim to put a hide over your shutters and drape a blanket across the doorway to keep out the drafts," Dorcus said.

"I am much obliged and take comfort in you all being here," Sarah said. "I warn you, the trip to the privy is cold, and lifting one's skirts in this kind of weather is most uncomfortable. I tend to put it off until nearly too late, so many times I must use the pot."

A loud sound shook the quiet cold.

"It was a tree down by the river, freezing and collapsing," Eli said. I hope we do not lose any of those big chestnut trees. They produce our best hog food."

Todd spoke from the flickering darkness of the cabin, lighted only by the log fire. "We are fortunate this is a calm night. If the wind was blowing, we would lose not only trees but some of our stock as well. I would like to pray for our safety and the safety of our animals."

The four of them prayed then, and each day for several days.

The cold lasted four days, nearly exceeding their endurance. The inside of the door behind the blanket was white with frost as were the shutters behind the hanging animal skins. Even the underside of the roof twinkled with ice crystals catching the light from the flames of the fire. Where the chinking between the rocks of the walls was thin, frost crystals built tiny structures of ice.

They exhausted their pent up conversations and silence settled. The women were sewing baby clothes, Todd read by candle light, and Eli was whittling a wooden elk to hang over the baby bed.

On the fourth day Todd and Eli examined the animals as they did daily, this time, joined by both Putt and Dare. The young couple acted well rested, and were glad to be checking and feeding all of the critters. The animals acted subdued and quiet, welcoming the attention of the humans. Even the fowl came forward to crowd around Dare as she spread corn on the sand of the pen.

As Dare tended the animals, Todd, Eli, and Putt walked to the hot spring as the bear ambled up the path and back to the mountain forest. Ice clung to the grass at the edges of the hot spring, and heavy steam formed over its center. The pool by the cliff looked unfrozen, but in reality, a thick layer of black, transparent ice covered it.

By midmorning of the fifth day, the clear blue sky clouded with the change in cloud direction. A south breeze moved in with rising temperatures. Putt and Dare moved back to their small log cabin, allowing Eli and Dorcus to take down the hangings on the shutters and door of Todd and Sarah's cabin and move back to their own stone cabin.

The stock ventured out of the shelter, finding some overlooked straw, dried weeds, and dried grass. Worms had burrowed underground to escape the cold, but the chickens found half-frozen bugs. The hogs were after roots and fallen nuts. so they had no shortage of food to return to. They headed toward the river and the grove of nut trees.

Todd and Eli saddled their horses, left the Bend, and headed toward the settlement. They found a dead cow near the creek and horses searching for food. Sam saw them and met them in the center of the small village.

"We lost no people," he said. "A few animals perished, but all the children did well, all burrowed in animal skins and blankets. Some of the men have frostbitten fingers from going out in the cold to make sure others had firewood and food. How is you men doing? Is the women survived?"

"We are fine. Eli and Dorcus bunked with Sarah and me to help with the fire and the cooking. Sarah is too big to do much. Putt and Dare kept warm by loving. The dogs are full of spunk as you can see by the way they are playing with your dog. Eli and I are about to go back to a dead cow that we found. It has not been dead long, and the animals have not yet started to eat it. We will drag the cow here and help you slaughter it. What else can we do to help you people?" Todd asked.

"I will tell you what we is needing most. Some of our folks did not have food or firewood in sufficiency. Next Sunday I want you to come to church with Eli and the two of you talk about being prepared. I know Sarah is too far along to come on horseback, but Dorcus can talk some also."

"Well," Todd said, "you having the store and all makes folks think they no longer need to prepare. Some of the newer ones have never needed to have enough to take care of themselves. Eli and I will think on the subject."

"Mayhap," Eli said, "you need to preach about surviving, and God intending we should be ready both spiritually and physically. Todd and I can do some talking. Dorcus will talk about putting food aside by gathering, drying, and smoking, and about the need for a garden even if they is town folks."

"That sounds good," Sam said. "Right now I will call some men to slaughter the cow where it lies. You men show us where it is and then go back to your families."

As the days warmed, the huge icicles crashed down one by one, smashing to fragments on the sand and boulders below. Putt shot off a dozen of them to make a safe path out of the cut.

With the warm weather came flocks of geese and ducks, gathering in the creek and the pond. Buds were ripening, the grass was turning green, but it was too early. There would be more winter to come.

CHAPTER 29

ROBIN

THEY WENT TO BED with the early darkness, expecting to wake to rain. Sarah woke Todd five hours later holding her huge belly and grimacing with pain. "I think the baby is coming. I have only little pains far apart, but I have a feeling it is time."

"Do you want me to go and get help from Lois?"

"I hate you should go out with rain and all. I do not know when the baby is due as it had opportunity to be made many times, but I feel it wants to get borned. I was planning to ask Lois soon but fear the time is arrived. Please ride for Lois. Before you go, open the bedroom door and let the warm get in. I do not want to have our baby on this narrow shelf."

Todd opened the front door to blowing wind and heavily falling snow. The bite of cold made him realize the weather required more than an oilcloth riders coat. He did not mention the snow or the cold to Sarah. He jerked a heavy jacket off a peg near the door, found a hat and gloves, and pulled a rider's cloak over his shoulders.

Sarah looked at him with an inquiring expression.

"It may be cold up on the rim," he said as he kissed her. Then he went out the door into the storm and headed to the horse shed.

Todd saddled his horse in a windswept, snowy darkness. Nothing appeared visible beyond fifty feet and the ground was white with snow. The temperature dropped overnight from spring-like to the dead of winter. It was early March and spring had been in the mountain air two days previously with a bright sun shining and birds singing. The buds on trees and bushes were getting plump, ready to burst into blossoms. The morning sun had dimmed, followed by a grey noon and a dark afternoon with thickening clouds and a rising wind. Now it was a blizzard.

He mounted and rode the short distance to Eli's cabin and awakened him, and then rode into the storm and up the trail to the rim.

The storm treated Todd brutally on the rim with snow pelting and the high wind trying to tear him from the saddle of his snow-covered horse. He rode the skidding horse down the slope. As he entered the woods, the wind lessened, broken by the trees and the land behind. In spite of the broken wind, the cold increased. The farther down the mountain he rode, the deeper the snow became as the storm thickened, buffeting Todd with cold, wind, and blowing snow.

The ride off the mountain was difficult because of the snow and the slippery footing for his horse. Luckily, the ground had not frozen before the snow so at first Eagle's hooves found some traction on the loose earth below. Once he was off the mountain and onto the high bald plateau the wind found Todd again, and the damp early snow piled up in clods under Eagle's hooves.

In good weather, he usually made it to Sam Lancelotta's cabin in less than an hour when riding alone. This night it took much longer in the cold, wind, and snow. Over the last year, he and Sarah had made the trip to the settlement several times to hear the preaching and have supper with the tiny congregation. Sarah and Lois became friends immediately, and each time they got together, they talked as if they had not seen another human in weeks. Husbands did not count as company.

Todd drew near to the cabin, cold and exhausted. A hound bounded out of the woodshed and dashed toward Hammer who ran ahead of Eagle.

"Sit, Hammer," Todd shouted. The dog responded as the neighbor dog circled him, and at a shout from the cabin, he tucked his tail and ran back to the woodshed.

"Sam, it is Todd, from up on the mountain."

"You is up early. Must be Sarah is having a baby."

"Stop the talking and saddle my horse," Lois shouted from within the cabin. "I've kept me a bag packed for this."

Sam hustled to the shed where the stock was sheltered and the horses tethered. As he led the horse out, Lois ran to it and mounted. Under her coat, she was an ample woman but mounted the horse easily. She settled the travel kit in her lap and turned to her husband. Her face was round but strong with clear skin and a shock of black hair falling from beneath her tied-down hat.

"You is now ma and pa both, as well as cook and school teacher. There is no telling the day I shall return home—several days most likely. Do not forget tomorrow is Sunday, so you need to get ready to preach."

After speaking, she turned her horse, gave it a nudge with her heel, and galloped into the storm and toward the mountain. She, Sam, and her children had visited Max Patch before and she knew the way.

"Much obliged, neighbor," Todd said with a wave and turned Eagle. He urged him into a gallop to catch up with Lois who had rapidly disappeared into the storm. He had to stop as Eagle began to falter because of the clogs of snow building under his hooves. The horse stamped and kicked. The clods came loose. He started Eagle at a trot and rode into the gloom. He found Lois, dismounted and poking at the ice stilts under her horse's hooves. Todd dismounted, pulled his pistol, and jabbed at the snow clods with its barrel.

They remounted and entered the forest. The colder feathery snow no longer clumped up under the horses' hooves. The wind, broken by the trees, was less tormenting.

The light of dawn did not arrive at its appointed time. The snow drifted deeply, blown by the wind, while the temperature continued to drop. Todd took off his rider's cloak and hung it around Lois as she hunched forward in the saddle. The final climb up the mountain was brutal. The horses struggled through the snow up the steep incline as the wind tried to force them back. Hammer was ahead, struggling through the snow, his body covered with white. He ran behind a rock, laid down and tried to paw the ice and snow from his eyes.

At the rim, the wind nearly stopped the horses from going forward. Todd was stiff with cold. Lois spoke with difficulty—her words slurred when he asked if she was able to make it a half hour longer.

"I am going to dismount and lead the horses down the path into the valley," Todd said as if he had a mouth full of mush. His stiff face made it impossible to smile. He slid off his ice-covered horse, holding the saddle until he forced his legs to function.

After Todd dismounted, he walked to the horse Lois was riding and took the reins.

"Hammer, lead horse. Lead, Eagle."

Todd could barely see the snow-covered Hammer but Eagle followed him blindly down the dangerous trail. Todd followed his horse and dog, leading the horse that Lois was riding. His feet kept slipping out from under him, but his hand on the horse kept him from falling. Slowly, they forged their way through the storm and finally made the last turn.

"Hallelujah," Lois muttered and raised her arms in spite of her stiffness.

Todd mounted his horse, urged it into a trot, and headed for the cleft in the rock and his home. Arriving near the front door Lois slid off her snow-covered horse, steadied herself with a hand holding the mane of her horse, and then walked stiffly through the open cabin door with her bundle in her arms. Dorcus greeted her and closed the door. Todd dismounted and led Eagle toward the animal shed.

Eli emerged from the whiteness leading Lois' horse and took Eagles reins, pointing Todd toward his cabin. With the eyes of both horses frozen shut with hoar frost, they had continued up the mountain and down the trail with an instinct unknown to man. Eli carefully brushed away the ice from their eyes, brushed off the ice from their coats, hugged them, and threw a blanket over each horse. He fed them oats and left them for Putt who had arrived to help.

Eli found Todd when he followed the sound of the barking of the usually silent Hammer. Todd was circling the large rock they used for a table. His eyes were covered with hoar frost and he walked clumsily. Eli took him by the arm and guided him to the cabin, jerked the latchstring that raised the bar unlocking the door, and helped him into the warmth.

Todd shook off Eli's help and staggered to the bedroom doorway. His wife lay in their bed with Lois tucking towels under Sarah's naked bottom.

"Out," shouted Lois. "If you is needed I will call. Eli, stoke the fire and put a kettle of water near the coals. When hot, make me a strong cup of Todd's coffee. Get this snowman undressed and in front of the fire. We will be having us a baby. Todd, I know you put your cover on me and you is about frozen. Thank you for the kindness. Now, get."

Eli helped Todd undress. As he lay down on his sleeping platform of warm stone, Eli covered him with the bearskin. He remained chilled and shivering so Eli called the fire-dried Hammer to join Todd under the blanket. Todd hugged the dog to his body. He dozed in spite of himself.

He awoke suddenly, hearing a muffled scream, soon followed by a small cry from an unknown voice, and a hearty cry of "Hallelujah" from Lois.

"Give me five minutes, Todd," she shouted, "and you can come in and see what present your wife has brought you."

"Are Sarah and the baby all right?"

"The baby is a girl, and perfect as is your wife," Lois said.

"A girl is fine," Todd said, spilling Hammer and the bearskin onto the floor.

The baby was nursing—the mother beautiful, with stars in her eyes. Todd's eyes clouded with tears that ran down his face. He wiped his eyes and grinned as he looked into Sarah's eyes.

"Hallelujah, indeed," he said as he kissed his wife.

"God is good," both Lois and Sarah said in unison.

CHAPTER 30

THE DIVE

SUMMER FINALLY ARRIVED. Todd sat in the sun on a flat rock, studying the pond and the creek feeding it. The creek started with a small spring on the far side of the valley and increased to a shallow stream five or six feet wide where it emptied into the pond. The creek grew by the addition of many small seeps that meandered out from the base of the cliff.

He and Sarah had swum the previous day as they usually did in hot weather. The day grew hot and by early afternoon, Todd, lathered with sweat, leaned his shovel against the fence and walked to the edge of the pond.

"Why doesn't the water rise?" he asked himself, as Sarah had asked on their holiday tour. He pondered the question a few minutes before stripping off his sweat-drenched shirt and taking off his boots. He dove into the water. Swimming down to the bottom, he found the tangle of a sunken tree up against the base of the cliff. The tangle of limbs collected old grass and other vegetation, forming a slimy barrier. His vision, blurred by the water, made the tangle of brush look dark and ominous. He surfaced, tilting his head back to look up the cliff, noticing a scarred area at the top. The tree had obviously fallen from the cliff where other trees were growing near the edge far above.

He dove down again. While examining the obstruction, he noticed that some of the slimy stuff hanging on the brush was streaming toward the cliff. He grinned and swam to the surface for a gulp of air. Now he knew there must be an outlet behind the debris.

Ever since he had first seen the pond and the stream he'd known there needed to be an outlet. He let Sarah believe she was the one who noticed the pond always looked about the same. He did not know if there was a crack in the earth, a sink of rubble, or an outlet through the cliff, but there had to be an outlet. Now, about to find out, a feeling of adventure flooded through him.

He needed to haul the brush out of the way to be able to examine the bottom and the cliff. He hitched up Bill, and led him to the pond with a length of heavy rope fastened to the traces of the harness.

Wading into the water with the end of the rope, he stopped, upended, and swam to the bottom. Fumbling in the murky water, he found a heavy limb, tied off the rope, and surfaced. He waded out, and clucked to Bill, who walked away from the pond. The rope tightened so he leaned into the collar and kept on going. A blackened tangle of limbs emerged in a boil of debris-filled water. Bill pulled it up the bank and into the field. Todd shouted "whoa" to Bill, who stopped immediately.

Sarah walked across the field and up to Todd, who was untying the rope from the traces. She did not look happy.

"Why didn't you ask me to help?" she asked. "It is not right for you to be diving in the pond by yourself. You have a responsibility now."

"You were busy with the baby, so I figured I would sneak off and do this. I' am a big boy, you know."

"No, you are a man now, a man with responsibilities."

Todd remained quiet for a minute. He remembered his father's advice, said many times, "It is never a shame to apologize." He really wanted to argue but knew she was right. He looked her straight in the eye and softly said, "I' m sorry. You are right. Will you help me check out the bottom now we have pulled out the tree?"

"The baby is asleep and Chestnut is guarding her, so I have an hour or so. Chestnut truly loves Robin and is a right good babysitter."

"To be honest, I am glad to see you. It was worrisome down at the bottom tying on the rope. If something had spooked Bill, it would have been a mess with me underwater and all tangled up in the brush. The Shipley's had all gone to the village to horse trade or I would have asked Eli to help"

"It is terrible to think about, but it is past. Just remember if you get hurt, your ma'ma is not likely to show up to doctor you as she did with the bear wounds. Also, as you said, all the Shipleys have gone to town horse trading so we are alone."

"I see your point, wife. Okay, let me take a swim and see if the bottom is clear. I am tying the rope around my waist, and you pay out the line to me when I pull on it."

"I will gladly help and am proud to see you have your pants on with the legs cut off. You are much less tempting with your britches on."

Todd chuckled and gave her a hug, a quick kiss, and turned to the pond. Her thin smile may have hidden a note of disappointment.

He swam to the bottom, but mud and stirred up debris blocked the visibility. He noticed a movement of water toward the cliff, but the water remained too cloudy to see anything. Rather than take a chance, he decided to surface and let the water clear. As his head emerged, he saw his wife waving at him.

"Come on, Todd, come out of the water before you shrivel up or turn into a block of ice."

He waded to the shore and stood next to her. "I cannot see underwater on account of the debris and stuff. It is a cloud of leaves and stirred up things."

"You lie down in the sun, Todd, to dry out and warm up. I will ride Bill back to the cabin and make us a lunch. I will come back with the food and our baby. We will eat and rest. The water will be clear, and I will help with the rope while you explore."

Todd was dry and warm by the time Sarah returned with Robin and with sandwiches made with fresh butter, and slices of smoked elk on thick slices of homemade bread.

They finished the sandwiches and lay back in the grass, their baby sleeping soundly. Todd rolled beside her and kissed her. She wrapped her arms around him and pulled him close as she returned the kiss.

By the time Todd returned to the pond, there had been plenty of time for the water to clear.

The rope went slack while he was exploring the bottom near the base of the cliff. He guessed Sarah was giving him some slack. He swam closer to the wall but saw only an assortment of sand and pebbles on the bottom. The dead leaves and small debris were gone. He saw a flash of something white and recognized his naked wife disappearing behind a large rock near the cliff.

He reached out his hand and grasped her ankle protruding from behind the rock. She jerked it from his hand, so he followed her and found her hovering near a dark opening in the face of the cliff. She pointed up and they rose to the surface clinging closely to one another.

"You found it!" Todd exclaimed.

"I went down trying to help and you attacked me, frightening me nearly to death." She giggled and pushed him away. "You know," she said, "it really is exciting. Give me the end of the rope and you go inspect the hole, but don't be squeezing in."

Todd swam to the hole and resurfaced several times before he swam to the edge and climbed out. Sarah remained naked but had pulled her dress across her lap and held an arm across her engorged breasts. The baby had obviously made many changes to her body and he liked them. She grinned at Todd and shook her head. Reluctantly he lay back down, thinking of the hole in the cliff.

"The crack is big enough to get through, and there is no current to speak of. My thinking is there must be an outlet back inside the cliff and its end must be level with the surface of the pond. I want to go inside!"

"No, sir! Here I am about to nurse your child. If you got sucked inside the mountain, what would I do?"

"First, you nurse my baby. Then I will tie on a rope and give you the end. If I get stuck you can pull on the rope. We can use Bill, and he is strong enough to pull me out if I get into trouble. He is right here handy.

"Or, I can signal by jerking the rope twice if needed, and then you pull. Tie the end to a big rhododendron so I cannot be sucked far. Besides, there is hardly any current."

"Todd, if you die I will never forgive you."

"Wife, if you will take of your shift and stand here naked I guarantee I will be back."

"That will not happen again so soon. Okay, the baby will be asleep for a while so go exploring.

Todd grinned at her, then turned and waded into the water with the rope around his waist and Sarah letting out slack.

He upended and swam to the bottom, holding some slack of the rope. He poked his head into the hole and eased into the darkness. He let out more slack and drifted deeper into the mountain. He looked up and saw a spear of light shimmering on the surface of the water—the only sliver of light in the darkness. Becoming short on air, he turned and pulled himself back into the pond using the rope, and swam up to the surface.

"No more!" Sarah shouted.

"Just one more dive, and it will be longer because I think that I found air. What a surprise! I am sure there is air in the middle of the cliff. Give me slack and do not pull unless you feel two hard jerks. Without waiting, he upended and dove to the hole and into the mountain. He found the light, swam upward, and burst into a dimly lit chamber within the cliff. Right at water level a shelf of rock led to a tunnel into the mountain. A shallow sheet of water flowed quietly over it and into the darkness. He breathed deeply and the air seemed fresh and cool.

Knowing Sarah would be frightened by the long time under water, he swam down to the bottom and out into the pond, swimming strongly to shore.

"Out!" she yelled. "You scared me to death. Please, no more."

"I found a cave with air," he blurted excitedly. "You can breathe in there. Come on, let me show you."

"No way I am diving; not today for sure. I have lots of work to do, plus, nurse your child."

Todd needed to do other things also, but his thoughts were on the room inside the cliff. He pondered the problem while working in the garden. The problem was how to take some kind of light into the room to let him explore the tunnel, or whatever lurked behind the dark shadow he saw. He wondered where the sliver of light came from that glinted on the surface of the water. It produced a faint light in the dark room.

Later, he scythed half an acre of tall grass and spread it out to dry. He was soon lathered with sweat but kept working for several hours. He loaded the hay on a stone boat, a flat structure of parallel poles with their ends shaped to keep the skid from catching on the uneven earth. His dad called it a float, and some called it a sledge. At school the professor said a sledge had two low runners on the bottom. His had no runners and he called it a stone boat

When he made it, he spiked a thick plank across the poles at the head and the foot, and then bored a hole to take a towing chain. It served him well in moving light stuff or bulky firewood. Eli was making a better one out of thick planks and bolts. Todd attached the chain to Bill's traces. He tied down the load and took it to the undercut shelter where they lived. He spread it in the sun to cure and went back for another load. He worked until late in the afternoon.

With the fresh cut hay put away to dry, he walked back to the pond and studied the cliff searching for a crack where light might enter. He saw none. He whistled for Eagle, who responded immediately. He mounted bareback and clucked the horse into a gallop. He stopped at the cabin and told Sarah he would be riding up to the rim to look around.

"Okay, supper about dark. Be careful."

When he gave Eagle a light nudge with his heel, he bolted into his fastest gait and headed toward the path to the rim. It became a lively ride with the dogs running hard, bellies near the ground, but slowly dropping behind. Reaching the rim, they turned south and around the lip of the cliff to a heavy stand of trees high above the pond. Todd stopped Eagle and slid off his back. When the dogs caught up, they sprawled in the leaves panting with streams of saliva stringing from their tongues. Eagle was lathered in sweat but acting nonchalant as he grazed, snickering at the exhausted dogs.

The ground was rocky with boulders and slabs of rock. Todd made his way through the rubble and the trees, trying to estimate where the room might be below him. He noted a large, flat slab of rock standing above ground level, with a space beneath. He dropped down on his knees to examine the situation and found four boulders of about equal size supporting the huge flat rock. He assumed someone in the past had formed the table for some reason.

He went about his search but found no cracks or holes letting any light down through the mountain to the room below. Discouraged, he returned to the table rock and sat down with his bare legs dangling over the side. The rock measured about eight feet on each side and was exceptionally smooth on top. He thought it would be fun to bring Sarah and Robin up here to have a picnic.

The day was warm, but cool air was striking his feet and lower legs below his cutoff canvas trousers. A slight movement of air disturbed a weed near his feet, but glancing up he noticed the trees around him were still.

Hammer explored the area with his nose to the ground. Chestnut, who was taking a break from baby-sitting, pretended to be on the trail of big game. She was usually at home with Sarah and Robin, but today she intended to make the most of her time off.

Todd called to Hammer, and he responded with wagging tail. Todd dropped to his knees to look under the rock, sending Hammer under to explore. The dog skirted something and Todd hoped it was not a timber rattler. He called the dog back and taking a stick crawled under the rock. He found no snake but did find a hole, enlarged by someone who had chipped away the stone. Surrounding the hole were ferns, reaching for the light but gently moving in a breath of cool moist air.

He gazed down into the darkness and could feel the movement of the air and the moist coolness on his skin. He lay on his stomach and reached down into the hole. Feeling a wooden structure, he found the top of a ladder made of poles. As he grasped the top rung, the structure crumbled and fell away into the darkness to splash, several seconds later, into a pool of water. The splash sounded muted, but there was no mistaking the sound of pieces of ladder striking water far below.

Todd realized that someone in the distant past had enlarged this hole as an entrance and an exit to the flooded cave below. From there they had access to the underwater tunnel and to the pond at the base of the cliff. When he had been in the cave below, he ha d seen the suggestion of another tunnel. But he was unable to guess where it may have led or what importance it might have to whoever had chipped the crack wider and built the ladders.

Todd slid out from under the rock, triangulated its location and called Eagle. Sarah worked at the grinding stone, watching him make his way down the cliff, across the meadow, and to her side at the cabin. He slid off Eagle, gave him a kiss on the nose, and a loving whack on his hindquarters, which he understood as being appreciated and relieved from duty.

Because of many chores, several days passed before Todd returned to the hidden access on the rim. Sarah went with him, taking Robin wrapped in a blanket tied to her chest.

Todd equipped himself with a whale oil lantern and several lengths of rope. He spliced them so that one was two hundred feet long and the other a hundred feet longer.

He would use the larger rope for climbing back up the chimney like tunnel. He tied both ropes to a nearby tree and tossed them into the hole. He put the longer rope between his legs and over his shoulder as he had been taught at the Academy for going down a cliff. The lantern swung on a short rope tied to his waist. The larger rope would be his safety line going down.

He also carried a cloth bag full of sap-rich pine sticks. They would serve as torches if lit by the lantern or a small amount of black powder and his flint and steel spark maker. If the lantern went out, he would light it again with his fire making tools and use the pine knots for emergency light. He was ready, but Sarah waxed apprehensive. She pleaded with Todd to give up the exploration. He held her tight and kissed her fervently. A moment later he ducked under the stone slab table and slithered feet first into the hole, taking care not to tip the lantern too much.

Once inside, he looped the rope under his thigh and over his shoulder, then lowered himself into the darkness. Ten feet down he found a shelf of rock and the remains of part of the ladder. Below were several more landings, some with intact but rotten ladders.

He stopped at a wide landing about half way down to let his eyes become accustomed to the faint light from his lantern. He continued until he stood on the ledge above the water where he had surfaced the first time he found his way in from the bottom of the pond. The light of the burning wick in the lantern did not penetrate the darkness for more than a few feet, so he decided to light a torch. He lighted a pine knot with a scrape of sparks from the flint and the flash of the added gunpowder. The pine resin ignited easily but burned with heavy smoke. As the torch burned brighter, the light improved. Todd looked about, but all around him still lay in shadows. Glancing up the chimney, he could make out the silhouette of Sarah's head as she looked down toward the flickering torch.

The light of the torch added to the light of the lantern revealed a large tunnel. The water ran slowly on one side in what looked like a shallow trough chipped out of the living rock in the distant past. He decided the trough acted as an overflow to keep the pond at an even level. After a rain, the trough would probably be full of rushing water, but the floor of the tunnel would remain dry. Why anyone went to so much trouble to keep the tunnel floor dry raised a lot more questions.

He shouted to Sarah that he would follow the tunnel but only as far as the rope would allow. The tunnel widened into a large room and branched right and left. The trough of water went to the right, so he followed the right-hand branch as it narrowed and widened again.

The black water flowed in a channel on his right. A deep blackness his feeble light barely penetrated lay ahead. He noticed a difference in the air. Squatting and then using his hands and knees, he inched ahead, holding the rope. Ahead he heard the fall of water and in the feeble light saw the stream drop into the blackness. Before him lay only a huge black void.

He noticed that a wide spine of rock crossed the tunnel and created the dam a foot or more high. The water tumbled over a lower area where someone in the past cut it down to the level of the bottom of the trough. His torch flickered in a strong breeze coming from somewhere off to the side. He added another stick to the torch and crawled forward to the lip, reaching down to feel the slick face of a cliff.

He scooted backward away from the void and headed toward the mouth of the tunnel.

Retracing his steps to the tunnel to where the tunnel forked, he stopped, but his curiosity took over so he took the left passageway. After fifty feet or more, he entered a large room, thirty feet wide and long, with the rock ceiling eight or ten feet above the smooth rock floor. On one side were the remains of piles of straw and several pottery jars, one partially filled with moldy corn, sorted through by mice or rats.

He was at the end of his rope, but in the gloomy light, he saw a dark area on the far side that looked like the continuation of the passageway. He wanted to go on, but his promise to Sarah that he would not go beyond the end of the rope rang in his conscience. He sighed and retraced his steps to the chimney.

Climbing up proved to be easy with the help of the large rope and the many good purchases for his feet. He concluded he would be able to climb without a rope, but he decided to leave one rope in place for further exploration.

He climbed upward towards the light and squirmed out from under the rock. As he stood, Sarah fell into his arms. Robin slept between them, bundled in a wrap tied around her neck.

CHAPTER 31

HORSE THIEVES

WHILE TODD AND ELI WERE CHIPPING THE ROCK to be used in enlarging the walls of the Shipley's cabin, a volley of shots spattered around them. They both dove to the ground and crawled around the mound of rock away from the direction of the shots

"That was a dangerous way to start a conversation," Eli said. "They must all have fired at once. I made out about six shots but I'm not real sure. It must be a gang of some kind."

Todd peeked around a corner toward the rim but he pulled back, his face streaked with blood and white powder from where the bullet hit the rock.

"With this range," Todd said, "the bullet arrives here before the sound. I was not hurt except where some rock chips scratched my face."

Two shots sounded from close by, and two more from off a few hundred yards, down in the bend.

"It is them women of ours, and my son and his girl, returning the lead," Eli said with a grin. "I bet those men on the rim got a start out of that. It would be helpful if they were hit, but it is a long way for even a good shooter."

"Sarah has a long gun from her daddy. It really reaches out and she knows how to shoot."

"I'm surely not fixing to do much good with just this pistol in my belt," Todd said.'I always carry a long gun but left it home today because I didn't want to have clay splashed all over it."

"Well," Eli said, "my guns are right over there in the cabin , but I do not see no safe way to fetch them. It is time to hitch up my trousers and make a run for it."

"I hate that you might be shot. Let us ponder this and see if there is any other way. For one, I can make a run for the back of the cave where there is shadow to hide in."

"Well, Todd, it is just as far to the back of the cave as it is to my wagon. I guess we should flip a coin, but I don't happen to have one."

"Todd," Sarah's voice called from the back of the cave. We have your guns and shot and a length of light line. Dorcus thought this up. She put a weight on the end so I can toss it to you and you can pull the guns and stuff over to you."

"Them is right smart women," Eli said with his usual grin.

The men retrieved their guns, then loaded and primed them. At their signal the women fired from the cabin. The men immediately looked around the side of the rock pile, and they saw the gunmen on the rim rise up to take a shot while the shooters in the cabin reloaded. Todd and Eli fired and the gunman on the rim clutched his gut and fell.

"It looks like we may have shot one of them, but it is a standoff right now," Todd said. "I have an idea we can use after dark, but it will be tricky. While I am laying it out, we can take an occasional pot shot. As long as they stay away from the rim, we aren't likely to hit anyone."

"This is a secret of mine. I do not think anyone in the world knows except for Sarah and some dead Indians. You know the pond over there by the cliff. Well, an underwater hole goes into the mountain with a stream of water and comes to a falls, and then it goes into nothing but blackness."

"I managed to swim into the hole, and after a few yards, I saw a tiny glint of light above. I swam up to the surface where I found myself in a place like the bottom of a well going straight up to the top of the cliff. It comes out about two hundred yards from where the trail goes down into the valley. I can climb to the top. The gang is probably right around the trailhead, so we should be safe if we don't make too much noise."

"How did you find such a place?"

"I found it by following a current of water going out of the pond. One day Sarah went with me. We found the opening at the top, and I climbed down from there and swam out the bottom into the pond."

"Todd, I ain't scared of much but don't cotton to swimming underwater into a mountain. If you need me, I will do it but I can t say it is anything to be looking forward to."

Todd laughed. "Here is my suggestion. We put together enough small line to reach down the cliff. I will take it to the rim by swimming into the mountain and climbing up the chimney, then dropping an end down. You tie it to the end of the big rope, and I will pull it up. After I catch the big rope you tie on some guns, powder, and shot on the end and I pull it up. I will let it back down, and if you are willing, you can start up on the rope with me hauling from the top.

"Eli, if you rather, and are so inclined, you can go through the underwater tunnel in the pond and climb up the chimney like me."

"Todd, I happen not to be so inclined. I have some experience climbing a rope and climbing cliffs but do not figure on getting any experience underwater if I can help it."

"That's fine," Todd said, "with two of us up on the rim and behind those shooters, we may be able to do some damage to them. I figure we need to shoot the leaders. If we just run them off, we will never have a good night's sleep again. They are sure to pester us and probably hurt one of us. The rest of them may not have a belly for lying up there waiting for a lucky shot at us."

"It is a good plan. Putt can keep the rustlers away from the rim, especially where you will be helping me climb up on the rope. The women can keep their guns loaded and back up Putt. That will keep the outlaws from entering the valley. Right now we should eat, and when it's nearly pitch dark, we need to start moving."

Todd stripped down, gave his clothes to Eli, and waded naked into the black water of the pond. With no light, he would have to go by feel and by memory. He was sure he would find the hole behind the boulder and once he entered the tunnel, all he had to do was swim. If he stayed near the top, as it turned upward he would be nearly to the air, but there would be no light to guide him.

It all went well in spite of a fear that tried to grip him in the cold, wet blackness. He controlled his fear by not giving it place and by concentrating on what he needed to do.

With great relief, he gasped down a lungful of air when his head cleared the water. He pulled himself out onto the small ledge and into the mouth of the tunnel leading to the falls. He found the bundle of torches and the flint and powder he had left for exploring the tunnel. He separated the torch into three small parts. After they caught fire, he stuck them into crevices in the wall. He tested the rope that was still dangling down the chimney and started climbing. Finger holds and toeholds were plentiful along one jagged edge of the crack. Where the rock was smooth, someone ages past had chiseled indentations serving as holds. Having the rope handy was a good thing.

The torches burned out before he reached the top, so he continued climbing the last few feet in complete darkness, feeling for handholds and places to put his toes.

It did not take long for Todd to make it through the watery passage, up the chimney, and crawl out from under the large flat table of rock.

Remaining silent, he listened. In the distance, he heard sounds of an occasional laugh and words too faint for him to make out. A fire glowed well back from the lip of the cliff. About two hundred yards away, the trailhead into the valley started at the huge boulder marking it. A slightly darker spot on the dark shape of the boulder was obviously a guard to prevent anyone from using the trail.

He dropped down some small rocks to signal Eli and lowered the still wet line to the bottom of the cliff. Eli tied on the heavy rope, and Todd pulled up the firearms and a bundle of clothes tied to the lower end, untied them, and then sent the rope back down. Eli took hold, and with Todd's help he made it to the top of the cliff by finding toeholds to help lift his weight. Eli coiled the rope and stuffed it under the table rock.

Todd slipped on some dry clothing. The men checked their weapons and eased off the rim into the forest and downhill a hundred feet. Then they crept toward the campfire. They heard the outlaws talking around the small campfire. Todd and Eli were too far away to make out the words so they began working their way toward the sound.

In the distance and downhill to the east, they heard the sound of a rock struck by something. The sound came from somewhere on the wagon trail Eli had made.

"Todd," Eli whispered softly. "Let me ease down the trail and see if maybe they have a lookout down there. I feel sure the sound is from a human or a horse. You stay here and keep an eye on those killers."

Fifteen minutes passed and Todd began to worry about Eli. A few minutes later Eli gave a low whistle like a night bird, then eased up to Todd with Sam and his neighbor Bud Simpson right behind. Both carried long barrel hunting rifles, but Bud also carried an Indian bow across his back with a quiver of arrows. Bud was large and muscular with bulging arms and wide hands soiled with grime. He did the local blacksmithing. Sam talked about him frequently, but Todd had not met him.

"Thank you for coming, Bud. I have heard plenty about you and how good you are with a bow. Let me give you men the lay of the land."

Todd told them the outlaws had set a guard atop the boulder at the trailhead into the valley. The rest were sitting around the campfire,

136

handing around a bottle and smoking. He had not spotted any other lookouts.

Bud said, "I've have some experience with this kind of thing. Let me get over near the lookout on the rock while you fan out and work into shooting range of the fire. The closer the better, but don't spook them."

"I agree with the plan," Eli said. "Being there is only three of us over here, I suggest we fire first with our scatter guns and use the rifles in case they run. We'll keep the pistols as protection while we are reloading. Todd has a double barrel with shot, so that will give us four quick shots from the scatterguns. As I said, if they start to scatter we'll use the rifles."

"It is a good plan," Bud said, "but if they is to start scattering in the woods it will be a tough fight. When you see the lookout fall, you start firing. After killing the lookout, I will come in from the west and shoot in a few more arrows and my two shots. Altogether, that will give us four shotgun blasts, four rifle shots, and four back up pistols and my bow. I make out about six outlaws, unless they have some others hid."

"Eli and I gut shot one and he fell out of sight near the big rock, so look out if he is still laying out there."

"I really need to give them a chance to surrender," Todd said.

"They did not give us no warnings," Eli said. "If you must, tell them not to move or you will shoot. If they move I intend to shoot without no more palaver."

"It's a plan," Todd said. "Let's move before I get more scared than I am."

"You ain't alone," Eli said. "All honest men is afraid at a time like this."

"Thanks. Let's go."

CHAPTER 32

THE PLAN

THE LOOKOUT ON THE BOULDER fell without a sound, an arrow in his throat and another in his heart. Sam, Eli, and Todd sighted their guns on the group around the fire.

"Don't move or you are dead," Todd shouted.

"Like hell," one man shouted back as he whirled around and pointed a pistol.

Two shotguns and a rifle fired nearly simultaneously, and one shotgun fired again.

The swarm of lead bullets and pellets cut into the men. Two men slumped over where they sat. Three Men jumped up to fight but a volley of rifle fire from two sides shot them down. One man, still on his feet, swore and raised his weapon to fire but never pulled the trigger. An arrow pierced his neck.

The four men closed in on the fire with pistols drawn, staying in the shadows and near the trees. Two men were dead. One soon bled out from the arrow that severed his juggler vein. The other was shot through the head and missing most of his brains. Three of the men were still alive but bleeding badly. One, shot through near the heart, squirted arterial blood. One held his chest and gasped for breath, a froth of blood on his lips. The fifth, a young man about twenty, sobbed, as he held his shoulder, blood drenching his shirt.

Three large dogs charged into the firelight, sniffing and growling at the bodies. Suddenly, Hammer lunged toward one of the bodies and sank his teeth into a raised arm a second before the gun in the hand fired. A ball of fire and sparks from burning wadding blasted harmlessly into the air—the ball rushed upward with no target but the night sky.

No one spoke as the sound of the shot echoed off the sides of the valley. Then Sam said, "Todd, the pistol was aimed at you. I seen it a second before the dog attacked. Hammer saved your life. I never seen a dog move so quick. I think he will be a might deaf for a spell."

Eli pried the gun from the man's hand, and Hammer released his hold at Todd's command. Eli rolled the man face down revealing the large exit wound on his back. "This one will bleed out in a few minutes and be dead for sure with a big hole clear through him."

"Too close," Todd said, wiping cold sweat from his forehead. His hand holding his pistol quivered.

Sam cleared his throat and spat before speaking. "We made a mistake not making sure they all was dead before we relaxed. While serving General Green, we stuck all the bad wounded with a bayonet to make sure they died and did not cause trouble. They often played possum and figured to stick you in the gut with a knife as you went leaning over them to check if they was dead."

"Well," Eli said, "looks like after the man dies there will be one left to hang. I do not know if we can or should save this one's life. If we let him be for a few hours, he will bleed out too. It is up to you, Todd."

"Eli, this man is about my age and only a year or two older than your son Putt. I think five dead is payment enough. Let's try to stop the blood and take him down into the valley on a horse."

"Seven," Bud said. "The lookout is dead and I found the body of the man you and Eli shot. Looks like both of you hit him, and he probably died real quick. His buddies left him lying there. Six dead and one wounded."

Sam and Bud began gathering up guns, checking pockets and making a pile of the stuff near the fire. In the pile were several gold coins, English money, and a few rough coins made in America. Besides the money there were sheath knives, tobacco makings, balls and powder, but no identification of any kind.

"No wonder they is thieving," Bud said. They was mighty poor except for the guy with the gold coins, and they, being shaved a bunch of times, were not worth much."

"Well," Sam said, "there may be some stuff in their saddle bags. We can give it all to this boy if he lives—if we decide not to hang him, and he can take it back to wives and such. If he dies, we can help some folk around here."

"Howdy, men. Looks like you done good." A voice came from the darkness."

They all tensed.

"Howdy, Son," Eli said. "Men, this here is my son Putt come a calling."

"I brung me some backup too," he said motioning to Sarah and his wife Dare astride horses behind him. Sarah carried a scattergun and a brace of pistols in a gun belt fastened over her dress. Putt's wife, Dare, held a Brown Bess and had a pistol on a lanyard around her neck.

"I am sure glad about your forward scouts. Hammer just saved my life," Todd said. Sarah slid down from her horse. Todd caught her in his arms and held her tightly against himself. The two dogs crowded around them.

"I might have figured gunfire would bring you folks," Eli said.

"It sounded like a battlefield and we worried," Sarah said as she turned in Todd's arms to speak. "Dorcus is home with Robin and a stack of rifles beside her in case things went bad. Shadow kept watching all around with her feet on the window sill."

"I figured Dorcus would never leave the child," Eli said.

"The fight turned out pretty much all one-sided," Sam said. "They didn't manage but only two shots. We gave them the chance not to fight, but they obliged us by pulling guns and turning to us to shoot. The leader moved first to aim his gun, but he got shot before he pulled the trigger so his aim was spoiled. After the fight was about over, a bad wounded one used his last strength to shoot at Todd, but Hammer got to him, and the shot went up into the sky."

"We have us a badly wounded young man here who needs more tending I stuck a little of his shirt in the bullet hole but he is still bleeding." Todd said. "All the rest are dead now. Some lived a while but have died. We need to try and save this one," Todd said kneeling beside the youth. The three women responded immediately and worked to staunch the bleeding.

"Putt, you and me need to round up their horses and lead them down to the valley. We'll take off their tack and turn them loose with our horses," Eli said.

"Just a minute, Eli," Todd said. "This ground up here is all rock. We will never be able to dig a hole or find enough dirt to bury them. Let's put them across their saddles and take them down to a sandy place in the valley where it will be better digging."

Before sunrise, they finished burying the horse thieves beside former Sheriff Grasty, then heaped rocks over their graves. Now they knew for sure that the men were after horses according to the wounded youth. The women had cleaned up the youth and he remained alive, holding his own. The saddles and tack lay heaped in a shed, and the horses were turned loose in the field.

Putt had worked with the men until they finished digging the graves. Afterward, he saddled his horse to ride to the village. He was riding to tell the wives of Sam Lancelotta and Bud Simpson that their men were fine and uninjured. The Max Patch people knew the sound of shooting must have carried with the breeze. It had alerted Sam to trouble because he had heard the first shooting down into the valley.

Putt returned after sun up with two heavily armed women following on horseback. Sam and Bud got to their feet from where they were sitting in the sand.

"They had decided to join their men and were mostly here. I met them on the trail part way down the mountain," Putt said.

Sam and Bud helped their wives dismount and faced toward the others. "As Todd and Sarah know, this here is my woman, Lois. The sweet young woman with a papoose on her back is Bud Simpson's wife, Alma."

Todd looked at the group and grinned. "Do you all realize what an army we mustered? In a while, we would have gathered two more. Us men had nine guns, and then came Sarah, Dare, and Putt with seven more. Lois and Alma arrived with two more. We had an army of ten with eighteen guns and three dogs. Let's keep our firepower in mind if there is more trouble in these parts."

"Todd, you forgot about the bow Bud brought. He killed two with it, and all us together only got four more and a hurt boy."

"Well," Eli said, "I for one am too tuckered out to reckon it all up. I'm going to sit back down in the sand and not even think about it."

"I've been thinking one thing," Sam said. "You know I ain't no preacher but have been doing the preaching at our settlement meeting place. I figure after we all rest up we have us some words over the dead men we buried. I'll do the honors and anyone who wants can add to it."

They all nodded agreement.

Two hours later the five women carried breakfast to the men who were lounging in the sand outside of the cabin. The women joined with them in eating the pile of ham, venison, and bear with biscuits, gravy, and lots of fresh butter. A long night full of tension and peril was past. The warm morning and a belly full of food made it easy to doze and forget the battle. Laughter, fellowship, and good food healed their tattered emotions.

CHAPTER 33

ROB WISE

THE WOUNDED HORSE THIEF told Todd that his name was Rob Wise and he came from Knox Town. He recovered slowly, surviving fever and infection; herbs, good food, and lots of care pulled him through. He exuded a bright and cheery nature inconsistent with his occupation as horse thief. It turned out to be a one-time job and a huge mistake on his part. He nearly died of his wound. When recovered, he also became a candidate for the noose. Horse stealing was a hanging offense.

He displayed youth, vigor, ate like a horse, and acted friendly and helpful to the extent he was able. Todd and Eli made no effort to restrain him while disabled, but with recovery at hand, they worried about the safety of letting him have free range of the valley.

Rob, a tall youth with broad shoulders and long blond hair, made friends easily. His well-muscled body and his wide, calloused hands made it obvious that he had grown up working the soil. He claimed only a smattering of education, but his brain was sharp and his disposition mellow. The people in the village and the valley liked Rob even though they were unsure about what he might do.

After a round table discussion including Putt and the women, the group decided that if Rob wanted to leave, he was free to be on his way if his story checked out. None of them curried the slightest desire to turn him in for a possible hanging. First, they wanted him to tell his story again to see if he would tell it the same as while injured. Todd and Eli agreed to invite Sam and Bud to bring their wives so all of them could confront the youth and sound him out.

Rob agreed to the meeting. It took place the following Sunday afternoon. He claimed the raid was the first criminal activity he had ever engaged in. He only did it because his dad had died in the war and his mother and five siblings were having a tough time. A rough-looking

142

gang had stopped at the bar where he did the sweeping. He had chatted with them as he worked. Later they had told him that if he rode with them they would help him earn big money quickly and easily. His only duties were to tend their horses, start campfires, and clean up.

"They claimed a trapper happened by Max Patch," Rob said. "He saw about twenty-four horses in the fields and knew several were of good quality and worth a lot of money. He said it would be easy to sneak in and take the horses during the night."

"He sure made a mistake," Eli said.

"They omitted to tell me their plan to shoot down into the valley and kill all the men and have their way with the women," Rob said. "They told me we came there just to take the horses. I sure am stupid."

"Horse thieves kill mighty quick if they are seen," Eli said. "Otherwise they will hang. All good folks hate horse thieves."

"Anyhow," Rob continued, "the gang and me escorted the drunk prospector out of town and left him with several bottles of whiskey and a few gold coins.

"On threat of death, the gang leader warned him not to tell anyone else about the valley. They planned to kill him, but the sheriff saw us all ride out of town together. They planned to send a man back to bushwhack him anyhow."

"Them was a bad bunch," Eli said. "We did a good thing killing all of them."

"You know how bad I was lied to? A jackass, green behind the ears and plain stupid," Rob said. "They said my job was just be the lookout when they went into the valley and I would not have to ride with them. They said they would give me a good horse when they took the horses out of the valley, and they promised to also give me the horse they loaned me. They said they planned to ride their way and I was free to ride back home."

Eli grunted. "I guess you have figured the only reward you would have earned was a bullet in the head once they managed to steal the horses. It is done many times. They take greenhorns to be scout, lookout, guard, tend horses and such, and kill them in the end. The gang members are always quarreling about the cut from the horse sale and even seasoned men are often left behind dead."

"I aren't no killer!" the boy insisted. "Ask the preacher in the town they intend to call Knoxville after some politician or general or such named Knox. We come there with my father before the war, and there was only a handful of cabins.

"One day a preacher come by and we set him up in an old cabin what was about falling down—left by hunters or trappers years before. We fixed the roof and he moved in. We let him use a log barn in town for preaching. He owned a book come from a doctor so he tended to us if we was sick or hurt. He shot his own meat, tended his garden, and helped others with crops. I worked with him lots of times, and he helped our family after word come Pa got killed."

Todd looked the boy straight in the eye. "Are you saying this preacher man will tell us he has never known you to go thieving?"

"Yes, sir. I ain't never done nothing illegal. I really was foolish agreeing to ride with that bunch. They said they were going to give me a horse just for riding with them. I knew it sounded wrong. Matter of fact, I never even loaded the old gun I carried. I could never have shot at you men, but do not fault you none for shooting all of us. Every one of those men was reaching for guns when you shouted not to move. The reason I only got hit in the shoulder was because of reaching down pretending to gather my gun."

"Son," Eli said, "We know you are speaking the truth about them all getting ready to shoot back. Once you have earned the reputation of being a horse thief, you know that if you is caught you are sure to hang. It makes them real mean, and they fight to the death rather than have their neck stretched."

"So what have you a mind to do?" Todd asked.

"Well, sir, I intend to go home and tend to my mom and the kids. I do not know if I will have to face the law but will do so if it is needed. As a matter of fact, there ain't no law in them parts except for some government men who come by occasionally—like this man named Knox."

"I'd not be in no hurry to tell anything," Eli said. "No one knows about this but us here. This Knox Town place is about fifty miles of hard riding from here, so they sure will not know anything."

"You can count on us not talking," Sam said. Bud and I is agreed that this boy will make a fine man. Todd, you should go to Knox Town with him."

"You are right," Todd said, "if I can work it out with Eli, Sarah and I will ride with Rob to Knox Town. We have a friend around those parts we will look up for a visit. We can talk with the preacher and your ma. We will not be telling all we know."

"The plan sounds good and I am grateful for the offer," Robb said. As I told you, my pa moved there some time ago when I was a kid, and I have met about all the folks living around those rivers. Maybe I know the name of your friend."

"He's an old soldier some call Max Patch."

"I know Max. He helps folks in need and has fed us more than once. It is said he fought Indians, fought red coats, even some deserters, horse thieves, and others. He is rough as a cob but sure has a big heart. He and the preacher are friends."

"He and my father fought all those folks together," Todd said. "It's agreed. We will go with you if Eli does not mind spending some more time in this valley."

Eli chuckled. "This here valley is horse heaven, so it makes me and Dorcus happy and content. Putt is so busy with his new wife he hardly knows what is going on except wife and horses. You need to take Sarah and Robin with you. We will be fine."

CHAPTER 34

KNOX TOWN

THE FIRST PROBLEM IN TRAVELING WEST was the river. Its gorge served as a barrier on the west side of Max Patch Bend. The gorge itself was virtually impassable with nearly sheer sides coming from high on the mountains down to the river. The steep downhill slant of the gorge created a river roiling around rocks and white water rapids stretched for miles.

Todd, Sarah and Robin and Rob rode north, off the mountain and onto the wide plateau, which brought them to calmer waters flowing west and joined by a smaller river merging with it. Between the two rivers stood a wide and rugged mountain, feeding both rivers from its multiple seeps, brooks, and streams. One place afforded a wide and shallow crossing where man, animal, or wagon might ford the river. The trail beyond became steep and washed out, heading west and descending into the flatlands.

From high in the mountains, this land looked flat. Up close there were rolling hills and dense forests. Now looking back, they saw the blue wall of mountain peaks that had made their way difficult for several days. It had taken them three days of slow going to reach the flat lands west of the mountains.

Todd rode first, riding Eagle and trailing a pack animal with their supplies and camping gear. Sarah followed, riding Thunder and holding Robin in front of her on the saddle. Rob Wise brought up the rear, riding a good horse that Eli had given him as a gift. Todd donated the saddle and tack. Rob was trailing the horse that the thieves said he could keep. The nag and its tack were not much but made a good town horse, and could be a passable workhorse. In Rob's saddlebags were the few personal items belonging to the horse thieves.

Rob figured it doubtful that the gang members came from the area, but he intended to make inquiries. Todd and Eli agreed that if Rob found any needy family of the gang members, they would pay them the value of the horse, guns, and tack. Eli intended to work the animals into his breeding program. Sam would sell some of the tack at his trading post and keep the money to help others in urgent situations. The guns, horses, and the rest of the tack would remain in Max Patch Bend until needed elsewhere.

After leaving the rolling hills, the party entered a flat plain— cutting through it flowed a wide and slow moving river. The traveling became easy as they followed the river, and the riding was comfortable for the horses on the brushless sandy soil of the river flood plain. On the fifth day, another river joined and soon they sighted a crude cabin set well back and on higher ground.

"That's the preacher's house I told you about," Rob said as he handed the line of his packhorse to Todd and galloped up to the cabin.

He came back slowly and looked worried. "He ain't there and it looks deserted. I saw no sign of him and there ain't none of his stuff. It is clean as a pin but no sign of Mr. Marshall."

"It might be that be your friend moved into some place larger. This place looks to be just one small room and we appear to be a spell from town," Todd said.

"I know. I have been gone for three months or more. I sure hope nothing bad has happened."

"Rob, I suggest we ride on to your mother's house. That is the most important thing," Todd said. "She will be sure to know about the preacher."

A short time later, they turned away from the river and up to higher ground. The town consisted of a scattering of cabins, a few people, and animals. Rob waved to several people as he rode to a cabin near the center of the village. Before he dismounted, three children rushed out the door and up to his horse. He swung down and embraced his sisters. His mother came to the doorway and behind her followed a tall man. The woman cried and the tall man grinned.

Mrs. Wise wrapped her arms around Rob and sobbed on his shoulder.

"Well," the tall man said. "I do believe my young friend has returned. I am mighty pleased."

"Rob, this here is my new husband as of about a month ago. I am now a preacher's wife. I want you to know we has been praying real strong for you after you lit out with those outlaws."

"You have a good son, Mrs. Wise,' Todd said. "He is no outlaw, but a fine young man. He got himself hurt but is now patched up and good as new."

"Please step down from your stallion while I help the lovely woman and child. She is riding a tall horse. My name is James Marshall, handyman, preacher, and husband to a real fine woman, the former Mary Wise."

"Rob has spoken of you often, and you may be a big part of why he is here now. This woman is my wife, Sarah, and the baby is our daughter, Robin. My name is Todd Casey."

"Oh my," Mrs. Marshall said."Look at the beautiful child. I am so excited I am forgetting my manners. You all come right in. James, put up the horses and help Rob unload. It looks like my boy has gained two horses. Oh my! I can hardly believe that he is home, bringing such nice people with him."

It took several minutes for the former Mrs. Wise to settle down. She took little Robin from Sarah's arms.

Mary was of medium height, thin-shouldered, and her long, well-used dress hung straight down to her shoes. Her rough red hands stroked the child lightly. She sat down on a large rocking chair, cooing and nuzzling the child as her three daughters crowded around. Mary was probably less than forty years old but looked much older. Sarah saw tears running down her cheeks as she looked up.

"You don't know how awful it was on hearing from James that the boy rode off with a gang believed to be horse thieves," Mary said. "Well, it kind of drawed me and James together, and we fell in love. I liked him a long time but needed to let more time go by after Tate, Rob's father, was kilt in the war. Us grieving together about Rob's riding off with outlaws made things right for marryin'."

"Mary," Sarah said, "there is no need for you to know all the details, but Rob was never an outlaw. We had a battle, the others died, and Rob was wounded. He never even loaded his gun. We took him to our place and he has healed. He feels bad about making the mistake he did but wanted to earn money to help you and the children. Nobody is looking for him, none of the outlaws survived, and nobody knows anything except what I told you."

Mary set the baby in the rocker and embraced Sarah. "The Lord has been real good to me. He give me a new husband and he brought back my son. I is blessed." Her face began to soften as the worry lines faded. Her eyes became alive and her smile deepened.

After the welcome words, things lightened up, and the women and girls set about cooking a feast to celebrate Rob's return. Todd brought in a quarter of smoked venison and a peck of his potatoes. The women put chunks of the meat into two Dutch ovens, stirred up the fire, and put the pots in the coals. Then they stirred rough flour with milk and lard to make a batch of biscuit dough. James contributed carrots from the garden, and Todd brewed a pot of real coffee.

"Sam Lancellota, our local trading post owner," Sarah said, "traded something for these precious beans and passed them on to Todd for this occasion."

The food was ready a few hours later, and James said the blessing. Talk and laughter filled the house as all ate their fill.

After the feast, Todd and James Marshall sat at a crude table in front of the Wise cabin, now known as the Marshall house. The place looked well kept and spoke of a lot of recent work by James. He was an excellent carpenter but passed himself off as a handyman and a preacher. Todd had not heard Marshals preaching, but was sure it would be as good as his carpentry. He liked the erect way the man stood, and his full chest and scarred hands. James looked like a man of character.

Todd finished telling James the details of the outlaw attack and of Rob's wounds, his behavior, and attitude. The man exhibited genuine love for Rob, with hopes for his future. He also displayed a deep gratitude for the care and love given Rob. He wanted to meet Eli, Sam, and Bud and thank them personally for their attitude toward the boy.

"Todd, you are welcome to stay in our barn with the chickens and cats," James said, "but I happen to have a snug little cabin down near the river. I would be proud to have you use it. It is a lot more quieter than here."

"Rob pointed it out to us, and he rode up there looking for you. He found it empty but as clean as a pin. We brought plenty of supplies so we can make do in your cabin right well. I appreciate the offer. We brought a piece of canvas to rig as a tent, but the cabin sounds much more comfortable for Sarah and Robin. Besides, if Sarah stayed in the stable all the chickens would want to sleep near her." Todd said with a laugh.

"I left an old rope bed there with a mattress stuffed with corn husks, but some mice may have moved in so be watchful. The ropes are fairly new and should hold you fine, but it will be right narrow for two."

"It will be fine, James. By the way," Todd said, "I have an old friend not too far off. Do you happen to know Max Patch McBride? He sometimes uses other names because he did some delicate government work during the war. Rob said that he knew him."

"Yes sir, he and the missus occasionally come to our Sunday meetings, and we have some good talks afterwards. His wife Claire always brings a big basket of food, as we share breaking of bread after the service. Most all folks bring food and she brings enough extra, as well as cookies to fill up all the children in town. She has a soft place for the little ones."

"We plan to go visit with Max and Claire in a day or two after we rest up."

"I do not mean to run you off," James said. "but have you been noticing how dark the sky in the southwest is? I am thinking we have a storm moving in from there, and the ones from the south are usually wet, windy, and last a day or two. Best you make for the cabin while you can. We will ride along and give you a hand unpacking the animals. Out back of the cabin there is a lean-to for firewood and a place for two or three horses if they is friendly."

"Let me go tell Sarah so we can be going. It is growing darker as we talk and I reckon the storm is closer, so we need to go. The wind will be sucking toward it soon and then it will hit."

Rob ran to reload the pack animals and saddle the horses. Todd and James tied things down and hurried Sarah to have Robin ready for the move. They left in only a few minutes with a rising wind at their back as they rode toward the cabin. James rode ahead to make things ready for their arrival, and Rob took charge of the pack animals to enable Todd and Sarah to ride faster.

The wind turned, and the rain fell in a swirling blur. Rob arrived wet with the rain sheeting down with such force it rebounded several inches into the air. He and James put up the pack animals and carried the supplies into the cabin.

The cabin was far too small for three men, a woman with a baby, and two dogs. James and Rob formed a circle with the Caseys, holding hands. James said a short prayer ending with, "We recognize the work and the hand of God. The prodigal son has returned, bringing some real nice friends. We thank you, Lord, Amen."

James and Rob rode away into the darkness of the storm. Todd opened the door to look out, but wind and driven rain met him. Todd closed the door against the storm, dropped the locking bar into the slots, and gathered Sarah into his arms.

CHAPTER 35

THE STORM AND THE VISIT

BY THE TIME THE CASEYS WERE SETTLED and their stock fed and put away, the wind turned some more and then came with vengeance from the south. James and Rob had ridden away as sheets of rain dropped from the roiling sky. The temperature dropped with the wind as pebbles of sleet mixed with the rain.

"Best we make a fire in the fireplace, Todd," Sarah said. "It will be getting cold with nightfall, and Robin needs to be warm. So do I. I am tuckered out and sure would like to stretch out warm."

"James has laid a fire so all I need to do is start it with steel and flint. He left a pile of soft stuff ready for a spark. I notice we have two wet dogs lying next to the fireplace ready for me to set it alight. Soon this cabin will be too warm and smelling like wet dogs, for there is no opening the shutters on the windward side. How do you like the sailor talk?"

Todd continued talking and Sarah stood there with hands on her hips smiling. It had been a long and exciting journey—with new people, a new town, and now a new place to cook and sleep. Todd was accustomed to things being about the same every day and did not adapt as fast as Sarah did. To her, having her husband, her baby, and a dry place to sleep was about all a woman really needed—for a few days.

"Todd, please get about starting the fire. You sound as wound up as I feel. I do not care about the smell of wet dogs. What I really want is to be warm and held by you in the narrow bed."

The storm pounded the valley with wind and water. At times the whole world disappeared, blotted out by the cloak of rain the storm cast over them. At first, the air of the storm turned cold, but it warmed as it pumped in from the south. The storm hovered over them all night and continued the next day. The river started rising and overflowing its banks. It rained over a wide area and much of it found its way to the river, Huge uprooted trees, green with leaves, rushed in the current. Debris of all kinds, mixed with red of mud, were tossed and churned as the river poured onward.

The roof of the cabin leaked in spots and the sound of drips falling into pans was a constant pinging. The Caseys dodged the leaks, cooked, and lay down. The narrow bed proved to be no problem at all. The rumble of the river and the howl of the wind continued steadily all day and into the night.

Shortly after dawn on the second day, James and Rob rode up to the cabin, shouted a hello, and dismounted. Sarah threw open the door and James rushed in. Rob took the horses to the lee side of the cabin that somewhat blocked the wind- driven rain, and tied them near the building. By the time he entered the cabin, his legs below the oilcloth were soaked and his boots squished on the plank floor.

"We is worried about the river. I see it is way over its banks but still out a spell from here," James said. "It sure is making a lot of noise and the wind is joining in. I am afraid the rain in the mountains will feed the river, and it will rise yet more. We in town is up high, but this is a lot lower. We need to keep a sharp eye on the river."

"I plan to stay in the shed with the animals," Rob said. "If the river is rising too much, I will help you all move out of here. I been living all my life by this river so I can tell if it is rising too high. Don't worry as it has a way to go before it floods this area."

"No shed for you," Sarah said. "I appreciate what you are doing, but if you stay it shall be with us."

"No ma'am," Rob said. "I will be in the shed and keep looking out. I owes you much, and I plan on keeping watch no matter what you say, ma'am."

"Only if you eat with us and come in to warm," Sarah said.

"I will, ma'am, and to chat some. My dad will be going home to tend to ma and the little girls."

"Rob has about said it all," James said, "but if you don't mind I will stay and talk a spell. I have been hoping to have another cup of the real coffee you brung. We has used roasted chestnut shucks, burnt grain, burnt toast, weeds and such, but nothing tastes like coffee."

The rain continued and the river flowed wide and fast, coming within a few hundred feet of the cabin. The cabin stood on higher ground, but it was frightening to see the turbulent river so close. Sarah looked out at the turbulence, convinced the water level was even with the cabin. Finally, the sun came out, but the river continued to rise.

The Casey's visited with James and Mary and met the town's people. The land was muddy and James thought that the local streams would be running too high for them to try and find Max. After two days, the water started to recede and the land to dry. The time had come to visit with Max Patch McBride and his wife, Claire.

The Caseys stopped by the Marshall cabin to inform them they might be away overnight. James met them at the door with Mary behind him in the doorway, three little girls clinging to her dress.

"I think it best I go with you," James said. "On the trail is several creeks to cross, and they will still be running strong with all the rain. I know where the safe fords are. Have you been in to McBride this way?"

"No," Todd said. "As a matter of fact, I have been there only once and followed directions from the north. I know it is a rough ride down out of the mountains because it sure was rough for me and Sarah going in. I did not want to take Sarah and Robin out the same way. Rob showed us the easier way to get here. The short answer to your question is, I have never been to Max's cabin from this direction. I was about to ask you if you might ride with us to show us the way."

"That settles it. We is riding together. I happen to have a kit on my horse and am ready to ride."

"Good," Sarah said. "Mary, are you satisfied with James riding with us?"

"Yes, honey. Now I have my Rob, we will get along fine. James has things fixed up around here. You all ride on and do not be worrying about me, but make sure you say hello to Max and Claire."

She and the children waved as the travelers turned their horses and trotted away. Rob stood proudly beside his mother and sisters, his flintlock pistol cleaned and loaded in the holster on his belt. He had left the village as a boy and returned a man.

The easy one-hour trip turned out to be three difficult hours. They encountered deep mud in the low places, heavily flowing streams, a few slides, and many downed trees. It took them until noon to arrive at the McBride cabin. Hammer and Chestnut ran beside the horses and raced ahead as they recognized the cabin and the rangy hound guarding the place. All three dogs barked with delight, bringing Max to the door carrying his rifle.

He shouted to his wife and rushed out into the yard to greet them. "Glory be," he shouted, "Todd, you even brung a preacher with you. Hello, Preacher Marshall."

Claire rushed out of the cabin and ran to Sarah's horse, reaching up for Robin and taking the child in her arms. "Max, help this woman down from this horse. Where has gone your manners? Is you goin' to just talk man talk?"

"Shucks," Max responded. "I plans to hug this young woman and is waiting for you to turn your back." He laughed as he handed her down and gave her a hug. Todd and James kicked their boots out of the wooden stirrups and swung down to the ground. They all talked at once, stopping only for laughter. The dogs were wrestling in the dirt, ignoring their people. Chickens were running for cover with long strides and outstretched necks, squawking, and running to avoid the huge new dogs.

Later, the women pulled together some dinner while the men fixed places to sit under an oak tree. The clear sky after the storm let the sun shine down so strongly that soon that they all soon moved, looking for shade. The dogs found it first. They reclined like lions, legs out stretched, but even the shade felt hot and muggy as the sun pulled the moisture from the soggy earth.

The men helped the women tote out the meal and place it on sawed parts of logs. They all dug in to the food blessed by a prayer from Preacher Marshall and a hearty "Amen" from Max.

Telling Max and Claire about the horse rustlers and the shootout took a spell. McBride wanted details. The part about the underwater tunnel and the chimney to the lip of the cliff fascinated him. They listened carefully to the story of the wounded Rob and the marriage of Marshall and Mary Wise. The marriage set the women atwitter as the men talked of guns and outlaws.

McBride leaned back and lit his pipe. He puffed some smoke into the air and asked Todd about Vinett Fine. Todd shook his head. "I don't know the man. What's this all about?"

"Well, a man coming through a few days back told me that near a settlement called Cataloochee by the Indians, a farmer named Vinett Fine ended up in a creek with an arrow in his back. It happened back in the winter when a band of renegade Cherokee Indians hunted in the area and caused trouble. Well, the weather turned very cold and the creek was freezing, so Mr. Fine got stuffed under a shelf of ice in the creek by his neighbors to keep him while they hunted the Indians. When they came back to the creek to fetch the body, Mr. Fine no longer remained under the ice. They looked all over and never found a trace of him. Some say bears took him and some say wolves. Others thought the raiding party come back and carried him off.

"This man passing through said the neighbors decided to name the creek after Mr. Fine. They stretched the name to the whole valley and called it Fines Creek. Anyhow, it must be near you, judging by the way that the man said he travelled. He said it happened only a few miles from a river in a gorge. It sounds like the one behind your valley."

"It may well be the truth," Todd said. "Two new friends, who live in a small settlement down on the hilly ground east of the Bend, told me that occasional raiding parties of young Indians, Cherokee, Shawnee, and even others, come through once in a while. You know most of the land on the west side of the gorge is Cherokee land, but you also know settlers. They have been moving onto Cherokee land just as you is on Shawnee land. The old chiefs tend to only talk and move back. The young ones want to fight, but it seldom amounts to much."

"Well, Todd," Max said, "you know the Bend was once an Indian village, so you is homesteading on Indian ground too. That chimney in the cliff was a flaw that someone long ago chipped out, as you said, to allow a man to use it."

"That is true," replied Todd. "When I first found the chimney, it contained a series of ladders made of poles. They long ago rotted, and they fell to dust when I disturbed them. Luckily, there is many good hand and toeholds so they were not really necessary, except maybe for women and children. At the top is a big flat slab of rock set up on four rounded stones to form a table that hides the chimney and is high enough to let a man out."

"The Indian I doctored, who had been shot," Max said, "often sat near the pool like he knew something. I think he wanted to tell me about the tunnel and the chimney, but considering it an Indian secret—he never let on."

"You know, I am not sure of telling you before, but the chief of the Indian boy we saved said he knew of you, and the man you saved has become a great man."

"I' m proud to hear it. I would like to meet him again someday. He was Shawnee judging by his arrows."

"As I recall," James said, "while serving in the militia, we fought a skirmish or two with Shawnee in this part of the country. This area is to go to the Cherokee and west is for the Shawnee. As Todd says, the lines were vague, and the settlers kept moving on west in spite of the government or the militia. We did not have much heart in it because most of us knew friendly Indians."

"Before," Max said, "Todd's daddy and me did some fighting with the Chickamauga Indians in 1779. Your daddy was off fighting about the time you started at the Academy."

Claire made a bed for Sarah and Robin in the cabin, and the men were assigned to the animal shed. Max Patch McBride laughed as he marched to the shed in his nightshirt and cap. "It seems my side of the bed has gone to a young woman and a child. My wife said to 'get,' and 'get' I did. It makes you wonder if you want much more company." He laughed, and the men laughed with him, as they shifted in the hay to make more room.

The next morning the men finished a breakfast of fried fatback with eggs fried in the grease. The women served huge slices of cornbread, hot from baking in a cast iron pot. The men smeared their bread with homemade butter and wild honey. Afterwards, Todd produced his bag of precious coffee and after grinding it with mortar and pestle, made the coffee by putting the grounds into a pot of boiling water. They topped their cups with cream skimmed from the milk of the cow. The surface of the coffee was thick with the fat cream.

"Does any of you remember the battle of King's Mountain in 1780?" James asked. "I served out west at the time, but one of my neighbors said he fought there. King's Mountain is located over in the foothills east of our mountains. Jed called it a hot battle because of a fight at Waxhaw. Tarleton's Loyalist army tangled with Buford, who commanded around three hundred Patriots. Buford did not even form up before Carleton swooped down and cut them down with Cavalry and troops. When Buford tried to surrender, old Tarleton kept his men fighting until there was hardly any men left and them he captured. Later, some called it a massacre."

"That is the first half of the story," James Marshall said. "Later, them Loyalist' wearing the red met up with some of our boys at King's Mountain, as you said. Tarleton got shot dead at Waxhaw, so Patrick Ferguson with the 71st Foot commanded the Loyalist. We was commanded by several fine men, but we followed Isaac Shelby. I say we, because Jed, the man Max spoke of, fought beside me. We was called the Over the Mountain Boys, because we come from around here and gathered in Abington to march to King's Mountain.

"We really whooped them because we got afraid of getting slaughtered like we hear about at Waxhaw, so we kept at it real fierce and we won. It is said the battle helped to win the war."

"I know," Max said, "that we could tell war stories all day long, but the girls want to take a picnic dinner and go somewhere."

"There is them falls not far away," James said.

"We is thinking the same," Max said. "We can put our picnic at the bottom of the lower falls, and them who wants can hike up to the upper one. Where we is going is bear country, so I recommend we take our guns as we may see one."

"You don't have to tell me twice," Todd said. "I tangled with a bear that came after my smokehouse and nearly died from it. Both dogs were torn open, and if Sarah had not killed it with her gun, it would have killed me in another few seconds. I am certain to keep a gun handy."

They followed an animal trail leading to the pond at the bottom of the lower falls. The water fell a hundred feet from the lip above and plummeted into the basin. Around the edge of the basin, the rock was gritty except on the downhill side where the water flowed in a shallow sheet smoothing the rock slick, and then forming into a stream that tumbled down the mountainside.

The air smelled fresh and cool because of the falling water, and the surrounding hemlock trees sweetened the air with their perfume. Birds were singing, a few frogs croaked, and overhead a hawk circled as it looked down for potential prey. On one side of the pool lay the remains of a huge rib cage and skull with a few long bones scattered about. Todd along with the three dogs examined it. "Get," Todd said. That universal word of dog language cleared them away.

"Do you know what this is?" Max asked. "Well, I'll tell you. That happens to be a buffalo. Indians have told me that there was hundreds of them in these mountains. The old boy mayhaps was one of the last around these parts."

Todd and Sarah sat side by side on the warm sheet of rock. Sarah kept glancing at the pool and looking sideways at Todd with a grin. He knew the thoughts going through her brain, and he too imagined them swimming naked in the cool water as they did at the Bend. He winked at her and she blushed.

After the meal, no one wanted to explore the upper falls except the dogs who found time and energy. The humans sat around or stretched out on the warm rock. Baby Robin slept. The faint odor of pipe tobacco and horses drifted in the air. The horses were off to the side, watching, whipping their tails at insects, or reaching for something green and moist. The weather provided a lazy afternoon with a cloudless sky and a warm summer sun.

CHAPTER 36

HIGH EAGLE

THE WOMEN WERE SITTING around the table sewing something for Robin and chatting as women do. The men stretched out on the ground in front of the house, and the dogs slept. They were all full of soup and cornbread, including the dogs. The war stories tapered off and the conversation slowed to an occasional thought about one thing or another.

The dog's quick movement surprised the men as the animals leaped up and rushed toward the woods beside the house. They barked as they ran into the woods, but suddenly the barking stopped. The men jumped to their feet with worry creasing their brows.

Two figures emerged from the woods with the dogs at their sides. A young looking man wearing typical colonial clothing with pants, shirt, vest, and a tri-cornered hat stepped forward. Walking beside him was an older man dressed in buckskins, a blanket over his shoulders. Both were Indians.

The younger man held up his hand as he stopped. "Hello, Mr. Casey. I do not know the other men, but from descriptions I would say Mr. McBride and Preacher Marshal."

"Oak," Todd shouted, and ran forward to shake the Indian's hand.

"My elder is now a great advisor to many chiefs and once the patient of Mr. McBride."

Max walked forward with a huge grin on his face and embraced the old Indian. They stepped apart and held each other's hand. Tears dribbled down the weathered faces of the two men. "What a great day," Max said. "I have thought of you many times and hoped you were alive."

"This man, dressed like a preacher on the way to church, is Oak." Todd said, "His father is a chief. And this tall man beside me is preacher Marshall"

158

"And Max, you and Gilbert Casey are well known by the tribes because of your fair treatment when you commanded soldiers," the old Indian said.

"Come meet the two women, my wife Sarah, whom Oak met on the trail, and Mrs. McBride. By the way, what name do we call the great advisor?"

"High Eagle," Oak said, "because he sees all things. He once had a name that Mr. McBride thought sounded like Max Patch—it's what he called High Eagle and what he named the valley."

"Come on. Come see Sarah and meet Claire McBride."

"First," Oak said, "let us tell you there are six braves in the forest who guard High Eagle."

"Bring them out, Oak, and join us. We may even have some soup left over."

"Our braves have a deer they will cook over a fire. We have plenty for all and much left over as a gift to Mr. McBride."

Oak spoke excellent English because of the education he received at an Indian school taught by a missionary lady. High Eagle had learned to speak fairly well, and the six braves knew enough words to make conversation. The gathering had grown appreciably, and laughter and storytelling abounded as the meat simmered over a fire in the front yard. Max always grew a plot of tobacco and handed out pipe fillings cheerfully.

Before nightfall, the braves retrieved their bedrolls and gear from the edge of the woods, setting up camp under Max's great oak tree.

In the morning, the braves provided their own food and the food for Oak and High Eagle. The three white men ate in the house and later joined the Indians under the oak tree. High Eagle motioned to McBride, and they walked off to one side. After a long talk, they returned.

Max looked disturbed. "High Eagle has told me about trouble between Gilbert Casey and Wellington Howe, who still insists he be called Lord Wellington. He also says Howe and his invalid son have hired a bunch of thugs to track down Todd and kill him. It seems that somewhere during their first search they came across a horse trader who sent them to an inn, and during the night, someone made off with all of their horses and tack."

"High Eagle learned they only found two of the six horses and are sure the horse trader stole them. Later, as they were looking for their horses, a trapper on the river told them he had seen a fine horse with a tomahawk blaze on its head. It was hobbled with other horses behind a point of land near where the horse trader holed up. They knew that it had to be Todds colt but they could do nothing because they had no horses."

"It seems," continued Max, "they somehow got hold of four new horses and found two of their own, still saddled but with no bit in the mouth. Four of them did not have much in the way of gear and the horses were not much. The horse trader had moved on, and they were not able to figure which way he went. They headed on back to Howe and told him about the sighting of Todd's young stallion with the tomahawk blaze.

"Unfortunately for Howe, and for the gang, the governor had appointed a new lawman who promptly identified the gang as they rode into town and locked them up in jail for two years. The new sheriff found out they had stolen the four horses, beat up the innkeeper, and tried to molest his daughter until they were run off by other patrons. Later, the inn mysteriously burned down. The innkeeper, his daughter, and several horse owners showed up for the trial. The men were lucky to miss hanging because the descriptions of the stolen horses were inconclusive, Most likely they were swapped for better horses that they stole along the way.

"Howe's boy Quincy, has gut problems and has growed so fat he cannot mount a horse, but his three friends from the Academy are still hanging around. Their fathers have all fled to England but send back money to provision the boys, who were all living in their parents' abandoned homes."

Max was out of breath from such a long statement, so he spent a few minutes loading his pipe and taking several drags of smoke. The listeners all fidgeted as they awaited the rest of the story.

"Well," Max finally continued, "a month ago the gang was released from jail. They went straight to Howe, who hired them again to track down Todd.

Hundley, a cadet a year older than Todd has a special hate for Todd. He returned from Canada and moved in with Quincy, Dills and Smathers. Howe grew tired of the four loyalist boys hanging around eating his food and drinking his liquor, so he sent them with the gang and they were glad to go with such a large force and the prospects of killing Todd."

"That's a lot of information. How in the world did he pick it all up and know it is true?" Todd asked.

"I was thinking the same thing," James said.

Oak stepped forward. "I can answer," he said. "We have been representing the Shawnee for a group of tribes. High Eagle is their main representative who speaks for the chiefs. He has chosen me to contact the government. Todd's father, Gilbert Casey, is on the committee to investigate Indian affairs.

"I have been in contact with him, and we became friends after I told him I was the Indian youth Todd saved. I told him I am a friend of the brave who killed Sheriff Grasty It drew us together and we have become close friends.

"Mr. Casey knew all about the gang being released and about Howe sending them out with Quincy's friends. He also knew about Quincy being an invalid and grossly fat. Grossly was Mr. Casey's word. One reason we are here was to bring word form Mr. Casey that the gang is on the loose."

"I thought that you were going to tell us that," Todd said. "One other thing you should know is that the horse trader who scattered the gang's horses is Eli Shipley. He now is a close friend and lives in Max Patch with his family."

"Well, it is a lot of information all at once," James said. "It sure looks like trouble, but I doubt they have any idea where Max Patch Bend is located."

"That ain't correct," Max said. "High Eagle says Howe found out Gilbert and I rode together. He also heard I spent time doctoring a Shawnee in a hidden valley somewhere in the mountains, just south of the Shenandoah Valley of Virginia. That cuts it down to about five hundred square miles."

"See what happens when you tell too many of your war stories," Todd said with a laugh. "This time someone must have believed one of them."

"I'll give you that, boy," Max said with a chuckle, "but I never said nothing about exactly where and gave no landmarks. That information I kept as a secret. Your daddy didn't even know where the valley lay as he never asked."

"Let me speak clearly," Oak said. "The reason I have not told you this directly is because I report to High Eagle. It is up to him what he does with the information. The reason he did not tell you this last night is because he was checking the lay of the land. You know, making sure this is the time and place for you to have this information. It is his way to say things and let others work out the details. He lets me speak for him because I understand more of your tongue and how you think about things."

161

High Eagle stepped forward and spoke. "It is because I trust this cub that he is given large things to do. It is my wish he will one day take my place as the one who advises the chiefs. Our chiefs are all brave men and fierce fighters, but they do not all see the larger picture. We are too few and can no longer hold our place with arrows or guns against so many. It must now be done with words and white man's ways."

"Max," Todd said. "Sarah and I better be go back to the Bend right soon. If those riders show up, Eli Shipley and his son, Putt, will not have much of a chance. It sounds like they have seven of the gang and three of the cadet friends of Quincy. I am also worried about you. They will try to find you first off and make you tell where Max Patch is."

"I can take care of myself just fine," Max said rather indignantly.

"Todd is right," James said. "I seen at King's Mountain what them loyalists did to a farmer to make him tell where our lines lay. If they was to get hold of your wife, Claire, they'd make you do their will right quick. We need to be thinking how to defend you if need be. Maybe you should move into the Bend with Todd."

High Eagle took Oak aside and spoke to him in their language. A few minutes later Oak turned to the other men. "High Eagle says he wants to help defend you, but he knows the peace with the Cherokee tribes is fragile and easily broken. He is afraid a band of Shawnee braves would not be welcome. He would leave men to scout but if seen in the forest they would probably be shot or hunted.

"We will leave at nightfall and will stop at the Cherokee village and talk with the chief. He may find a way for them to help. The chief is peaceful—it is the young who are wild. The chief is a friend of many white men in this area."

"Let me ask you something, Oak," James said. "How have you managed to travel to northern Virginia and back with High Eagle and the six braves?"

Oak laughed. "I met High Eagle and the braves two days ago where the two rivers meet, not far from here. He and the braves will visit a few days with the Overhill Cherokees and return to the far west near the great river. I will travel with him, and after he meets with the chiefs. I will take their answer to Gilbert Casey and possibly to the provisional congress.

"As you see, I dress like a white man, speak his language, and have the rank of a military scout. I ride a Cavalry horse with a military saddle and if stopped, have letters to prove I am on a mission for the government."

"That is explanation enough for me," James said with a laugh.

CHAPTER 37

KIDNAPPED

HIGH EAGLE, OAK, AND THE SIX BRAVES left at dawn after a meal of baked potatoes and the leftover venison. Their farewell was warm, and the old Indian had tears in his eyes as he said a goodbye, probably for the last time, to Max Patch McBride. The dogs did not bark at the Indians but sat quietly near them as if bonded. Perhaps they sensed the natural odor, some primordial memory, or the Indian's understanding of animals.

Todd, James, and Max finished breakfast and sat under the tree sipping Todd's precious coffee.

"Our life is changing again," Max said. "Me and Claire live here real peaceful and have done such for several years since the war. I've had enough activity to last for years. I don't cotton to being under the gun, as they says, with this bunch after me and Todd."

"I know your feelings," Todd said. "We have done no war fighting, but Sarah and I have seen our share of troubles, and there is a bunch of dead men in our shadow."

"I know the shadow you are talking about," James said. "I do not know how many of my musket balls found a man but do remember a few men on my bayonet, and them troubles me. I want to shuck off killin,' but it looks like this gang that is after you two may involve me too."

"James," Todd said, "you look after Mary and the girls. Let the worry be on Max and me. No need for you to be troubled."

"Sounds real fine but it ain't the truth," James said. "You two are my friends, and we is in this together."

"Look," Todd said. "You did your fighting and so did Max, but he got involved by being a friend of my dad's and me."

"Boy, you made my point. I happen to be a friend of both of you so that makes me involved by your reasoning."

163

"Listen to me," McBride said with authority. "We has a problem and instead of all this talk, let's go to the heart of it. Me and Claire is in the gun sights, and Todd and Sarah is even more so. Once the gang finds the Bend, they is going to mount an attack, which, if it catches you in the open will kill you in about two minutes. They has at least ten guns from what we hear. They could fire all ten at once and probably have more loaded and ready. Our problem is to stop that from happening.

"I have one idea," James said. "Over in the mountains near the Bend is a settlement a bunch of British Loyalists tried to take just before the war ended. The King's men pulled along a cannon, aimed it at a group of cottages, and they prepared to fire. A flurry of shots come from the high ground, and most of the cannon crew dropped dead. Them that lived ran from there and never fired a shot. The men hooked the cannon to three teams of horses and dragged it to the piece of land the town come to be built around—all six cabins and a general store."

"Sounds like the village east of us," Todd said.

"It's the one if they has a cannon. Now, what if we was to borrow the cannon and put it into the Bend. By firing a shot, it would alert the neighbors that Max Patch is being attacked. All the folks within ten miles could hear it and come running," James said.

"It might be a plan for Max Patch Bend but how about McBride? If he stays here, it will just be him," Todd said.

"You know, we have about eight boys from ten-to fifteen years old, who march around town with sticks and drums pretending to be militia. The three older boys have some old rifles and shot. They pretend to wipe out dozens in their path and do not seem to know the war has ended, and we was the winner. What if we harness their energy and have them watch McBride? They would camp out near here and keep a watch like him being General Washington. They could take turns and make a game out of it.

"If the bad guys show up, they can sound the alarm and the neighbors on farms scattered around here would come in."

"I might accept if they didn't steal all my eggs and scare my cow dry," Max said.

"I will be the general and keep them straight," James said with a chuckle. Right now I am riding to town with the Casey's to collect the kids and to send Rob back with them. I have promised to help an old veteran this afternoon. I will see you tonight or tomorrow, Max. Right now we need to say good-by and head out.

The kids accepted readily, not knowing several men who fought in the war had agreed to back them up. The signal to respond would be to light a big fire on the ridge that all could see. The fire would be the first responsibility of Rob Wise, only he knew he that intended to ride to the Bend at a minute's notice, if the gang showed up and moved on.

No one expected the gang to appear for at least several days, and the second day turned hot and dragged on with no threat of any kind. The youth guarding Max were growing lax and joking around.

Hundley rode up to the field near the cabin where Max was working on the third day. He had graduated a year before Todd, and like Quincy, he carried a grudge. He was unchallenged—all the youth were in the pool by the falls. Hundley caught Max unaware and put him under his gun. The McBride dog sniffed at Hundley, turned, and streaked into the woods. Hundley laughed and prodded the rifle into Max's back.

Hundley whistled, and his two Academy friends moved in and ringed Max. A minute later the gang rode into the field. Hundley was angry because of the gang's approach. He had ordered them to stay in the woods.

"Mr. Max, or Patch, or whatever your name is, you are surrounded and we need to know where we might find Todd Casey. We have heard tell of your secret valley and need directions. Otherwise, we will move on to your cabin and play games with your wife." Hundley pulled his crop as he had done with Eli Shipley and whacked Max across the face.

Max glared at Hundley and then said, "I predict that the next man you strike with your crop will kill you. Mark my word."

Hundley snarled but did not strike again.

No one noticed as Max's dog, George Washington, sneaked out of the woods and into the cabin. Claire knew the signs of a dog with a message and taking down her Brown Bess moved slowly to the field and saw what was happening. She fired the gun into the air hoping to attract attention, then quickly retreated into the woods. She reloaded and fired again. Hundley ordered his men into the woods as he fired point blank at the defenseless Max.

Claire pulled her pistol and took down the first to approach. Cadet Dills was not able to raise his right arm because of the injury at the ambush. He was slow with his left hand and died before he was able to raise his pistol to fire at Claire. The second to die was one of the outlaw gang who crashed through the brush and into the jaws of George Washington. His screams caused the others to hesitate.

Suddenly war hoops filled the air and musket balls flailed the underbrush as the youth moved in. Hundley rode boldly into the forest, scooped up Claire as she was reloading, and bolted into the thick woodlands, his face bleeding from where her stubby fingernails had raked his face. The others scattered at a command from Smathers. Horses bolted through the underbrush and another of the gang fell from the saddle, struck by two musket balls.

Rob was riding to find good defensive positions when he heard the sounds of battle. He rode to the field to light the signal fire. The fire ignited as he shot into the kindling, then he galloped into the upper field, where he found the wounded and furious Max. Rob helped the wounded man into the saddle and mounted on the rump of his horse. He rode toward town at a gallop, holding Max.

Neighbors met him and formed up to search the woods. They found the dead Dills and two dead gang members. The others had vanished with Claire as their hostage. James ordered the youth to circle the settlement and to help the old men defend it if attacked.

Rob left the wounded and quarrelsome Max with his mother Mary, Sarah, and her baby. Max had lost a lot of blood, but by the sound of his voice he seemed in fairly good shape. Rob told them about the Claire's kidnapping. Then he mounted and rode to find James who was at a distant cabin helping an old veteran. After giving James the news he rode to catch up with Todd who left town immediately after Rob told him of the attack, and after making sure that Max was taken care of. Todd assumed that Hundley would try to force Claire to give directions to Max Patch. He would not know that he and Sarah were in Knox Town.

James turned the defense of the town over to one of the old veterans. He checked on Max, finding him well cared for, then mounted and rode on to catch up with Rob, who rode ahead of him by an hour or more. James did not know the way to Max Patch and lost a lot of time trying to follow Rob's tracks.

Rob knew the way and pushed at a fast pace into the rugged wilderness of the foothills. Three hours later, he caught up with Todd. The horses were winded and needing to rest. Both men dismounted and stood on high ground surveying the land below.

Below them, two horsemen backed their animals into the shadow of the trees "Gag the woman," Hundley ordered Smathers. "It looks like the fight is up to me and you. I saw this woman shoot Dills. Him with his crippled arm, should have been sitting at home on the couch with Quincy. What a joke, crippled by a dirt farmer and shot dead by an old woman. Dill's spirit sure will not rest easy. We will let the scum rape this woman as a tribute to Dills. We need to keep a tight rope on her.

"I want you to know I plan kill the dirt ball Snick, who commands the gang. He knew the plan was for just me, you, and Dills, going in. I ordered Dirtball and his men to stay hid. Instead, they stirred up those kids by getting seen up by the water falls."

"Yes, sir," Smathers said. They are only five now but they are mean."

"I don't care about them. All I want is Todd Casey, and you can have the woman of McBride if you want her before I give her to the gang," he said as he prepared to lower her to the ground. "She is old, but she may yet be useful, so put her on your saddle and keep her alive. As he lowered her roughly to the ground, Claire bit him on the hand, drawing blood. He swore, lifted his crop to whip her face, then remembered Eli's words years before about killing him, and thought of Max's prediction. He stopped the blow, but hated the defiant look on her face.

"If I ever meet that horse trader or whatever he was that I hit with my crop, I plan to whip, him and then shoot him."

He had a score to settle. Eli had shamed him and so had Max. They would be made to pay.

"See those two horsemen on the ridge?" Hundley asked, trying to cover his fear of striking Claire. I think they is riding to warn Casey. They went galloping out of town right after our fracas. They were no doubt sent to warn Todd. If we follow them, they will take us to his valley."

Todd saw a movement in the valley below, and his dog Hammer growled. Rob was with him, but there were just the two of them and Hammer. Chestnut remained with Sarah and Rob's mother, who was doctoring Max.

Hundley, Smathers, Dills, and the gang were far too many to try to fight in the mountains. They did not know that Dills and at least two gang members were dead. There were still too many. Todd was sure that the best hope of survival was to lead the gang to Max Patch Bend where he and Rob, with the help of Eli and Putt, could mount a good defense.

Todd and Rob knew that the gang was following, and they made life as difficult as possible for Hundley and the others. Another day passed leading the gang and their leader, Hundley, deeper into the mountains. One died with his horse when they fell from a narrow trail on a steep mountainside.

Todd and Rob deliberately rode past the small settlement where Sam Lancelotta lived. Sam went to the door of his store, but Todd rode past in the woods a hundred feet away without acknowledging him. He hoped Sam would be suspicious and bring some men with him to find out what was happening. That would put them behind the gang. Todd knew that Hundley followed at a distance, watching as Todd rode through the village. Todd did not want to start a fight in the dark, much less in the village with women and children. The gang followed him by keeping well back in the woods as they passed the settlement. Darkness cloaked them as they followed Todd across the bottomland and up the mountain.

On the evening of the third day, Todd and Rob were on the hip of the mountain, near the lip of the Bend. They eased down the trail in darkness and into the valley and rode to Eli's cabin. Eli, in turn, carefully made his way to Putt's cabin.

CHAPTER 38

THE SIEGE

IN DARKNESS, Todd, Rob, and the Shipleys quietly set up defenses covering the trail down into the valley. Before dawn, two scraped and wet women crawled into the shooting position behind a big boulder.

"Sarah, where did you and Mary come from?" Todd asked in surprise.

"We came to help," was Sarah's simple reply. "We caught up with the outlaws on the side of the mountain, left our horses, and walked up as they were making camp up near the trail head. We could not use the trail down into the bend because of the outlaws," Sarah said, "so we went down the chimney in the dark. Max and James are up there to find Claire and rescue her. Max is shot in the shoulder but is only thinking about saving his wife. Chestnut is up there too."

"How about Robin?" Todd asked.

"She is with Mary's neighbor and a bunch is guarding the town— both men and boys."

"We started riding a few minutes after Rob left. Max refused to be stopped from coming. He continued bleeding, but at least he let Mary Marshall put some balm on it and bind it up. We was in the saddle about an hour later after we took care of Robin and Mary's girls," Sarah said, taking a deep breath.

"Max reads signs real good," she continued, "so he kept us behind the gang by several of hours. Then he took a short cut and put us right behind them. Coming through the settlement, we saw Sam gathering men, so we told him what was going on. He said he would arrive here by first light. Like Mary and me, their horses will have to stay well down the mountain to keep from being heard."

"We saw Claire on the back of one of the outlaw horses several times, so they is saving her for something," Mary said. "If we keep them varmints busy, Max and James may be able to rescue her."

"As soon as it is light enough, we will take a few shots at them to attract their attention," Todd said. "I sure hope Max's shoulder is not becoming infected. He has been on the trail nearly night and day for several days now."

"If we live through this, I will fix him up," Mary said. "Right now, I is wet and still too scared to pee. That chimney, as Sarah calls it, was a bad dream, and black water in the tunnel turned into a nightmare I will never forget. I come up in the pond and into air to breath. I wanted to shout, 'Praise the Lord,' but did not, except in my soul."

Dorcus arrived, shook her head, and hugged the two wet and bedraggled women. "Best get dried and into some fresh clothes. I have some things that will fit Mary. Then we need to get us some guns," Dorcus said. As she spoke, Chestnut came out of the darkness and sat beside Sarah, panting. Her face lit up with a smile as she petted the big animal.

"He must have slipped by them men in the dark," Sarah said. "Now let us put on dry clothes and fetch us some guns, as Dorcus said."

The battle started at first light. The gang ringed the top of the cliff and fired into the three unoccupied cabins. No one occupied them at the time. Rifle fire answered from a variety of locations. Hundley ordered his men to pull back, reload, and then go forward on their bellies. He broke the men into two groups so that the rifle fire could be constant. It became obvious to him that it was a standoff.

Hundley strutted outside of the line of fire and ordered Smathers to form a raiding party and ride down and take the valley. No one moved because the rifle fire from below remained constant and accurate.

"Smathers," called Hundley. "As you are a coward, grab the woman and bring her here. You will march behind her down the path ahead of us with your pistol to the back of her head. They will not dare fire at us."

Smathers returned in only a few minutes. "She is gone! The ropes is in a pile. Snick is the one who tied her. Before dawn I seen a big dog some ways off. I seen it on the trail a time or two and think it is the one that was at the McBride cabin I think we has company up here."

Hundley flushed livid with anger. "I have to do everything myself to get it done right. Snick is going to die with a belly shot so it will be slow dying. We will find the woman and kill her later. Forget the dog. It was probably just following the woman. Right now we have work to do."

"Yes sir," Smathers said with a sharp salute. He recognized the killer mood rising up in Hundley.

"All of you men," called Hundley," go to the lip and pour the lead down. Kill the men, kill the women, kill the horses, and kill the cows. Kill all that moves."

"Hold it, men," shouted Snick, the leader of the gang. "We ain't shooting no women or no stock."

Hundley turned and drove his sword into Snick's chest, twisted it around, and, jerked it out. The man struggled to raise his pistol toward Hundley but dropped it as he grimaced with pain, falling face down. Hundley straddled him and plunged his sword repeatedly into the man's back, then began hacking at his neck and slashing his back.

Even the hardened gang members watched with horror as Hundley mutilated their leader.

"Begin firing!" Hundley screamed as he pointed his bloody sword at them. They fired from the edge of the cliff, fearing the guns below and fearing Hundley behind them. They found it hard to see in the grayness of dawn, but they fired at the spurts of rifle fire from the rocks below. Hundley stood behind them with a drawn sword in one hand and a pistol in the other.

Five guns fired into the valley one after the other. They reloaded and fired again.

Suddenly the sound of echoing shots changed. One gang member fell dead, shot through the head. Another reeled backwards and fell, writhing on the ground with a fifty-eight caliber slug in his chest.

"To the woods, take cover," Hundley ordered with raised sword. He was the first to run toward the stand of trees.

In the woods several muskets fired, then fired again as wives handed men a second gun, recharging the first. The four remaining gang members found cover and returned the fire. Smathers fired from behind a tree, and Hundley fired while crouching behind a rock. The gunfire continued for several minutes. Suddenly two horses and a dog charged from the trailhead.

"Surrender," shouted Todd. "You are surrounded—surrender!"

"Truly you are surrounded. Surrender or die," shouted the preacher.

"Let me at them. I will kill every one of you with my bare hands," the words bellowed in a gruff voice that echoed off the cliffs.

"Last chance, throw down your guns," Todd shouted.

Hundley sprang from behind a boulder, waving his sword "It's Casey. Charge or I will kill you myself."

The remaining men jumped to their feet, confused and frightened, but started to charge. They fell without taking more than a few steps, caught in a deadly crossfire. Hundley ran towards Todd with his sword upraised.

Hammer struck him immediately, knocking him to the ground. The dog trailed skin and shirt from his mouth as he struck the ground and rolled to his feet. Hundley leaped up, his tunic torn and his chest red with blood. He raised his sword to chop it down on Hammer, who lunged again. A large slug hit Hundley in the chest just before Hammer struck him with his hundred-pound frame. A cloud of smoke drifted away from where Sarah leaned against a boulder, still sighting her long rifle. Chestnut stood beside her with hackles raised and teeth exposed, ready to fight.

Todd leaped from behind a boulder with drawn pistol and ran to where Hundley lay, the large black dog astride him snarling. "Off, Hammer," he told the dog, who obeyed instantly. Todd looked down at Hundley who gasped, barely alive, losing blood rapidly.

"I'm sorry, Hundley," Todd said.

"You is still dead, farmer boy," he rasped as he choked up blood, "Quincy will finish the job."

Hundley died full of hate, with wide-open eyes and a grip on the fancy hilt of his sword.

Smathers hid himself behind a tree. Seeing Todd leaning over his friend, he gathered his courage and sighted his rifle on Todd. As he squeezed the trigger, an arrow plunged into his exposed side, driving through ribs and flesh, lodging within his heart. His body stiffened and his finger tightened involuntarily. Smoke and the shot from his rifle went upward into the branches of the tree.

His legs twitched for several minutes after he fell. Blood poured from his torn heart and filled his body cavity. His eyes blinked as he stared up toward the Indian brave. His eyes remained open, without luster. He was dead.

The Cherokee stepped forward. Sam ran over to him. "Canoe," he said. "You saved the life of my friend, Todd. I saw the gun barrel a second before you shot him with the arrow."

"Todd, meet Canoe," Sam said. "He is the one who warned us about the gang a comin' our way. I did not understand you not talking to me when you rode through town, so I started gathering some men, and soon Canoe came. He had seen the men following you. The Cherokee chief, as a favor to High Eagle, sent him to keep watch because the gang was after you. Later, Sarah come by and explained things."

Eli was standing with James. "Hold everything," Eli said, "James and me has been studying this. We need to count bodies and make sure all is dead before we celebrate. Remember the last time when Hammer saved Todd's life because one was still alive."

Seven men lay dead. Three others had died earlier. The smoke of powder drifted through the trees and the banks of rhododendrons. Rob rose up in the bushes, as did Sam, Bud, and several other neighbors. Their wives were powder-smeared; each of them looked around, counted their friends. They were two short until Claire came from the woods, struggling to hold up Max. His wounded shoulder wound had broken open and drenched both him and his wife with blood. He straightened up and smiled as Rob rushed to relieve his friends exhausted wife.

Another battle won. Now only Lord Wellington Howe and his son, Quincy remained. Their hate had caused nineteen deaths. Other men died and Quincy lived.

Six new graves were dug, and filled near the graves of the horse thieves, and of the former Sheriff Grasty. Hundley's fancy sword marked his burial mound. Sam Lancelotta and James Marshall did the burial service and then took turns thanking the Lord for the great deliverance of the defenders of Max Patch Bend.

Claire and James met the town people and the Shipleys and Everyone gathered around the front of the Casey home as the women began to cook amid a constant chatter. The men walked around the farm and then gathered around the big flat rock when the women called them for dinner. In the middle of the afternoon the village folks started back home, Todd and James accompanying them up the trail to see them off.

James, Mary and Claire stayed several days to give Max McBride a chance to heal up. When they were ready to go Sarah and Todd went with them to collect Robin who was still in Know Town.

As time went by, several of the village folks who needed a horse or a saddle received one. The money and valuables in the saddlebags would help others. The rest went into the tack room, armory, barn, and into the herd of horses in Max Patch Bend, to be given away eventually.

Hundley and Smathers were riding fine horses that would become part of the breeding operation run by Eli and Putt. The horse that Dills had been riding was excellent horseflesh and was given to James to replace his, which he gave to Mary in place of the nag given to Rob by the horse thieves. The three Marshall girls gladly received the nag.

Life settled down. The settlement prospered as a steady stream of families moved into the area. The Bend flourished with gardens, horses, and cattle.

CHAPTER 39

RUFUS

SAM SHOUTED "hello the Bend," from the rim of the valley, the sound of his deep voice echoing from side to side in the high walled valley. Todd acknowledged the call with a wave of his hat, and Sam began his descent into the Bend. Todd finished his work, called Eagle, mounted bareback, and rode to meet his friend. Sam was at the main corral talking with Eli and Putt as he rode up.

"Hey, Todd," Sam said with a wide grin, still mounted on his black horse with four white feet. "I brung you a present."

He reached into a sack tied to his saddle and withdrew a ten-pound, dappled grey, white, and black puppy. He held it by the scruff of the neck and handed it to Todd, the dog patiently hanging by the grip on his spare neck skin. Todd pulled the dog to his chest and let the animal plant his hind feet on the horse. He grinned at the dog, and the dog reached up and swiped a wet tongue across his mouth.

"See, I knew this was your dog when I laid eyes on it."

"Sam, I have never seen this dog."

"Well, I know as he just arrived, but you have three huge hounds what fight bears, desperadoes, and stuff, so you need one that digs out woodchucks, ground squirrels, and other hole makers. He will help to keep your and Eli's horses from stepping into holes and breaking their legs."

"I never seen any dog look like that," Putt said.

Todd swung off his horse with the dog tucked under his arm. He set it on the ground in front of Hammer, who sniffed the pup from stem to stern. The little pup stood perfectly still, quivering some, but with head and tail held high. Finally, the pup growled.

Hammer took a step back, unaccustomed to anything growling at him. Shadow and Chestnut reached out their noses to take a whiff of the new dog. The dog stood eight inches high, a miniature compared to the three huge hounds around him.

"I ain't never seen a blue-eyed dog," Eli said. "I has heard of dogs way up north that work with Eskimos, or such, have blue eyes. This dog is built different from other dogs. It has a huge head, a full chest, heavy shoulders, and little short legs. Its hind end is narrow with slim hips. I has heard there is dogs that digs out foxes and things and are strong on the front end. A man once told me they are big on the front so if they can work their shoulders in a hole the back end won't get stuck because it is smaller and able to back them out."

"I heard," Putt said, "the big head is so they have strong jaws that will not let go."

Todd laughed. "I think you Shipleys better stick with horses and not count too much on your dog knowledge."

"I can agree with that," Eli said. "Where did this animal come from? I have not laid eyes on nothing similar."

"Some folks come into my store a wantin' to trade," Sam said. "They was hungry and had little ones. Them was a thinkin' the mountains had game falling out of the trees and berries on every bush. They offered me the dog, and when I said I would not take their dog, they said they was embarrassed anyone should see this dog. The dog lay there acting like it expected to be hit."

"We don't like it no way, and have got no use for it. It hunts rats but we has none. You can have it for a dollar in trade."

"Them words is about what they said, but they was from up beyond England and hard to understand. Someone gave the dog to their kids on the docks in Charlestown on the day they arrived.

"You could tell them kids was hungry," Sam said. "There was a baby trying to suck, but the woman's teats was all slack from lack of food. I give them about ten dollars worth of corn meal, other things, and some fatback. I took the dog, seeing it had a bad future with them. I also give the man some gunpowder and shot as they was all out. I took it out of the Max Patch account we keep for giving away, and give them one of the saddles from the horse thieves. They had an old horse pulling the wagon and another old riding horse but no tack. Someone sure cheated them on horses."

"So what is the name of this blue-eyed dog?" Todd asked.

"They said the name speaking Irish or Swede, or something sounded like R's , F, and S so I call him Rufus, and he likes it. He has been called worse, I am sure."

"You need to take him, Todd. If he digs out ground animals, we can sure use him in the Bend," Eli said.

"You are the horse man so better you take him," Todd said.

"No, this Rufus will belong to Max Patch, and we will all take care of him," Eli said with a wide grin crinkling his long scar. Me and Putt will build him a dog house between the keep and the chicken coop. That is where most varmints go to steal.

"Eli," Sam said, "I am glad that you men have settled the dog issue. You is for sure a horse man. I have never seen better, so I have a question for you. I have been studying this question and a watchin' horses real close but cannot answer it. It is this. Most horses can walk, trot, canter, and gallop. Some few has other gaits. Now, I want to know what happens to the feet that changes the gait they use."

"Me and Putt has been studying too, and has a few answers. Now, as you know it is downright confusing trying to watch the movement of a horse's hooves so we might be wrong. When a horse walks, it lifts a front hoof and then one on the opposite side at the back, then the other front, and the other back. The horse always has three feet on the ground.

"Now, when the horse starts to trot, two feet is always off the ground, making it one front and an opposite hind—and repeated with the other two feet. It makes for a rough ride."

"I have often studied this too," Todd said, "and about understand the walk and trot, but how about the canter—some calls it a lope."

"Now here we is up into the air with all four feet. Let us say it starts with the left hind foot lifted, followed by the right hind, along with the left front, and then the right front pushes off, and the horse goes airborne with all four feet off the ground."

"Amazing," Sam said. "Now I must put this to memory."

"Let me tell you about the gallop," Putt said. "First the left hind followed by the right hind, and then the left front. The right front pushes off, and the horse is airborne as Eli says."

"Do you want us to explain how a horse backs up?" Eli asked.

"No, my head is about to explode, so I will not bother about that information," Sam said. "I want to thank you. Now I better mount up and head for home. Enjoy your new dog."

Rufus was soon earning his keep, busy from dawn to dark digging out all sorts of hole digging animals. The valley resounded with his distinctive bark. Hounds ruled but they all respected the blue-eyed hunter. Because of his diligence and his mellow disposition, Rufus was loved by all and quickly rewarded attention with a slurp of his long, wet tongue. Soon he weighed fifty pound but remained a short dog.

Rufus grew longer but kept his short legs. He considered himself in charge of all the other animals except for a big yellow tomcat that trucked no interference in his life. Rufus was also careful to keep glancing at the big hounds, suspecting—but not ready to admit to himself—that they were really in charge.

MOSES, THE BLACK CAT, had a new name. The name Moses that Rev. Asbury gave her no longer seemed to fit after she had a litter. She was renamed Molly. Later she had more black kittens by a wandering black tomcat named Jake. They roamed the valley with a batch of yellow cats that Sam dropped off. There was no longer a mouse or rat problem in the Bend.

The hawks carried away a few kittens and baby chicks, but Sarah's long gun soon cleared the sky of scavengers. The balance between the domesticated animals and the wild predators was hard to keep. About the only thing no animal or bug wanted much to do with were the gourds that grew on fences. When dried, they were used for mugs, dippers, measures, birds' nests and baby rattles. Gourds were not weeds; they were a necessity. Todd kept away the weeds until the gourd plants began to climb.

Todd and Eli often commented on the smell of smoke. Wild fire occasionally roamed the mountains but was not a threat to the Bend. To the pioneers, fire was a good friend when handled properly. They used it for warming, cooking, and giving light in one form or another. Most settlers kept a fire going night and day, all year long. They used fire to clear brush, kill off vines, burn out stumps, keep warm and cook dinner.

The men and women in the Bend took care of their guns and made most of their own shot. They bought black powder and kept a good supply. Lead shot and black powder were essential, used to gather food and repel enemies, both human and animal. Pioneer life would hardly exist without guns.

Families like the Caseys and the Shipleys gathered carbohydrates and protein to carry them through the winter and the next spring. They gathered, stored, pickled, preserved, dried, smoked, and cured. Protecting their food was always difficult. There was always something attempting to find and devour it. Most mountain families made brandy or liquor. Converting corn into liquor made it a convenient product for cash or barter. Wine would store a few needed minerals and calories, but liquor was the best cash crop. Liquor making was an art and many folks had a still. There was no law against making alcohol in any of its forms, and most settlers thought it a normal part of life.

There was no still in Max Patch. Sarah knew the problems of alcohol after working with her mother in the saloon. Dorcus was a Bible reader from a religious family and took heed to the Scriptures about hard liquor. They did make a little wine from damaged fruit and berries. Neither Todd nor Eli were drinkers, and both would rather use their time developing the valley than tending a still. They did like sweet stuff and kept a few hives of bees. Sam found them a sorghum press so they could make their own strong syrup.

New people with ideas from all over Europe began to settle in the mountains, bringing music and dance. Putt and Dare were learning to play on some homemade instruments and sang songs they picked up in the village. Eli knew a number of songs from marching with the troops and taught the melody to the musicians. Sam traded for a fiddle and learned to scratch out a few notes. Todd made a box and by stretching dried gut across it, he was able to plunk out a few deep notes. Put and Dare were learning dance steps.

When the people of Max Patch Bend began to sing, dance, and play their instruments, the animals drifted to the far side of the valley and the dogs howled.

Life was becoming easier in the Bend because of its foundation built on years of hard work. All of the adults were diligent and orderly. They knew what to do, when to do it, how to do it—and they did it. Dare added two children, so there were four new voices echoing off the valley walls.

CHAPTER 40

WICKS

A SHOUT OF "HELLO, THE VALLEY" drifted from the lip with a rider waving his hat. Putt recognized the rider and waved back. Todd heard the shout, too, and knew that the rider would head to the main corral. The shed at the corral had developed into being a greeting place for visitors with two long benches and several stools.

Bart finished what he was doing, called Eagle, mounted bareback, and galloped to meet the rider he knew was his neighbor and friend, Sam Lancelotta. When they met, they laughed and traded insults. Then Sarah arrived with questions about Lois and the children. Soon Eli and Dorcus joined the group. Dare rode up on a horse that she had been training.

"Todd, what I come to tell you is there is a man asking a lot of questions around town. He says he is looking for a Tranthem to serve a warrant of arrest. We got a few of them back in coves in the mountains so did not think much of it. Course, no one give him any information. He says he's been looking for this Tranthem girl for several years because she stole a bunch of stuff from an attorney's house. Well, sir, when he said 'she' and several years,' I perked up my ears, and he goes on to say this Sarah Tranthem is a bad one according to the attorney who hired him to serve the warrant."

"Sounds like Tate Wicks is the one behind this."

"That is the name the man mentioned, Tate Wicks, Attorney at Law. And I seen it on the papers he was a holding too."

"Is he still around? Todd asked.

"Most likely not. I sent him off in the wrong direction to a cove where some real rough folks live. They are so far back into the mountains the sun comes up about noon and sets an hour or two later."

"Talking about Wicks makes me want to ride to Wicks Junction and see my aunt. She is my only relative, but if Wicks found out I would surely be arrested," Sarah said.

"Tell you what," Putt said, "me and Dare will ride over there someday and act like we is looking for kin. When your aunt is alone, we can talk with her and tell her about you being married to Todd, about your baby, and such."

"Putt, it is real kindly of you to offer, but be prepared for a long ride. Wicks Junction is out in the flatlands past the mountains. My aunt's name is Rachel. She is real sweet, and the black couple that works for her is Hattie and John. The bad one is Tiny. She is short, small, and slight, and looks about fifteen but is probably twenty-five. You will need to stay clear of her."

"Let's all sit down and plan this out," Todd said. "First, Sarah, you need to help me write a long letter to Rachel telling all the news. You need to write some of it to show her how well you are doing with your reading and writing. In case Putt is unable to see her without Tiny, he can slip Rachel the letter. Let' think this situation out as it could be dangerous to all of us."

Putt and Dare returned three weeks after leaving the Bend, riding to Wicks Junction, and meeting with Rachel. They considered it a vacation and did not mind either the hard riding or the camping along the way. When they returned, the families met for dinner at Todd's home.

"We enjoyed a great time," Dare said. "Putt said I will do most of the telling because I am much better at talking. Well, Rachel is fine, her daughter finally married a rich trader, and has birthed two children. One come a few months early, following the wedding. I can tell the women more of the gossip later. Putt says to stay on the path and not talk like a scattergun.

"Well, hear this, first. Tiny was away tending to Mr. Wicks while he traveled to Richmond on business. Rachel was glad having them gone even if he was bedding the girl.

"The big news is that this Wicks is working with Wellington Howe in some fraud to make the land grants from England look like transactions with colonists. They have dummied up deeds and such. Howe and Wicks is partners in the deal.

"Rachel received this information in a visit from Wicks' assistant. This man, you is unlikely to believe, is the brother of Potts Riddle, who the dogs killed. His name is Gerard Potts. He told Rachel he and Potts sprung from different fathers, but they do not know who they were. Their mom died long ago. Potts was really large and rough, but Gerard is frail and a bookworm type. He doesn' t much like Wicks but is paid well, so he has buried his conscience and does his work."

"This story is dragging out awful long," Putt said.

"It is fine," Todd said. Sarah and Dorcus nodded their heads in agreement.

"Putt, you interrupted just as the story is getting good," Dare said. "Well, Gerard heard enough to believe Wicks may have killed Sarah's father, Judd Tranthem. Mr. Tranthem worked as a government man, as you know, sniffing out corruption. He caught on to what Howe and Wicks was doing, and they managed to kill him before he made his report to the government. Is you believing this? They took his report out of his saddlebag, and it is in the safe in Wicks' office. Can you believe the gall of them saving the report to gloat over? Gerard says he can steal it if we can use it. Naturally, they might kill him for double-crossing them.

"Now, the last of the information is this. Gerard recognized Gilbert Casey's name. He said Mr. Casey was helping Mr. Tranthem gather information on the Tories and the suspected smuggling and such by Wellington Howe."

"This information makes a lot of things easier to understand," Todd said. "I never understood the depth of the Howes' hate for my father and me. Dad never mentioned Judd Tranthem by name. He said he passed on rumors and a few facts about Howe to a government man. Dad's name must have been in the report. I am not surprised Howe was in on the killing of Judd Tranthem and saw the documents. It all happened a long time ago, but it must still be fresh in at least the mind of Howe and probably in the mind of Wicks."

"This really saddens me," Sarah said. "If what we think is true, those two men need to hang. I believe their own guilt explains the hate of both Howe and Wicks toward us. Remember me telling you how Wicks turned on Ma and me about the time Pa was killed."

"I never in my life seen such a coincidence," Eli said, "as Todd and Sarah meeting and being married when two evil men are connected to both of them and have tried to kill them."

"This here Wicks sounds like an evil man," Sam said. "I best get on back to the village. I will let you know iffin I hear more of this man."

Chapter 41

Independence Day

THE SOUND OF SINGING AND LAUGHTER arrived before Todd saw the wagons stopping near the edge of the Bend. He waved his hat and mounted Eagle, who stood quietly waiting. Eli and Putt were ready, their horses harnessed to a travois, as Eagle was. A travois was made of two parallel poles and a hammock made of skin. One end of the poles was attached to the saddle, and the other end dragged on the ground. They started up the path to the wagons, dismounting at the top to welcome the crowd of men, women, and children. Sarah appeared on her horse with a coil of rope, dismounted, and hugged the women. Barking orders like a general, she lined up the children and mothers, interspersing older girls and the mothers between the younger ones. All the children put a hand on the rope, and Sarah started them down the path, keeping them all near to the inside of the trail. Her horse took up the rear, patiently following the group down the cliff. At the bottom, the older girls collected the little ones and marched them across the field to a smoking pit and a series of tables and benches, and if needed, the two privies that the men of the Bend had set up.

With the women and kids out of the way, the men sat down in the shade of a wagon and swapped news. Later, the men loaded the supplies, tents, and bedding on the three travois. Todd, Eli, and Putt led their horses with the men walking near them, still swapping news. Later, Putt and Dare unhitched the dray horses and led them into the valley, releasing them to graze on the lush grass.

The blacksmith set up several spits for cooking the various meats—a large one reserved for the soon to be roasting pig. Todd had previously lined the pit with rocks to hold the heat from the fire that was burning into coals. Later, the women would use the fire to heat their dinners, and then the men would recharge it with large chunks of wood to burn all night and create a deep bed of coals.

Todd unfurled a yellow flag with a coiled rattlesnake. The words below read, "Don't tread on me." He placed the staff into a hole and tamped the earth firm. As Todd unfurled the American flag, Max shouted "Attention." The children quieted, turned to look, and stood at attention as Todd placed the staff into a hole and tamped the earth around it.

When Max called out "at ease," they all relaxed and began to chatter. The children resumed their play.

Sarah was the only woman who knew how to swim, other than Mary who could dog paddle, so she took charge of the pond with Mary's help. Dare sat in the warm mud on the edge of the hot pool as the children played around her. The men wandered about, some checking out Eli's string of horses, some looking over the cows or the large flock of chickens and ducks.

Max led men towards the stand of nut trees where the hogs contentedly rooted. Beyond the trees, they stood on the high bank and looked down into the roiling water as it passed over rocks in the narrow confine of the cut. Several of the women joined them, watching the river, and admiring the stand of huge chestnut, black walnut, and hazelnut trees.

"Todd has expanded the flock of animals, especially these pigs," Bud Simpson said. "The farm truly looks prosperous."

"Most of it is thanks to Sam Lancelotta, who has been trading with the newcomers and then with Eli or me. The pigs all came from just one sow that arrived pregnant and later delivered sixteen shoats. A few months later she disappeared for about a week, returning pregnant. In a year's time we went from one pig to thirty. Now who knows how many we have and how many we have smoked or given to the folks in town."Eli multiplies horses, Sarah multiplies cows, and the pigs, ducks and chickens multiply themselves. We arrived with one duck that mated with a wild duck and now we have a flock of ducks. Chestnut has pups and Molly found a mate in the bulrushes who has come to live with us."

"Our town is growing too," Bud said. "We has growed about three times in three years. We now has fifteen cabins on the bluff above the creek, and the coves round about is filling up. Sam is doing good at the trading post. He and I are building a grinding mill down on the creek, and my blacksmith work is nearly steady. Now that the trail will take wagons, I am about to go to Virginia and fetch me a load of coal to use in my forge. With you and a lot of others helping, we finally have a wagon trail about twenty miles to the Shenandoah Road. We cannot call our path a road, just a wagon trail, and mighty rough."

The children ate their supper in late afternoon and by dusk were falling asleep. The little ones went to sleep immediately, but the older children talked among themselves.

As darkness fell, Eli and Sam stoked up the fire while Todd rolled up the flags and put them away. The men smoked a final pipe full of Todd's tobacco before going to bed.

Sunrise arrived late in the Bend. The high cliffs, and the mountains behind, blocked the first rays. The camp came to life, filled with new energy and the expectation of the feast to come. They found the two flags in place, a pig roasting on a spit, and a breakfast of hot biscuits, slices of smoked ham, and a basket of eggs ready to cook. There were skillet-size rounds of fried bread to tear apart and dip in sorghum syrup. There was fresh butter, jars of various jams, and more jars of jellies. Lois Lancelotta put a bowl of honey on the table right near the hot biscuits and butter. With pride, Todd brewed a large pot of real coffee.

While the women cleaned up and dressed the children, the men loaded Eli's stone boat with as many stones as would fit. He had made it out of several wide, thick planks placed side by side and fastened with cross planks. The ends of the planks at the front were slanted upward to keep it from digging into the earth. It was a much stouter boat than the one Todd made. A chain was attached so that a horse or a team of horses could pull the boat. The boat lay flat to the ground to make it easy to roll rocks, or stumps onto it while clearing a field. Without wheels, it created a lot of friction, making it hard to pull if loaded too heavily. The men heaped it up with rocks and hitched Bill to the chain.

The men gathered around as Todd guided the horse to tighten the chain. He spoke to Bill, rubbing his nose. Then he stepped away and clucked his sound for "go."

Bill thrust into the harness as it tightened against the load. He leaned forward, his huge feet digging into the ground. The stone boat moved. Todd yelled encouragement as Bill's hooves tore up the sod, slowly moving the load faster. When he was unable to pull any farther he stopped, his flanks quivering and his nostrils flared, sucking in huge amounts of air.

Todd stepped to Bill, saying words of appreciation and patting the massive shoulder muscles. The horse relaxed and the chain went slack.

All the men were cheering the heroic effort as Todd unhitched the chain from the harness.

Several other horses attempted to move the stone boat but none succeeded. After removing several hundred pounds of rocks, the unsuccessful horses tried again. One of Sam's horses moved the stone boat a few feet, becoming number two. The men lightened the load again, and one of Eli's dray horses became number three.

The women lined the kids up, each with both legs in a grain sack and the child holding it in place with both hands. At a shout, they headed toward the finish line, staggering, bumping one another, and sprawling on the ground. One twelve-year-old girl, hopping like a scared rabbit, made it to the finish line. Following the bag race there were sprint races, broad jumps, and beanbags thrown at a bushel basket.

The smell of the roasting pig and the other hunks of meat filled the air. Two turkeys impaled on upright iron rods seeped juices as they cooked, while sweet potatoes and onions slowly cooked near the coals. A pot of beans simmered near the fire—hunks of fatback spreading a deep layer of grease on the surface. Slabs of side bacon in a small iron pot were rendering fat to pour as dressing on spring greens.

Todd and Eli placed stakes with a cloth flag at various points around the field. In the middle of the field, they set out a straight row of flags on shoulder-high sticks. First up was a bareback slalom—no saddle or bridle allowed. Dare, Putt, and Sarah were the only riders. Sarah led off, crossing the start line at a full gallop, weaving in and out of the poles, using only her voice or her knees to guide the horse. Her knee hit the seventh flag.

Putt did a professional job, his movements fluid as water. He hit the last marker as he urged his horse to move closer to the pole. All ninety pounds of Dare on her Indian pony beat the elapsed time for both Sarah and Putt—her time was the best and she hit no poles.

The grand finale horse race began forming. The only rules consisted of passing a horse's length from the marker poles and stopping when waved off at the end of the race. Max disqualified Todd's Eagle and Sarah's Thunder. Max assigned Bill to Sarah and one of their dray horses to Todd. Everyone hooted and laughed. Eli assigned the teenagers the slowest horses in his stable. The rest of the adults each picked a wagon horse. Just as the tension was building and the race was about to begin, Max requisitioned Thunder for Claire, and Eagle for himself. The spectators laughed with tears in their eyes. The old fox had effectively put Todd and Sarah out of the race and put Claire and himself on the two best horses.

Max was the official starter, held his pistol in the air and nodded to Claire. Her horse, Thunder, bolted, and Eagle followed, after a nudge in the ribs from Max. A horse length later, he fired the starting gun and leaned over the mane of the tall stallion. The riders and the spectators shouted foul, but Max and Claire took the lead and held it half way around the course, a few others close behind but most straggling.

Todd put two fingers to his lips and whistled twice. Eagle stopped so abruptly that McBride slid over his head and landed on the ground. He jumped up and remounted, but Eagle stood rock still as the other horses passed him on the right and left.

Claire, still in the lead riding Thunder, was waving her hat and shouting as she saw the last post not far ahead. Todd put his fingers to his mouth and whistled a different signal. Thunder slowed and swerved into the infield, dropped his head and grazed, Claire beating him with her hat.

Eli pulled the same trick, sending both Dare and Putt's horses out of the race. The workhorses and Eli's slowest horses forged ahead, nearly neck and neck. As they approached the finish line, Sarah maneuvered Bill to block the leaders as a thirteen-year-old girl crossed the finish line, screaming with joy.

Todd whistled twice more. Both Thunder and Eagle responded, charging back into the race. Claire beat Max, who came in a distant last. Everyone was laughing so hard tears ran down their dusty faces. Max made an angry scene, shouting that Todd cheated him. Todd signaled to the other riders to close in around Max. Eagle glanced at Todd, and he gave the horse a hand signal. Slowly Eagle sat on his rump, leaving Max at a steep angle and sliding backwards. Todd signaled again, Eagle responding by sitting up straight with front hooves in the air—sliding Max off his back, landing him in the dirt. His anger was all a show and he sat in the dirt laughing, looking up at the ring of horses.

"Dinner in two hours," Todd shouted above the laughter. The group broke up, some to the hot pool and some to the cold pool. Some left for a nap and some went to the horseshoe pits.

Evening approached as the sun diminished in light and heat, settling behind the mountaintops to the west. Coolness trickled over the edge of the cliffs and into the Bend. Everyone was full of food, the kids were tired, and the adults chuckling over the activities of the day. Max kept shaking his head and laughing. Never before had anyone so thoroughly fixed his wagon. He was a kidder and a prankster, but Todd got the better of him this time.

Todd called Max to stand beside the flags with him. Everyone quieted.

"In honor of this day, I will read you the opening paragraph of the Declaration of Independence. Max will read a section, and I will conclude the reading. Sam Lancelotta, our storekeeper and preacher, will say a closing prayer that doesn't have to be too long because he gave us a big dose when he said the blessing." Todd chuckled and everyone grinned." I know you will be leaving early in the morning to ride home, so let me thank you now for a wonderful celebration. We are blessed to live in these mountains among such fine people."

> "In Congress. July 4, 1776. The unanimous Declaration of the thirteen United States of America."

> When in the Course of human events it becomes necessary for one people to dissolve the political bands which have connected them with one another and to assume among the powers of the earth, and separate and equal station to which the Law of Nature and of Nature's God entitle them, a decent respect to the opinions of mankind requires they should declare the causes which impel them to the separation.

"Thank you, Todd, for giving me the really good part to read," Max said.

> We hold these truths to be self-evident, all men are created equal, they are endowed by their Creator with certain unalienable Rights, among these are Life, Liberty and the pursuit of Happiness—to secure these rights, Governments are instituted among Men, deriving their just powers from the consent of the governed,...

"Let me finish," Todd said, "with this last sentence."
Sam stepped up beside Todd and Max.

> "Divine Providence is interpreted to be the hand of God," Sam said. "I firmly believe this country is

ordained by God to become a beacon to the nations…And for the support of this Declaration, with firm reliance on the protection of divine Providence, we mutually pledge to each other our Lives, our Fortunes and our sacred Honor."

"Amen," a chorus of voices said.

Sam stepped up beside Todd and Max and began to speak. "Divine Providence is interpreted to be the hand of God," Sam said. "I firmly believe this country is ordained by God to become a beacon to the nations. Each of us is no less important than another. Lois births our babies. Bud Simpson makes our tools and fixes our stuff. Without him and the support of his wife, Alma, with her bent toward inventions, our life would seem much more difficult. If a scythe breaks in the middle of reaping, your wheat would rot except for Bud. Eli and Putt raise excellent horses for our reliable transportation. Max is a soldier who fought for the document we have read. Our women are strong, keeping our homes, making our babies, and tending our needs. This little group is the future. We represents the future, and we will spend our lives building it.

"Let us not forsake our God. He is Divine Providence—he is the bedrock of our nation and the bedrock of our dream. Make him the bedrock of your life. Let us acknowledge him in our lives as we go forward on this great quest. Without God, we will not succeed. Only with God will our nation be birthed. Amen."

CHAPTER 42

GOOD NEWS—BAD NEWS

A YEAR PASSED and Sarah birthed a second child. Lois delivered their son, and Todd named him Anthony.

Todd and Sarah continued making money from the things they grew and the animals they raised—Eli prospered from the breeding of horses and the sale of colts. Max healed from the gun shot to his shoulder with only a moderate loss of motion in his arm.

Life remained hard but peaceful, and it could all have gone on forever, but the news changing their lives came with the arrival of Max Patch McBride. He told them that Gilbert Casey, Todd's father had been arrested for sedition.

Todd and Sarah listened quietly to the news, tears streaking Sarah's face as she held her baby. Placing his hand on his wife's shoulder, Todd listened carefully, a grim set to his square jaw. After Max finished speaking, Todd turned and looked into Sarah's deep eyes.

"Sarah," he said, "I need to go to northern Virginia and help defend my father. The one thing in the world Gilbert Casey would not do is to turn his back on his nation or lead an insurrection against it. Howe must be somehow involved. A long time ago, he must have realized something happened to Hundley, Smathers, and Dill and his party of outlaws. Howe is surely working on ruining my father's image and arranging to have him hanged. Quincy is no doubt goading him on."

"Todd, I am surely going with you, but we have two children now and both are too young to travel far by horseback. You will need to find us a carriage that will not jar our brains out as a wagon does."

"I would gladly take you and the children, but I fear that time is important. By myself I can ride nearly day and night."

"Surely you will not go alone," Max said. "One reason is that I am going too, and the other is there is not much hurry. They arrested your dad about five weeks ago, and the judge set the trial three months ahead. That gives us right at seven weeks to reach Richmond. From what I hear, no one is anxious for a trial except Wellington Howe. And the judge is dragging things out so that he can keep his own name in the news. He wants to use this trial to assure himself of reelection."

"The arrest of your father changes things," Sarah said. "It will take us several weeks on the trail, leaving us three weeks to make ready."

"You're right, Sarah. We will need a buggy with two seats to make room for the four of us and all the gear we will need to take with us. We will need in case we do not find much on the way.

"We will also need to sew a tent of some kind out of that sailcloth we brought with us years ago. We may be able to occasionally find cover in barns and, hopefully stop at inns. But we need some kind of cover in case we are caught out in the country by a flooded creek, a broken wheel, or something.

"Todd, let's go find Eli and Dorcus and talk about what we will need and what kind of rig to buy," Sarah said. "They lived several years in their covered wagons."

"Their wagons were built strong and were heavy as stone. You remember how we let them down the cliff piece by piece. I am sure Eli will have ideas about what we need for the trip. He can pick out dray horses for us an extra team, or whatever he thinks is best. We will take our riding horses and maybe a packhorse or two. We can work it all out."

Todd placed Robin on his shoulders while Sarah hoisted Anthony to her hip. Max walked beside them. They found the Shipleys sitting in front of their cabin.

"Folks, Sarah and I have decided to go to northern Virginia to see my father who has been arrested for sedition, and to try to help him get acquitted from the ridiculous charges against him. We need your suggestions about what kind of wagon to look for, how many, and what kind of dray horses and other provisions we need to take with us."

"This business don't sound right, Todd. your pa is a fine man," Eli said.

"We are guessing Howe is behind this," Todd said.

"I knew you would decide to go help your dad, Todd, and I have a hankering to go with you," Max said. "Howsoever, I have not done much with fancy carriages and such. I know only about cannon trucks and supply wagons, so I better quit talking and let the experts speak."

Eli laughed. "I m not much of an expert, but my family and I have spent a lot of time in wagons. We do know about horses as much as anyone does, so it is no problem. You can count on me to pick out good matched horses from my herd and Todd's. That should be easy. You will need to take your riding horses, and you have two of the best so that is no problem either. Let me study on the kind of wagon you will need and where we might find one. Will you be wanting a carriage too, Max?"

Dorcus grinned and leaned forward toward the group. "I have been thinking about giving you one of our wagons, but neither of you is padded enough to stand the bumps and jars. Them is mighty strong wagons, but they is meant for freight, not for people."

"Them will not do," agreed Eli, "and I am not sure we want to haul them up the cliff if we don't have to. Besides, Dorcus is right. You can buy much more comfortable wagons."

Sarah sat down on a short section of a log used for a seat. She shifted Anthony to her chest, flipped a shawl over her shoulder and over the baby, and opened her dress to suckle the infant. After he had his fill and became quiet, she spoke.

"I believe we should let Eli sketch out what we need. Then we can ride to the village for a visit and ask Sam if he knows where such a rig might be found. With all the talk about North Carolina becoming a state, folks are flocking into these parts. There is a lot of stuff for sale once they settle down on some land and begin to build."

"It's a fact," Dorcus said. "I been a talkin' with Sam's wife, Lois, the other day at church. She said there is all kinds of things available from settlers trying to gather money to homestead."

"Right," Putt said. "Me and Pa have bought some fine horses from the settlers. Many brought in two teams and now just need one. Some of the dirt farmers will sell their saddle horses and keep one workhorse to pull a plow and such. But I Don't recall seeing any traveling wagon."

Sarah spoke again as she adjusted the baby to her other side. "Sam mentioned he has made contact with traders down off the plateau in the flatlands where people have been living for some time now. Possibly there may be a carriage maker down there, and it is a more likely place to find one of those fancy outfits with iron springs."

Max spoke up. "I have seen some politicians go through my town. They come in real nice and comfortable buggies because the road up the valley is now good enough for lighter built rigs. As Sarah said, someone must be building buggies or carriages up in the Shenandoah. After me and Claire return home, we will ask around. A bunch more folks use the valley road than is coming into these mountains. Before we come up here, they was streaming west."

"Well," Eli said, "iffin' you find a rig, you will have to bring it up the valley and into the mountains. Once you are off the Shenandoah main road, it is tough going by wagon. Me, Dorcus, and Putt nearly had to carry the wagons to get them through. I reckon it is some better now with all the travel, but count on it being rough."

"I'm a thinkin," continued Eli, "Bud Simpson in the settlement is a blacksmith. He and me might could make us a buggy. Me, Dorcus, and Putt made our wagons. We traded for some heavy wheels, and we built the rest of it with blacksmith's help. A cook-pot fixing man—he called himself a tinker—came by one day with a bucket full of bolts and nuts in his wagon. Some man in New Jersey made a machine to cut threads on the bolt and a die to cut threads in the nut. It's why my wagons didn't shake themselves to pieces."

"We studied some at the institute," Todd said. "They also told us about bolts with slots forged into them so you could put a wedge-like piece in and drive it in to tighten the bolt."

"My plan," Eli said, "is tomorrow me and Putt goes to visit the settlement and see what we can find out. More than likely, it will take two weeks to pass the word around. The delay will give Max enough time to check the town where he lives and trading places on the main road at the end of the valley."

Todd stood from sitting on a large rock. "Sarah and I will be sketching out some plans. First, she and Dorcus will talk together, gathering ideas and making plans. The distance to Richmond is about 250 miles to where they are going to try my father. If we make twenty miles every day, it will take two weeks at least. We don't need to ride like royals, but I do not want to addle the brains of my family.

"I can do like Eli did and keep to my horse, but Sarah and the kids will have to be in the wagon. Let us see what we can find or build. We need to hurry. I sure Do not want to arrive there after they hang my father."

"Let me correct you," Eli said. "You cannot plan on making twenty miles a day. A flooded creek or river can stop you for a week. A few days of rain will turn the trail to deep mud. A breakdown can make for a long delay.

"I would figure ten miles a day to be on the safe side. That would be twenty-five days. Call it a month. You might have luck and do better."

CHAPTER 43

SHACKLES AND LEG IRONS

ROB RODE TO THE BEND to inform Todd that Max had found a good buggy and was ready to travel. Todd was ready too, and set the date and the meeting place down off the mountain. Todd asked Rob to deliver the message and then return and help Eli and Putt with the animals and the last of the harvest. He was pleased with the offer and would return as soon as he spoke with Max

The Caseys met the Mc Brides at the Shenandoah Road at the foot of the mountains. The roads were dry and dusty but smooth because of the wagon travel over the summer. The fords over rivers and creeks were at low water and easy to cross thanks to a long drought. The weather held mild and dry but with a touch of fall.

Todd kept them on the road from dawn to dark. The large carriage Sam located proved more comfortable even than Todd's saddle, so he rode most of the way beside his wife with a child in his lap. What suited him even better was Max and Claire following in a fine rig pulled by a matched pair of white horses.

The travel went so smoothly, and with so few real problems, that Todd started to worry that things with his father would go the other way. Sarah refused to think negative thoughts as Mrs. Casey had instructed her during the family visit to Max Patch when Todd was recovering from the bear attack. She was a very positive thinking woman.

To keep life from becoming dull, they swapped positions from carriage to carriage and from carriage to horseback. Even though they moved from place to place, two and a half weeks of bouncing from dawn to dark took its toll on their bodies.

To give everyone a brief rest, they stopped at the McGinnis farm where Judith had killed Deputy Snipe. They spent the afternoon and the night with the Sergeant and Judith. The scout had been working with Sergeant for a week or more as he waited for Todd to arrive. It was afternoon when they arrived but the Scout saddled his horse and he rode through the night to tell Todd's mother that they were two days behind him.

The travelers only took a total of eighteen days to reach the Casey's farm. As they approached, old memories and emotions welled up in Todd and his eyes moistened. He reached for Sarah's hand. He rode away as a youth many years before with a posse approaching the farm. Now he returned as a man with a wife and children. In a way, he dreaded the thought of accepting the reality of his father's arrest. Seeing the buildings, and the land his father had poured his life into, brought his thoughts into sharper focus.

The Sergeant was riding beside Todd's buggy. His wife remained home to tend the store. He had been telling Todd all the latest news and pointing out the improvements that Gilbert had made to his farm.

Inside the gateway sat an ancient dog. As soon as Hammer saw his mother, Anvil, standing at the gate waiting for him, he sat down and howled. His friend Chestnut and the McBride's dog, Washington, sat beside him and howled with him. The old girl trotted out and stood nose to nose with Hammer, then bowed before him in an invitation to play.

She had been a tough customer in her youth and still demanded attention, which she always received. All four of the dogs trotted side by side ahead of the horses toward the Casey farmhouse. Lucy Casey ran to the door to greet the dogs and a minute later to greet the two carriages carrying her grand children, son, his wife, and Lucy's old friends, the McBrides.

In the evening, the dining table was ladened with hams, roasted chickens, fresh pork loin, baked potatoes, and bowls of vegetables. Lucy had known it was about time for her son to return and had gathered her food together, baked her pies and bread, and made ready for his arrival. The Scout's news that Todd was two days away had given her plenty of time to prepare.

They feasted and laughed, with the women making over the children and helping with the meal. The men sat on the veranda smoking their pipes and swapping news. The women joined them after doing the dishes and putting the children to bed. Lucy finally burst into tears and with sobs, recounted the story.

"They came after dark," she said. "A large party of horsemen surrounded our house and called us out. Gilbert and I both went to the door and faced Lord Wellington Howe, who identified Gilbert to a man standing by the doorway.

"'This here man is carrying a warrant for your arrest', he said to Gilbert. 'Mr. Tate, this man standing before you is Gilbert Casey. Please serve him your warrant.'

"'Mr. Casey,' the man said, 'my name is Elwin Tate. I have been commissioned by the council to serve you these papers and to transport you to Richmond, where you will be interrogated and placed on trial for sedition and treason.'

"I started crying as I held my husband. From the expression on Howe's face, it became obvious he received great satisfaction from the situation."

Unknown to Lucy, hanging Gilbert Casey was the first step of Howe's carefully laid plans. The second step would be to find and kill Todd. He would let his own son do the killing. In his warped opinion, Quincy deserved the honor after suffering for so many years because of the injury he received in the failed attempt to ambush Todd.

Lucy continued. "Tate drew a pistol and held it pointed at Gilbert's chest. He said to me, 'Woman, move back.' Talking to Gilbert he said, 'Because you are charged with such serious charges I will transport you in my carriage, shackled both hand and foot. The men now surrounding your house will stay near you both day and night with orders to shoot to kill if anyone attempts to rescue you. Is it understood?' he asked Gilbert.

"Your dad said to the man, 'you are understood, and you are also badly misinformed. These charges are ridiculous and were contrived up against me, probably by the man standing beside you.'

"Both Tate and Howe laughed and Howe spoke. 'Dirt farmer,' Lucy continued the narrative. 'You are now in the hands of your betters and I suggest cooperation or you will deserve a beating. Is that clear? The trial is set for three months from now to give you time to think about the hanging.'

"'I am sure you will make things as difficult as possible,' your father said. 'That is what I would expect from any justice you are involved with, Mr. Howe.'

"Tate called for the shackles and two men attached them to Gilbert's wrists and ankles. He asked for a moment with me, but they scoffed and jerked him away, leading him to a carriage and driving away with him, surrounding him with gunmen."

Todd had waited patiently for her to finish. He stood and gathered his mother into his arms, holding her tight against his chest. Sarah and Dorcus surrounded her, murmuring woman's words of consolation and encouragement.

On the ride to the Casey farm the Sergeant' had filled Todd in on many details of what happened after the arrest. Todd talked with friends and neighbors gathering more of the details, so he knew that what she was saying reflected what had happened.

According to a neighbors, as soon as the gang left with Gilbert, Lucy had saddled her horse, and ridden to the home of the Scout with instructions to inform the local men what had happened and then to ride to the Sergeant, then on to Max McBride, finally to ride with him to find Todd.

The Casey's oldest son was campaigning with the army, and would surely hear the news. She sent her daughter, Nancy, to their closest friends to tell them what happened and to ask them to meet at the Casey farm.

By dawn, a group of a hundred or more gathered to hear what had taken place. Hearing they took Gilbert away in irons, charged with treason, infuriated all who knew him. They were doubly incensed by the fact Wellington Howe was in the arresting party. To them, Gilbert remained a paragon of the Patriot cause, and he remained above reproach. Most remembered the trouble with Quincy Howe, and they suspected Wellington Howe had hatched the plot to get even with the Casey family and to drive Todd into the open.

The friends of the family all knew that the gangs sent out to find Todd had not succeeded. Most remembered that Sheriff Grasty and Deputy Snipe both rode out of town to search for Todd. Only Snipe returned—dead, tied to his saddle. Dills and Smathers rode out with Hundley and never came back. Rumors at the time hinted that Hundley hired a gang of cutthroats who were never seen again. In the opinion of all, the area was much better off without those who were missing. No one even knew about the six horse thieves who died or the three who intended to hang the Indian boy.

Unfortunately, the judge who Gilbert worked closely with in the past lost his reelection to a coalition of unsavory people, including Wellington Howe and his friends. Most people decided his loss resulted from vote fraud on a large scale but never proved it conclusively. The new judge proved to be as crooked as those who put him into office.

Unfortunately, he was the judge that would hear the case against Gilbert.

Old soldiers told of their service with Gilbert, and neighbors applauded his success at farming. The merchants knew him as an honest man and one who paid his bills. The parson of the community church lauded his Christian virtues and his generosity in helping others.

The Sergeant arrived two days after the arrest, tired and dusty after twenty-four hours in the saddle and leading a spare horse. After hearing all of the details, he took charge by standing on a barrel and shouting in his best command voice.

"I want you to know Lucy has sent the Scout to find both Todd and Max McBride—it will be six or eight weeks before they can get here. Now, all this fine talk will not help Gilbert one bit unless we put it into a funnel and pour it out in Richmond," he boomed. "I say we choose six good men who can take some time off from farms and work and can ride to Richmond right soon. As I see it, we need to tell the real story to the papers and to all the politicians and important men we can reach. You work it out as you will. I will be ready to ride in the morning."

With that, the Sergeant had jumped down off the barrel and led Lucy Casey into the house. He explained he had left his wife Judith at home to tend the trading post. He would go to Richmond to see Gilbert, but he would have to return home in a few days.

He told Lucy he needed to know about the visit they received from Benedict Arnold.

He had heard a rumor that in the fall of 1787 Arnold came by one night with a band of sailors from one of his ships. He heard Arnold remained a few hours and soon rode back to the coast and sailed away in his ship.

"If I heard about it, you can bet Wellington Howe heard about it too. He might even have been involved. I need to know what happened," he had told her. Then he repeated his words to Todd on the way to the farm.

Lucy had reminded the Sergeant that Arnold and Gilbert were fellow officers who fought many times side by side. Gilbert did not much like Arnold as a friend but admired his ability as a commanding officer. He said that they spent a lot of time together making plans and such. Gilbert said that Arnold remained mannerly to him and he admired him as a military man. Arnold was haughty and argumentative with all the other officers.

Gilbert told Lucy that Arnold had come to try to explain why he became a traitor. He said he knew it bothered Gilbert and may have hurt Gilberts reputation, after being so close up in the Wilderness.

"I knew all that," the Sergeant said to Todd. "I told Lucy that I served with Gilbert through all fighting and understood the relationship. I might even understand Arnold wanting to apologize. We do know there are no charges against him now, and he lives in St. John, Canada. It is north of the top of Maine. I do not see anything illegal about his visit."

"Here is more of what Lucy told me and I am telling you. Arnold asked Gilbert to switch over to the British side and help him lead a new force down from Canada to retake the colonies. Gilbert said Arnold's plans might have worked. Of course Gilbert told him no. Lucy said she heard a few loud shouts, and Gilbert ordering him off the property or he would call out their workers."

She told the Sergeant that Arnold left upset, shouted at Gilbert, and rode away at a gallop. Gilbert was so mad he could hardly talk. It bothered him deeply how the man could even think he would turn against his own country. After he cooled down, he even wondered if maybe Arnold had gone crazy.

The Sergeant said that he believed Wellington Howe was responsible for the whole situation, and Arnold might have been making a desperate attempt to gather a band together and play general. He knew Arnold had never made a full general, and it bothered him badly.

In the morning after Gilbert was taken, eight men showed up. The Sergeant knew all of them, and in his opinion, they were right for what needed to be done. After a long discussion, the men rode off, leaving Lucy waving her hands from the front steps. She wanted to go with them to Richmond but had work to do on the farm. She knew the Sergeant and the other men would do what they could to help her husband.

CHAPTER 44

RICHMOND

AFTER THE ARREST of Gilbert Casey, Lucy made several trips to Richmond to see her husband. The eight men who had travelled with Sergeant moved Gilbert to better accommodations and demanded the removal of the leg irons over the objections of Mr. Howe and his son, Quincy.

The Howes' accommodations in a fine new house with several servants were nothing more than what they considered their due. The thought of Gilbert in jail without shackles was an affront to them. They were also furious with the judge for stalling the trial. They wanted to see Gilbert swinging from a rope.

Wellington Howe was drinking heavily as he and Quincy rehashed their gripes hour after hour, with Quincy consuming food relentlessly. His father sat red- faced, bloated with liquor, and puffing out clouds of acrid cigar smoke. Their servants made it a point to avoid their besotted and angry employers.

While the Howes sank into their opulent misery, the delegation from Max Patch Bend was arriving at the Casey home in the Shenandoah Valley of Virginia.

The party only stayed one day and the next morning they were ready to travel. Lucy climbed into her buggy and invited Anvil to sit beside her as she snapped the reins on the back of the matched pair of black geldings. The horses, eager to travel, set a brisk pace in the lead for several miles. Lucy finally slowed her team and took her place behind Todd's carriage. Her horses still held their heads and tails high as if still eager to run. Lucy handled the reins well. The grand hound Anvil beside her and the two lively horses under her command left no doubt that she remained a strong woman.

During the years Gilbert fought various battles before, and during the war, and even some after the truce, she had run the farm, expanding and improving it as it prospered.

Stopping on the bank of a wide shallow ford, Todd called for a break to water the horses and eat the lunch the women had prepared. The air was dry and cool; the mountains around them appeared green up close and blue in the distance. The road ran fairly straight and smooth. Since there were only a few wagons on the road, it remained a fine day for travel. By late afternoon, they were in Richmond.

The men who had preceded them met them and took them to a large home owned by a woman whose husband, Col. Levi Lasseter, had died in the war. Eva Lassiter remembered her husband speaking many times about Gilbert Casey. She gladly gave up her home to Lucy and moved in with her own sister. On Lucy's arrival, Eva met her at the door to help Lucy familiarize herself with the home and the two servants. She was gracious and the two women bonded immediately.

On previous visits to Richmond, Lucy had taken rooms in a rooming house. On learning about Mrs. Casey taking rooms, Mrs. Lassiter had made it a point to contact one of Gilbert's friends to extend the invitation for Lucy's next visit. Her invitation included all those traveled with her.

"It is so good to hear children's voices and to hear little feet on the floor," Eva said. She turned to Claire McBride. "In addition, you, Claire, are practically a legend among militia wives. I have heard stories of you sneaking into the front lines to make sure Max was alive and well. Some say you brought with you a wagon full of food."

"In case," Claire said, "you want to meet the old coot I am married to, this here stump of a man is Max."

"Max is another name I have heard many a time. What an honor to have all of you in my house. My sister is planning on giving a party for all of you with her friends, whenever it is convenient with you."

"We will surely let you know, and we thank you and your sister for the invitation. Right now," Lucy said, "I need to visit my husband. The men arranged it so I can visit Gilbert any time I wish. Wellington Howe and his gang are losing credibility now that some truth is spilling out.

"Howe has spread all kinds of lies about Gilbert and about Todd," continued Lucy. "He is claiming that during the past years all Todd has done was ride around killing people, including the sheriff, his deputy, and Quincy's three cadet friends Never mind they were the ones hunting Todd to kill him, financed by Howe himself."

"Well," Eva said, "it appears to me they have the wrong man in jail. I am sure that scoundrel Howe is behind this trouble. My husband was suspicious about him and his shipping company. He said he knew things, but he never shared them with me so I would not be in trouble for knowing. Howe still has a lot of influence for some reason. It is hard to understand."

CHAPTER 45

THE PRISONER

CLAIRE AND SARAH took over the household duties while Max and Todd's sister, Nancy did the baby-sitting. Todd and, Lucy, walked the few blocks to the Virginia Colonial Prison. It was an austere brick building with few windows. Its one heavy front door was covered by only enough roof to keep the rain off the wooden steps.

A gloomy interior met them as they entered a small receiving area where a man sat at a desk. After listening to their introductions and taking a ring of keys from the wall, he opened another heavy door. The odor of unemptied chamber pots struck them with the smell of men and sweat. Four cages made of iron, each twelve feet by twelve feet, lined the right and left walls. In them, men either sat on the plank floor or lay on narrow wooden benches.

The jailor took them past the cages to another door and opened it. He stood aside as Lucy and Todd walked in. Gilbert Casey leaped to his feet at the sight of Lucy and his son. He embraced them and led them to several straight chairs in a semi-circle near a coal hearth.

Todd guessed the room would measure twelve feet by sixteen feet, with a bed against one wall and a circle of chairs. A table at one side held a pile of books and writing material. An oil lamp stood between the books. On one wall was a barred window opening but with no glass. Two shutters lay flush with the wall on the inside to close against cold or rain. The opening faced toward the south with a view of the dusty main street and several buildings. A patch of blue sky was barely visible above the rooftops.

Gilbert went to the window and pointed across the street. "You can see Shockoe Bottom from here. It is the big slave-trading center for the South. The word is we have about ten thousand white folks in the area and six thousand slaves. If the wind is right, you can smell the slave quarters."

The room remained uncomfortably warm after a day of summer heat and sun. High on the wall opposite the window there was a narrow slit a foot wide and three feet long. It too had bars and was fitted with a shutter. This allowed for a slight cross movement of air and siphoned off the heat from the ceiling.

The family chatted for nearly an hour, catching up with the happenings at the Bend and the harvest on the Casey farm. Soon the conversation turned to the upcoming trial.

"Todd," Gilbert said. "I am sure you have heard of the visit I received from Benedict Arnold. He said he sailed his privateer down from Canada to the Chesapeake, then stopped somewhere on the James River that comes up to Richmond. He may have been carrying slaves for all anyone knows.

"He told me he had business in Richmond and rode over to our place to discuss his turning sides. He really came mostly to ask me to move to Canada, up around St. Johns, and join him in an attempt to raise an army and reinvade the Colonies. He claimed to be heading to England to raise support for an invasion from Canada. He wanted to capture the cities of the Northeast and down the coast to Norfolk. He claimed to have it all worked out but needed a general to command the land troops. He offered to make me a general with good pay.

"Well, I ran him off!" Gilbert said making a fist. "I want no truck with going against my country, and I told him so plainly. Arnold had a tear in his eye as he said goodbye. He is an egotistical man, a traitor to his country, into privateering and possibly slave dealing, but he was a fine military strategist. We worked together for a long time as fellow officers and I respected Arnold's military abilities. But I disrespected many of his personal traits.

"That brings me to something only your mother and I know," Gilbert said. "It is time to tell you and possibly the other men if you agree. Back in 1781 before Arnold turned sides, he came to see me at the farm. He may have been negotiating with the British, but up until then he had reached no agreement with them. He hinted at it but did not say it outright.

"Arnold asked me if I ever considered going over to the British and I ordered him off our property for even asking such a thing.

"He said I misunderstood what he wanted to say. He said he wondered if a man would even consider such a thing and wanted the reaction of a friend. He showed a hurt look on his face as he said it while backing out of my house."

Gilbert looked at the crudely planked ceiling for a moment. "I thought about reporting the conversation to our governor, but I realized that Arnold never directly said he might turn traitor. I knew he was upset about not receiving a full general's rating. Others had been given full general rank, but for reasons unknown to me, they passed him by. I did know that Arnold was a proud man, quick to become offended, and prone to violent emotions."

Gilbert got to his feet and looked out the unshuttered window for a few seconds, and then turned and continued, "I did not think Arnold would turn on his own country. I honestly thought it might be his pride talking, that he would get over it and go on with the war. He was born in Connecticut. He fought in the war from the time of the tea party in 1776 to his visit in 1781. I served with Arnold to take Fort Ticonderoga and pull the cannons back to hold the British in Boston. I served with him when a ball struck his leg in our attempt to take Quebec. I lived near him in the wilderness for months, and later we visited George Washington in Valley Forge. How could I believe that Benedict Arnold would betray the country for which he had fought and shed blood?"

"Dad," Todd said. "I believe you one hundred percent and know you are completely truthful. Now we need to figure how we can present it to the court so they will believe you. Your friends will be character witnesses, and Max can give some battle history, but no one was there to hear any of your conversations."

"I was there," Lucy said. "I didn't understand all their words because they were in another room, but I did hear the raised voices of the argument after Arnold suggested Gilbert might be interested in changing sides in the revolution."

"That is not good evidence, Mother, coming from his wife," Todd said. "I am sorry, but so far all we have is Dad's story and several friends telling us what a fine man he is. That defense will not work!"

"Wait," Lucy said and looked at Gilbert "You mentioned to me one time that Howe might be involved with slave trading. You also hinted he was involved in supplying the British soldiers while pretending to be a privateer for the colonies."

"More speculation," Todd said. "We need something concrete. We need witnesses."

"I know the problem," Gilbert said. "I have been racking my brains for something concrete."

"Well," Todd said, "I am headed down to the James River to see what I can find out about Howe and his trading. He is sounding so righteous in his accusations—what if he is a slaver?"

Gilbert thought a moment. "We might be able to impute misbehavior to Howe, but that does not directly apply to the charge of treason he has lodged against me."

"I do not want to terrify you," Gilbert said looked at Lucy and then at Todd, before continuing. "It looks like the gallows are in my future. I see so no way to counter Howe's charges."

"But Dad! His evidence is only what he himself says. He has no case unless he has some kind of independent witness, letters, or something else solid."

"According to our friends from home, there is talk on the street Howe has an eyewitness who will testify to the conversation he heard."

CHAPTER 46

THE TRIAL

TO GILBERT'S FAMILY AND FRIENDS it was obvious that the eyes of Blind Justice were wide open, and no justice would come from the court.

Gilbert's attorney called for a three-day delay. The judge granted only twenty-four hours. One of the men supporting Gilbert finally managed to obtain an appointment with Governor Randolph. He had just returned after several months in Philadelphia working on court reform. He found the governor was acquainted with the Casey's trial, but he did not know the background of the situation or any the facts. He did know the presiding judge and immediately involved himself. He dismissed Gilbert's friend with the promise that he would look into the case and communicate his findings.

Governor Randolph did say that the Continental Congress continued to debate provisions of what they were calling the Judiciary Act. It was an attempt to establish a federal supreme court, under it an appellant court, and below a lesser federal court. On a state level, there would be a similar three-tiered system of courts. He implied he was in favor of the act because the state courts were in disarray, including Virginia's.

In fact, the governor did not communicate further with Gilbert's friend, his attorney, or with Gilbert himself. After the twenty-four hour delay, the court convened in a hall packed with people and grey with acrid cigar smoke. The judge was arrogant, tilting his head back and looking down his long nose. He repeatedly sided with Wellington Howe and with his attorney. He often used the appellation, Lord Wellington Howe.

The testimony engaged hot and on target. The prosecution did everything in their power to prevent Gilbert from speaking, while at the same time making much of the hearsay evidence presented by

Wellington Howe on behalf of the prosecution. By the noon recess, the Casey defense was overwhelmed and discouraged. Gilbert and his friends felt defeated. The judge did not allow any points in Gilbert's defense. The situation looked hopeless.

At the end of the lunch recess, the judge mounted the bench, hammered his gavel and demanded silence. "This court will now be in session, hearing the treason and sedition case of Gilbert Casey."

A well dressed, and dignified looking man walked boldly to the front, opened the gate, and stopped directly in front of the judge.

"Sir," he said in a loud oratorical voice. "You will not preside over this trial and will immediately vacate the bench."

The sound of murmuring voices surged through the room as many recognized Governor Randolph. The judge on the bench jumped to his feet. "Get out of my courtroom," he shouted.

"Sheriff," the Governor said forcefully, "remove this man from the bench. If he causes a disruption, put him in jail. I have many charges the State can bring against him."

The judge recognized his eminent peril, quieted, arose from his seat, and stalked out of the courtroom.

"I object to this interference," shouted the Howe's attorney, Tate Wicks.

"Silence," the governor shouted toward Wicks, "or you will join your friend the judge in jail."

Todd was stunned to hear the name Wicks. Now he was beginning to understand the vendetta against his father and himself.

Governor Randolph turned to the courtroom. Three men lined up beside him. "The Continental Congress is debating judiciary reform. I have decided this is the time to make reforms in Virginia," he said. "I would first say that a state cannot try the charge of treason against the federal government. Only a federal judge can hear such a charge.

"However, in these changing times I have arrived at an interim solution. I have with me a state judge of impeccable character, a judge from the state supreme court, and a judge from a federal court. This will be a three-judge panel. I am asking these three judges to preside because of the disarray in the system between state and federal judiciary practice. In this way the federal judge can speak for the colonies, and the other two judges can speak for Virginia."

Applause and shouts erupted from the court's spectators, with much moving about and murmuring. The Governor allowed the assembly time to settle down.

"Gentlemen, please mount the bench. You will note that my aides have positioned two more chairs. Please call the court to order at your convenience and proceed."

The three men seated themselves with the federal judge, George Addington, in the center holding the gavel. He cracked the gavel once on the desk and called for order.

"This court in the case of Howe vs. Casey is now in session. First, since this is a three-judge panel, we will now dismiss the jury. You may step down now. Secondly, an individual citizen may not bring a case of sedition or treason against the federal government. The federal government must bring the charges, and the individual must defend himself.

"In this case, the court knows of no such charges made in a federal court. Therefore, we dismiss the previous trial, and we will call this session a hearing of facts. If the court sees a clear course of evidence for either sedition or treason, we will so charge the accused, and the federal court will proceed."

Judge Addington struck the gavel on the desk again. "This is a very unusual situation," he said, "but let us proceed. The court calls Gilbert Casey to the witness stand. Please take a seat, sir."

There was murmuring in the courtroom and the sound of surprise and excitement.

"Mr. Casey, you are not on trial. I understand they took you from your home in shackles and imprisoned you in the local jail. I wish to apologize. Their action remains a misguided and probably illegal act, and we must rule that the action is not in accord with any law we know of. You may have a personal legal action against the responsible parties.

"We have been briefed on the accusations presented in the illegal trial this morning. As a matter of record, please recount your arrest in detail and give us the details of the two meetings you entered into with Benedict Arnold. I might add there were no convictions in his case, and he had a legal right to talk with you on both occasions. If necessary, we will hear your witnesses later in the hearing. Please proceed."

Wellington Howe sat with his attorney, Tate Wicks, conferring with him often. Wicks appeared furious because of the takeover of the court by the governor and the instillation of a three-judge panel. He knew none of the judges and had no influence with any of them.

The judges sat without comment, listening to Gilbert Casey tell the story of his arrest and the two visits by Benedict Arnold, and his previous dealings with Mr. Howe. There was a question and answer session, and then the court adjourned for the day.

On the second day of the hearing, a group of armed sailors surrounded the exterior of the courthouse. Benedict Arnold entered courtroom. He courteously introduced himself and stated that he wished to testify. The three judges welcomed his presence, and public interest required that they listen to his testimony. Whether traitor or not, he remained a free man with the right to give testimony.

Tate Wicks jumped to his feet with an objection, but the court ordered him to sit down. He was no longer a big fish in a small pond; he was jist a minnow in the ocean. His face turned livid with outrage, sweat running from his scalp, down the side of his pudgy face to his soaked collar.

"Gentlemen," Benedict Arnold said. "Before you find a righteous man guilty of an offence against the colonies, let me say a few words. First, men from the crew of my ship are standing outside of this building to help assure my safety. I recognize my actions have angered many people."

"This is unusual, General Arnold," Judge Addington said. "Under the circumstances, we welcome your testimony, but first, let me warn Mr. Wicks not to jump up with objections or he will be removed from the courtroom. Please proceed."

"In 1776 and for several years following, I served with Captain Casey. Again, let me repeat my men who surround this court intend no disruption. I am here to state to you that this man is guiltless. I am disgraced, but my words remain true that this man is a patriot, and an attempt has been forwarded to prosecute the wrong man.

"This man, Gilbert Casey, is guilty only of being the most patriotic man I know. The man who accuses him, Wellington Howe, is guilty of many and far more serious transgressions. His attorney, Tate Wicks, is a shameful man and may have participated in the murder of a government officer, Judd Tranthem."

Shouts of anger rang out and the audience murmured among themselves. The judges rapped their gavels, demanding order. Tate Wicks, jumped to his feet, protesting loudly.

"Once more, Mr. Wicks, and you will be in contempt of court and removed to the local jail."

With order restored, Judge Addington leaned forward to speak directly to Mr. Arnold.

Howe jumped to his feet shouting. Tate Wicks was pulling at his coat, trying to make him sit down.

The judge pounded his gavel and spoke directly to Mr. Howe. "Sir, conduct yourself properly or I will have you removed."

"Your honor, I am not on trial here. We are confronted by a traitor who is supporting a traitor and I am being impugned."

"The situation is unusual, Mr. Howe. You are not yet on trial but your testimony is. It looks like your attorney, Mr. Wicks, is not above suspicion either. This court will hear Mr. Arnold," Judge Addington said. "At least he was a patriot and spilled his blood before he turned. You, on the other hand, have never been a patriot from the rumors that I have heard. Now sit down or I will have you removed. Please continue, Mr. Arnold."

"Your Honor, you have heard Mr. Howe's testimony that a rider—who was with my group on both visits to Mr. Casey's home—confided to Howe that Captain Casey and I sat and discussed military plans concerning a potential invasion from Canada. He claims he heard that we were laying plans for Captain Casey to defect to the British. The allegation is that I negotiated the rank of general for him along with a sizable sum of money.

"You have heard Mr. Casey admit to the two visits. I want you to know that I did not receive any indication of his willingness to defect, and in one case he ordered me out of his home. This, I am told, he related to you in some detail and accurately reflects what took place.

"On my first visit, I used him as a sounding board to help me make my final decision. He so forcefully rejected the idea of anyone defecting, that it gave me pause. On the second visit I was indeed, as he suspected, attempting to lure him to my side. I received a firm and resolute rejection."

Howe jumped to his feet, objecting to the testimony. Again the court ruled, this time sternly that after his next outburst he would be remanded to jail. Arnold continued.

"Your Honors, outside of this building are five men who rode with me on the second visit. If you ask, they will testify that they maintained a perimeter fifty feet from the house. They saw no one and heard nothing. They will testify I never spoke of the visit to any of them. This supposed witness of Mr. Howe either fabricated his story or has learned it by heart from Mr. Howe. I can prove to you that no one man accompanied me on both visits to Captain Casey. That makes Mr. Wick's witness a liar."

"I object, Your Honor," Wicks said contritely after receiving a nod of permission from the court.

"Noted, go on Mr. Arnold."

"Thank you, sir. On my first visit to the Casey farm, I arrived as an officer with the United States Army. As such, six men accompanied me from my command. Three were later killed in action, but three remain. I will give you their names so you may call them to testify if you wish. The fact is that they too remained at a distance from the residence, just as on my second visit, and heard or saw nothing. I did not discuss my affairs with them or reveal to them the subject of my visit."

"I am sure the court is knowledgeable about the bad blood between the Howes and the Caseys. That is not an accurate understanding. In fact, the bad blood remained all on the side of the Howes. This entire episode was formulated in the mind of Wellington Howe. I know that to be a fact as he expressed to me his desire to destroy the Casey family."

"Howe is my silent partner as a political convenience. He is a slave trader. Ask around Shockoe Bottom—ask at your slave market. You will find many who know him."

A rumble of surprise coursed through the room.

"Interrogate the crew of his vessel," Arnold resumed in a loud voice. "You will find that when he was masquerading as privateer for the Colonies, he frequently engaged in aiding and abetting the British in many ways. He, your Honor, should be on trial here for treason!"

The courtroom erupted with many voices.

Judge Addington rapped his gavel for quiet.

"Mr. Arnold, please remain before me in case you can add to what I am about to tell the court.

"I have in my possession a report written by a federal agent," Judge Addington said. "It testifies to numerous charges against both Mr. Howe and Mr. Wicks. To those charges, I will add the charge of murder," the judge said firmly. "The late federal agent, Judd Tranthem, was murdered while conducting an investigation of two men, Wellington Howe and Tate Wicks. Mr. Tranthem was assisted in the investigation by Gilbert Casey."

The courtroom erupted again in loud voices and movement. The Judge let the disturbance go for a full minute and then he gaveled the courtroom to silence.

"Let me continue," Judge Addington said. "Judd Tranthem wrote a detailed report, identifying Howe and Wicks as criminals.

"This document came to us directly from the office safe of Mr. Tate Wicks. It was given to us by Mr. Wicks' assistant who will swear to the authenticity of the document as well as to other facts surrounding the murder of Judd Tranthem. He will also testify about the attempted murder of Tranthem's daughter, Sarah who is now the wife of Todd Casey. Wellington Howe's agents also made several attempts on Todd Casey's life."

The courtroom filled loud voices and confusion. The judge pounded his gavel. Wellington Howe jumped to his feet calling out loudly. Tate Wicks stood waving his arms to attract the attention of Judge Addington who was demanding order.

In the chaos of the courtroom, Howe pulled a pistol from under his coat and aimed at Benedict Arnold who was still standing before the bench. As Howe moved to obtain a clear shot, Max McBride jumped over the rail that separated the attorneys from the crowd. He lunged into Howe, deflecting his aim away from Arnold but the pistol by chance fired into Tate Wicks chest.

Todd lunged too and tackled Arnold, knocking him to the floor as Howe pulled another pistol.

Gilbert jumped from his chair and took several quick steps toward the bench where Howe leaped away from Max and was raising his drawn gun again toward Arnold. Gilbert ran forward but he was too late to surprise the gunman. Howe turned toward him, an outstretched pistol only a few feet from Gilbert's chest. An animal scream of rage burst from the lips of Wellington Howe as he jammed the pistol into Gilbert's chest, near his heart. A shot rang out as Howe stood before the bench, jabbing Gilbert with the gun. Smoke from the shot drifted among the judges.

Howe collapsed, blood spurting from his shattered head. Judge Addington laid the smoking pistol down and rapped the gavel in the stunned silence. Wellington Howe and Tate Wicks lay dead before the bench of justice.

"This hearing is adjourned," Judge Addington said in a loud, stern voice.

CHAPTER 47

HEADLINES

JUDGE EXECUTES TRAITOR read the front page of a Richmond newspaper the next day. Many gasped, thinking that Gilbert Casey had been found guilty and was quickly hanged. Luckily, most knew the whole story and knew in fact that the right men died, that Gilbert Casey was innocent and free.

At the end of the trial, the Casey family had shaken Arnold's hand and wished him well. No one liked what he had done, but he'd had made his choice.

When the three judges filed out of the courtroom at the end of the hearing, each had given a slight bow to Arnold as they passed. His men had formed up around him as they mounted horses and galloped away toward his vessel moored in the James River.

"Well," Sarah said, "I guess that ends our problems with Howe."

"I'm afraid not," replied Max. "I saw Quincy hobble out the back door of the courthouse and head up the street. He did not even look at his dead father bleeding on the floor. He had an angry look on his face. He was furious, pushing people aside with his hand on the hilt of his fancy sword. We had better keep our eyes open. In my opinion he is more dangerous than his father was. He probably goaded his father to keep his hate alive."

Todd said, "Dad, we need to go by the sheriff's office and tell him about Quincy, warn him he may try to start a fight or shoot us from cover on the way home."

"I wish to go with you," Sarah said. "I need some air."

As they entered the sheriff's office, the sheriff jumped to his feet, bowed slightly to Sarah, and shook the men's hands. He apologized for the way they had treated Gilbert, saying that Wellington Howe and Tate Wicks and had misled him with a pack of lies.

"I knew Howe was into slaving, piracy, and helping the British in many ways, but I found no real proof. He had a haughty attitude that drove me crazy." He pounded his desk and then apologized to Sarah for his outburst. "I'll tell you what," the sheriff continued. "To help make up for my being buffaloed and to help clean up the town, I will tell Quincy to leave and not ever come back."

"You have a deal," Todd said. "Everything you did is forgiven on my part. You did what you thought was legal."

"One other thing, Mr. Casey," the sheriff said. "In all the confusion you may not have noticed but Tate Wicks wife Rachel, was way in the back of the courtroom with her house girl, Tiny. Tiny went crazy when Wicks was shot, and ran screaming to his body. Mrs. Wicks showed no emotion at all and quickly left the courthouse. I saw it myself."

"I saw that black girl but never gave it a thought in all the confusion," Todd said.

"Well," continued the sheriff, "this morning Mrs. Wicks came to me and said Tiny had run off during the night, then asked me not to arrest her if she was caught."

Sarah nodded and said, "I guess we all suspected she was sleeping with Tate when Rachel was not around, or when he took Tiny on a business trip as his servant. She grew up in the Wick's home so Rachel probably does not want to harm her, just wants to let her go."

"Mrs. Wicks was upset about to how to handle the burying of her husband," the sheriff said, "and traveling back south to her home by herself."

"You may not know this," Todd said, "but Rachel Wicks is the blood sister of my wife's mother."

"That explains something," the sheriff said. "She mentioned that she had relatives nearby but was too embarrassed to go to them."

"She is in fact my aunt and I love her, Sheriff," Sarah said. "I assure you my husband will take care of my aunt. We will invite her to travel south with us and to stay with us for a spell. We were once close, but Wicks kept us apart. Please tell me where she is staying, and I will go to her at once."

CHAPTER 48

THE PRIVATEER

HATE ROILED THROUGH QUINCY'S BRAIN, enlarging, and replaying images of the past week, interpreting what happened as insult and hate. His brain seethed with plans of revenge, and images of the slow and painful death he would personally inflict on Todd Casey. First he would even the score with the governor and the federal judge. Then he would personally kill both Todd and his father.

Three days before, he had seethed with fury as he watched the trial—that had turned into just a hearing—from his seat in the back of the courtroom in Richmond. He was red-faced with furious dismay at the turn of events and then seethed again as Benedict Arnold gave his testimony. He knew he and his father no longer possessed any evidence to support additional charges.

In Quincy's mind, the purpose of the trial was to force Todd out into the open so Quincy or his father would be able to kill him. He did not know that his father had murdered Judd Tranthem, Sarah's father, and was afraid that Gilbert Casey could expose him.

Quincy's second goal was to hang Gilbert Casey, to discredit the Casey family in the eyes of the people. He and his father had planned to wait until Gilbert was sentenced to death and then to kill Todd. They had failed. His father was dead and the Caseys were alive and free.

His father had even arranged for the local newspaper to print a scathing rebuke of the Casey family, and in the event of a not guilty verdict, the article would suggest the trial was a sham. It would demand a new trial before a local judge who Wellington Howe could influence. Indeed, one judge even had shares in their privateer and slave ships.

Nothing had gone according to plan. The trial turned into a hearing before real judges, and the newspapers learned the truth they were no longer able to avoid. Gilbert Casey had become a state hero.

For Quincy, the outcome of the trial delayed his dreams of revenge and killed his father. In his eyes, the fault lay with Gilbert and Todd. It was all a conspiracy made possible by the arrival and testimony of Benedict Arnold. Why would anyone listen to an admitted traitor? Why did the court even allow him to speak? Why did the judges permit Arnold to make accusations against his father, accusing him of murder, treason, and slave trading?

The trial was dismissed and never happened. The hearing was over, and his father dead. Even Tate Wicks, his father's attorney died. The end came so suddenly and explosively that Quincy remained mentally stunned. He found it impossible to think that his father, an English gentleman and Lord, had died in a courtroom, accused of murder and slave running, and shot by the judge. It proved again to him that America was the backwater of the world—a slime pot of ignorant people.

In his warped mind, the country made Quincy its enemy—stabbed him in the guts. It had run off his mother and sister, then killed his father. After all that disgraceful treatment, the sheriff ordered him to leave town and never come back. America, his sworn enemy, would pay. He would even that score first.

Quincy watched the departure of the Casey family as they loaded their carriages with things to take home. Gilbert took his place in the lead carriage, driven to Richmond by his wife. Lucy. She proudly sat beside Gilbert, and beside her sat the noble dog, Anvil.

Sarah drove the second wagon with her daughter, Robin, beside her. Rachel rode in the second seat with her nephew Anthony. Beside the carriage trotted Sarah's hound, Chestnut, and her horse, Thunder.

Max Patch McBride held the reins in the third carriage. Beside him sat his wife, Claire, and Todd's sister, Nancy. Behind them rumbled the freight wagon driven by a friend of the family. It was loaded with the clothing and other gear amassed over the months of Gilbert's imprisonment.

Todd, mounted on Eagle, rode beside his father. Hammer, ever vigilant, trotted on the off side of the horse.

Sergeant McGinnis, and the old friend always referred to as the Scout, led the large group of friends who worked to make Gilbert more comfortable and had advised him about the legalities of the trial.

Those in the traveling party smiled and joked as the group formed up and headed out of town. Many of the townspeople lined the streets and waved. Even the sheriff and members of the court were there to say good-bye. The governor, mounted on a fine stallion, waved his tricorne hat.

Quincy Howe watched too. He sat behind a lace curtain in his home, looking down on the procession. He sat alone except for several servants going about their business downstairs in the ornate house. His mother and sisters remained in Canada since they had moved there with friends two years previous. They had grown ashamed of both Quincy and his father. They knew their "Lord Wellington Howe" was just a treacherous man without a title. They would soon learn that he was dead—exposed as a murderer and slaver—and killed by the judge to save Gilbert Casey's life. His mother and sister learned earlier that Quincy had fallen on his own dagger while attempting to kill Todd. Both Dills and Smathers had admitted as much.

Anger and a dark ugly mood settled around Quincy. He smelled his own nervous perspiration as he heaved himself to his gout-infected feet. He winced at the pain and wavered as he took several steps to his closet.

Hanging inside the closet door were two light blue velvet dress coats that hung down below his hips. Beside each uniform hung a cranberry colored ruffled shirt. The trousers were a stiff white knee length material with a clasp at the bottom to hold up the cranberry colored knee socks. On the floor were new black shoes with large brass buckles.

He labored into one of the uniforms with the help of his manservant. He could not reach his feet, so the servant put on his knee socks, tucked them under where his pants were gathered at the knee, and helped him on his shoes. Quincy checked himself in the mirror. He knotted his sash around his waist and over it buckled his sword belt, jeweled scabbard, and gold leaf sword hilt. Placing the matching blue tricorne hat on his head and grasping the heavy cane with the gold ball on top he struck a figure and liked the results.

The tight pant legs and stockings accented his scrawny appendages, but his huge torso held the jacket well away from his thighs. The visual result appeared much like two toothpicks supporting an Easter egg. It is certain he saw an entirely different image in the full-length mirror.

He waited for the Casey procession to leave and for the well-wishers to go about their business. He called for his servants to finish his packing and to help him down the stairs and into the carriage house. They hoisted him into a closed carriage pulled by a team of dappled gray horses. The servants loaded two large trunks of clothes and personal objects.

He pulled the curtains across the windows, then told the driver to take him to his father's favorite ship, the Lord Howe, berthed on the James River several miles east of Richmond.

The vessel, a brigantine, carried two masts with square sails, and fore and aft sails, along with a long bowsprit supporting several jibs. She was of shallow draft, the kind of vessel pirates loved. With her shallow draft, she only needed a few feet of water to sail in. She was able to dart behind reefs and up shallow rivers to hide or avoid a stronger vessel. Her rigging had been simplified, so she could sail with a small crew of twenty men. On each side there were three gun ports and behind them nine-pounder cannons. The captain's cabin consisted of only one room but a comfortably large one with a sleeping area, a desk, and a dining table that would seat six.

The Lord Howe earned the reputation of being a fast vessel and much easier to sail than the longer version. A large hatch amidships accommodated the cargo, trade goods, or humans. The vessel gave off the faint smell of human waste and corruption. The three officers lived in tiny cabins below the captain's quarters.

Quincy commandeered the captain's cabin. It was one room across the stern of the vessel that opened directly onto the aft deck. It was a fortunate arrangement because he was too fat to fit through the hatch to the lower cabins. He called upon the carpenter to make him a heavy chair and spike it to the deck outside of his cabin under a canvas fly.

The captain moved below to one of the three tiny officers cabins, which forced the boatswain into the forepeak with the seamen. Quincy's personal servant and the cook slept on the floor of the galley.

The vessel put to sea after notifying the port authorities they would sail to the islands to procure rum and spices. When Quincy could no longer see land, he told a seaman to pull down the American flag and hoist the British flag. Captain Snow objected but was overruled. When the Captain informed him that the vessel was one hundred miles off shore, Quincy demanded they sail back and forth, north and south. Because of the truce with England, his father's letters of marquee were no longer in effect, but Quincy's intentions had nothing to do with French or English shipping. He intended to hurt America. His hate seethed within him day after day as he sat in his fancy uniform and surveyed the horizon with his glass.

Quincy acted in an imperial and demanding manner, without humor or a smile. An angry frown creased his forehead as he issued sharp orders to Captain Snow. His own personal slave served as his cook and body attendant. Quincy was alone in the large cabin at night, eating and drinking.

He remained surly to the crew and obnoxious to the officers. He acknowledged no one but the captain, whom he treated as a cabin boy. Quincy spent his days in the chair on the aft deck, issuing needless commands while consuming huge amounts of both food and wine.

Captain Snow marched around the decks, angry and perplexed. He was a short man but thick and hard. His face wrinkled and deeply tanned from a lifetime on the water. He resented some of the compromises Wellington Howe had forced upon him as the owner of the vessel, but was afraid that working for his son, Quincy, would be intolerable.

The crew, like the captain, tolerated the father because he seemed reasonably competent. This fat, egotistical oaf of a man, acted as if he were captain of a ship of the line, with a crew of hundreds, serving three decks of guns. In reality, the vessel carried six small nine-pounders and not enough crew to both man the guns and sail the ship at the same time. That fact escaped Quincy's limited understanding, and no one intended to enlighten him.

On a bright and cloudless day with light wind, a speck of sail appeared on the horizon. It grew as the two vessels approached one another. Finally, its hull appeared. The masthead lookout reported a small navy sloop. Captain Snow recognized it as the Swallow, a carrier of dispatches and mail, making the run from London to Richmond. The Navy owned her, operated her with Navy sailors, and sent her on official government business. She flew a huge American flag from her masthead.

All the men on board the Lord Howe, knew this vessel and her young captain, Lieutenant Snow. Her reputation for speed had increased after the navy removed her four nine-pounders. Since the end of the war, she sailed in friendly water and needed no armament. No privateer or pirate would waste his time on so small a vessel, especially one that only carried mail and dispatches.

The ships closed the distance. Quincy ordered a signal be flown to 'heave to' so the two vessels would ride side by side to swap news. The Lieutenant in charge of the sloop recognized Howe's vessel, Lord Howe, but his pride in his first command would not let him take any chances.

Besides, the Lord Howe, was registered as an American vessel and should not be flying the British flag. Something was amiss.

"Load the cannons and prepare to fire," screamed Quincy from his chair on the afterdeck. He waved his pudgy hand in the air as he scowled through jowls puffed with indignation. His corpulent body hung over the sides of the chair as his spindly legs braced him in place against the gentle rolling of the ship.

"Keep the gun ports closed until I command you to fire. On my command open the gun ports, run out the port battery, then fire at my signal."

The captain stormed aft to confront Quincy only to stare into the muzzle of a brace of pistols.

"Do as you are ordered, mister. Keep the gunners out of sight."

The use of the term, mister, was a spiteful slap in the face to the captain. He turned on his heel and walked quickly to the gun deck. He muttered orders to the first mate who commanded the guns. The guns were loaded and made ready to fire.

As the two vessels sailed abreast, port side to port side, the distance narrowed to a hundred feet.

"Open the ports and run out the guns," Quincy screamed. "Fire as you bear."

The ports banged open and the guns rumbled out. The sloop became an easy target.

"Fire, Fire, Fire," screamed Quincy as he struggled to his feet and raised his sword.

The brigantine rolled as a long swell passed under her keel. The guns fired on the downward roll and a cloud of smoke and burning wadding rushed toward the sloop. No cannon balls struck the sloop.

"Reload and fire again," Quincy shouted as he struggled to remain standing, waving his sword with his right hand and aiming his pistol with his left hand at the captain and crew. His second pistol tucked into his sash with the butt protruding.

The sloop sailed close enough for its captain to understand the words and the intent of .the Lord Howe's master. Quincy was incapable of understanding that young lieutenant Bacon, the captain of the Sparrow, did not intend to allow a renegade to destroy his vessel. The Lieutenant reached below the bulwarks and placed a heavy object in a socket in the cap rail of the bulwark. He aimed it toward Quincy who he now recognized and had heard him giving the order to fire another salvo. Lieutenant Bacon jerked the firing lanyard. The swivel gun belched a dozen musket balls streaking toward the attacker and striking Quincy in the chest, tearing him to pieces. The impact tossed him across the deck to smash against the starboard bulwark, his stick-like legs, kicking in death, the ruffled cranberry-colored shirt torn and bloody.

The Captain of the "Lord Howe" jumped to the mast, loosed the flag halyard, and the British flag fluttered to the deck. He and the crew rushed to the rail with their hands raised.

The first mate on the sloop was reloading the swivel gun as Lieutenant Bacon picked up a speaking trumpet and hailed the Lord Howe.

"Captain Snow, is that really you? Are you surrendering?"

"Aye, Lieutenant Bacon, this was not my fight. Mr. Howe, who commanded that we fire upon you, deserves the responsibility but will have to pay from hell."

"Captain, I noticed you forgot to load ball shot. All you gave us was smoke and wadding, and you fired on the down roll so even that went into the sea."

"It was our intention, Lieutenant Bacon. We did some slippery work during the war, but we are now only interested in legitimate cargo hauling."

"Captain Snow, can I trust you have no shot in your starboard batteries?"

"They have not been loaded, sir."

"And your port battery—I saw your men reloading."

"Only loaded with powder and wadding as before."

"Captain Snow, lower a boat. Come over and let's have a talk. You loose your sail and we will lower ours. I want to hear the story as to why this attack occurred. I want to know why Quincy Howe was giving commands."

The two men met on the deck of the Swallow, the crew holding rifles and keeping an eye on both Captain Snow and the men still lining the bulwarks of the Lord Howe.

Lieutenant Bacon and his vessel were on the return trip from London when Gilbert Casey stood trial before his accusers. He knew of Gilbert's reputation and his service to the country, but he could not fathom why Mr. Casey should be tried in a court of law. He stood amazed, hearing the news that Wellington Howe died at the hand of the judge. It was nearly beyond his comprehension that there was a trial in the first place, and the ending startled him. The presence of Benedict

Arnold seemed unusual, but he agreed that Arnold had acted as a person of honor by defending Gilbert Casey.

"I know that there festered bad blood between the Caseys and the Howes," Lieutenant Bacon said. "I met with Captain Casey's older son, Major Joshua Casey, up near Boston. He was serving with a unit searching for pirates believed to be hiding somewhere on the coast. I took Major Casey and several of his men to search the coves and islands.

"He told me about the fight his brother, Todd, had with Quincy and how Quincy stuck himself by falling on his own dagger. The Major said that Quincy had sent out parties of cutthroats, and even his cadet friends, to find and kill Todd. I am sure his daddy, Lord Wellington Howe, as Quincy called him, financed the search."

"I know the past history," Captain Snow said. "This attack today is part and parcel of the hate for Todd Casey that consumed Quincy for many years. With his daddy dead, I guess he realized the Caseys had won, and he turned his hate on the whole country. That must be why he wanted to sink an American ship.

"He never lifted a finger in his whole life and did not have a clue about shipping or anything else. He came aboard dressed like an admiral and sat in the big chair the carpenter made and nailed to the deck. The crew could tell that the operation of the ship was a mystery to him, and he did not know a stay from a halyard.

"He was spoiling for a fight," continued Captain Snow. "He told me he was the last English ship captain fighting and said he had never surrendered. Luckily, he picked you and your sloop. We would all be dead if he had challenged something with a 24-gun broadside. I do not think he even thought he could be defeated. The wad of shot that blew him apart must have been a great surprise to him."

"What about your future, Snow?"

"Well, sir, me and the men were talking after Wellington Howe died. We will try to buy the vessel from the estate. His missus moved to Canada, not wanting anything to do with him. I know because I sailed her up there to be with friends. I plan to see if she will make me a deal if she inherits the ships. She has an inheritance from her own family so does not need a shipping business with three old ships.

"Especially, she does not need a ship that carried slaves. I guess you know the Lord Howe was a slaver pure and simple. I want no part of slaving. I will be glad to help Widow Howe sell the other ships. I sure would not trust Mr. Howe's factor to handle any business for her. He is as slippery as Howe was."

"Captain Snow, let's forget this whole incident. I will have to write it up, but I will make it clear that I killed Quincy and that you did all you could to keep from hurting my crew or ship. Let us take you back to the brigantine. I want you to sail behind me back to port. As soon as we anchor, I will tell the authorities what happened and they can take off Quincy's body. That should be the end of it."

CHAPTER 49

THE END OF AN ERA

TWO HOURS AFTER LEAVING RICHMOND six riders in uniform galloped toward the Casey group, waving their tricorne hats. The seventh man, riding ahead of the others sat tall in the saddle, astride a stately white horse. He was not in uniform, his clothing stylish but with little adornment.

Todd raised his hand to stop the train of horses and wagons. He wheeled his horse to face the approaching horsemen, his hand resting on the pistol at his side.

"Son," his father shouted, "the man in the lead is George Washington." Todd quickly removed his hand from his pistol. He sat straighter in the saddle.

Gilbert Casey and Max McBride jumped down from the carriages and stood beside Eagle. Todd dismounted and stood near his father. Within seconds, the Sergeant and the Scout rode up and stood by their horses to the right of Gilbert and Max.

General Washington dismounted, approached Gilbert and embraced him. He shook the hands of the others, all old comrades in arms. He turned to Todd, took his hand in a tight grip, lingered, and then released it smiling broadly.

"You have another good looking boy, Gilbert. Now, let me meet the ladies. After that delightful task is finished, I need to have a word with you and Todd. By the way, my friend," he said turning to Gilbert. Congratulations on avoiding the noose. I would never have let them hang you but refrained from interfering before the need arose. I did know your new judges and believed them to be honorable men, in contrast to your accuser. Howe has always been an obstacle to our quest for independence and the establishment of a nation."

Gilbert introduced his wife and the other women in the company. General Washington spoke graciously and put them all at ease with his friendliness and humor. At the proper time, he turned aside and nodded to Todd and his father to step into the shade near a stand of trees.

"Gilbert, you have served your country well and have spent several years on the field, in battle, in cold and hunger. I can ask no more service from you. Even now, your son Joshua is serving our country, ferreting out pirates and smugglers.

"What I do ask of you is to allow Todd to serve with me. The time has come for qualities not specifically needed for battle. We are now faced with the daunting task of building a country."

"Sir," Gilbert answered, "Todd must make his own decisions. He now has a wife, two children, and a fine farm he carved out for himself. He has defended it with his life—and taken the life of those attempting to kill his family, friends, and himself. He has more than earned his manhood."

"Those are the qualities needed. I have also communicated with his old professors—friends of mine—who speak highly of his intellect and his patriotism."

"Thank you, sir, for the compliment," Todd said.

"Here is what I have in mind," General Washington said. "I need a man on my staff who can find his way through many and sundry situations—mostly political. He must be a man of honor, one who earns the respect of others. Sometimes your duties will be open for all to see, yet on other occasions secrecy will be paramount. You will not have a specific posting but will carry the rank of captain with my personal vouch-safe in your kit.

"We will be mindful of your family, trying to keep you near your wife and home as much as is possible under the circumstances. I assure you, your children will not grow up with an absent father. Your father was not so fortunate and with his companions spent years in the field."

Todd opened his mouth to say something, but General Washington held up his hand for silence.

"Todd, you must think this over and discuss it with your family. I will need to have your answer within one month. Enough said."

After saying hearty goodbyes to all, George Washington mounted his white horse, turned and cantered off, his men catching up and clustering around him.

The Casey family sat in the shade of the same tree and pondered the offer George Washington made.

"Todd," his father said, "I will not interfere in your decision, but I do want to say you have been offered the second best job in the colonies. The general offered you the chance of a lifetime, but it will completely alter, rearrange, and redirect your life, and the life of your wife and children. You have the rare chance of being in the heart of the action as this country of ours organizes into a nation."

Gilbert called to the others in the party and asked them to come and sit in the shade. He proceeded to tell them what General Washington had proposed, asking them to pray about it and to feel free to make any comments they might have to Todd.

At the end of the discussion Gilbert stood as a signal that they were about to move on. "One more thing," he said, "is that Quincy Howe being alive still worries me" The others nodded agreement. No one knew that two weeks later a rider would reach the Casey farm with the story of Quincy's death.

Later, as the wagons and company of friends neared the Casey farm, Max Patch McBride rode up beside Todd and Sarah. Sarah was riding Thunder close beside her husband. Claire and Rachel were driving the wagons.

"Just so you know, me and Claire has a hankering for the mountains. Flat land near the rivers does not suit us anymore. We have been thinking of asking if you would welcome us to live in Max Patch Bend."

"It would bless my heart to have you live in Max Patch Bend. In addition, I believe you will soon find a fine house vacant in the Bend. It would be yours until you build your own."